THE
SCENT
OF
HER SOUL

B. ALLEN DAVIS

BOOKS BY B. ALLEN DAVIS

The Reapers Trilogy
Reapers
Beyond the Gateway
Reaper Reborn

Time Echoes Trilogy
Time Echoes
Interfinity
Fatal Convergence

Dragons in our Midst
Raising Dragons
The Candlestone
Circles of Seven
Tears of a Dragon

Oracles of Fire
Eye of the Oracle
Enoch's Ghost
Last of the Nephilim
The Bones of Makaidos

Children of the Bard
Song of the Ovulum
From the Mouth of Elijah
The Seventh Door
Omega Dragon

Dragons of Starlight
Starlighter
Warrior
Diviner
Liberator

Tales of Starlight
Masters & Slayers
Third Starlighter
Exodus Rising

Standalone Novels
Wanted: A Superhero to Save the World
I Know Why the Angels Dance

**To learn more about these books, go to
www.daviscrossing.com**

Facebook - facebook.com/BryanDavis.Fans

Published by Scrub Jay Journeys
P. O. Box 512
Middleton, TN 38052
www.scrubjayjourneys.com
email: info@scrubjayjourneys.com

ISBN: 978-1-946253-30-9

First Printing – May 2018

Printed in the U.S.A.

Library of Congress Control Number: 2018901867

AUTHOR'S NOTE

The Scent of Her Soul is a novel for adults. The story includes sex-trafficking, a scene of brutality, and a smattering of profanity.

Although the content is relatively tame compared to what is readily available elsewhere, as an author of several series for youth, my concern is that this novel might fall into the hands of readers for whom the content is not appropriate.

Therefore, I am publishing this book under **B. Allen Davis** instead of **Bryan Davis**. Perhaps this change will be enough to eliminate *The Scent of Her Soul* from searches for my other books.

I shifted my normal genre and audience hoping that this story will raise awareness of the evils of sex trafficking, inspire people to pray for and help those trapped in its clutches, and give aid to those who are out on the streets trying to make a positive difference.

CHAPTER ONE

THEY GAVE ME her shoe—Nike, size six, typical for a twelve-year-old.

As a human bloodhound of sorts, I had been asked to smell a variety of items. A shoe was not one of my favorites. Yet since Amy wore it when she was abducted, it was the best scent source possible.

I sniffed the inside. The odor carried her essence—pungent sweat, a trace of blood … and the scent of her soul.

As I exhaled a stream of white, a frosty breeze sent the vapor up through the glow of a neighborhood streetlamp and into Spokane's nighttime sky. Through my ski mask's breathing hole, I inhaled fresh, crisp air and let my membranes absorb the elements. The particles of a thousand Amys filtered in, along with a thousand Alyssas, Aarons, and Andrews, but only one matched the sample. The missing Amy was out there … somewhere.

I turned to the weeping mother. I couldn't remember her name or the name of the father who held her close, both bundled in heavy coats on this dark night. No matter. I knew Amy's name. And I could provide them the assistance they desperately needed, a service the police could never hope to provide.

"I can find her," I whispered.

The mother swiped a tear from her cheek. "You mean …" She swallowed down a sob as her hopeful eyes sparkled. "She's alive?"

"She's alive … for now. But if traffickers got her, she's living in hell." I pulled my trench coat close. Even with a sweatshirt underneath, the bone-chilling air cut to the skin. "Do you have what I asked for?"

"Right here." The father extended a small canvas bag. Light from the streetlamp revealed its purple color. "I sold my Mustang to raise this money. Getting Amy back …" His voice faltered. "Well … no sacrifice is too high."

"Amy's photo is in there, too," the mother said. "It's from just three weeks ago. Also Fred's business card so you'll have our phone number."

I took the bag. "And what keepsake for Amy?"

"A stuffed bunny she named Beans. She sleeps with him every night."

"That should work."

The father's lips firmed. "Look, I get why you need Amy's rabbit, but why the purple bag? We couldn't find anything purple on short notice, so we had to dye this one."

"It's personal." I gave them a nod and forced a confident tone. "I'll keep Mahoney up to date. Send all communications through him."

Just as I turned to leave, the father grabbed my arm. "Uh … just a sec." He released me and cleared his throat. "I'm not sure what to call you … but …"

I offered a mechanical smile. "The media has several names for me. Just pick one."

"Guardian Angel," the mother said.

"Sure. That'll work." The father averted his eyes. "I just wanted to say that we guarded Amy. You know. Internet rules. Don't talk to strangers. No skin-tight or revealing clothes. That sort of thing." His jaw tensed. "She was taken while walking home from school." His voice pitched higher as he struggled to finish. "It's only three blocks away, for God's sake. This is Spokane, not Seattle. We didn't do anything wrong."

The mother patted his coat sleeve with a gloved hand. "He knows, honey. He read the report."

"Right. Right." After a heavy sigh, he made eye contact again, his own tears sparkling. "So … we aren't bad parents. That's all I'm trying to say."

I gave them both the most sympathetic look I could muster. "Trust me. I believe you." Without another word, I turned and strode down the sidewalk and into darkness, clutching the purple bag by its throat.

As I walked, I inhaled deeply once more. The cold air froze my nostril hairs, but I needed to keep Amy's scent locked in place. In the early days, I had lost other girls' scents, including the scent of the most important girl. That would never happen again.

When I neared my rental minivan, parked as far away from streetlights as possible, I reached into my pocket for the key fob and pressed the unlock button. I got in, fired up the engine and heater, and set the bag in the passenger's seat next to a bottle of Excedrin. After glancing around for any onlookers, I peeled off my ski mask and laid it by the bag.

As I drove toward the neighborhood access road, I set my phone on the dashboard's mount and said, "Call Mahoney."

Within seconds, Mahoney's distinct New-York-flavored voice punched the air. "Mike? You got the Castillo girl already?"

"No, I skipped to number two on the list." I heaved a sigh and mentally recited my mantra. *Every girl is unique. Every girl is loved. Every girl needs a hero.* "Amy Horowitz. White. Twelve years old. Blonde. Blue eyes. A prime target."

"Then they'll find customers quick." Static crackled through a short pause. "I'll add the new info to the file, but what about Castillo? She's got the look, right?"

"I saw the photo. She's close, but her history checks out. She's not Emily. Besides, Horowitz is younger. A clear case of abduction. It's my call."

"As always. But Castillo was last seen in Seattle, and now you're in … Here's the file. … Spokane? What is that? Three hours from Seattle?"

"More like four. Still close enough to head back after I find Horowitz."

"Okay, boss, I'll see if I can rustle up a handoff there."

I glanced at the GPS screen and followed its directions toward Interstate 90, the main east-west artery through Spokane. "You got anything else for me to do while I'm here?"

"Just a suspected brothel. The address is in your mission list."

"A brothel? That's police work. Why don't they raid the place?"

"They did. No one there. That's why I said *suspected*. It's an abandoned motel. Police said it was probably once used that way, maybe not too long ago."

"What's that got to do with me? I'm not into busting brothels."

"The informer said the girls are underage, like the teenagers in one of those pimp motels. They call them stables or ranches. It's all in that article I sent you last week. I thought you might want to check it out."

"Sniff around to see if any girls are close by?" I nodded. "All right. After I find Castillo, I'll come back to Spokane."

"Good man." Mahoney yawned. "What time is it there?"

I stopped at the side of the road near a junction to the Interstate and glanced at the dashboard clock. "Four twenty."

"So it's seven twenty here. I can barely see my clock. Coffee is the only reason my eyes are open at all."

"Too early to contact a handoff in Spokane?"

"Nope. To get on my list, the candidates have to be on call twenty-four seven." Mahoney slurped something, most likely his coffee. "Just give me a buzz when you get Amy. I'll have a handoff by then."

"No fan girls this time." I inhaled and looked both ways. The scent led to the right. As usual, the sensation wasn't truly olfactory, though it entered through my nostrils. "Any other news?"

"The typical overnight load. Five more super-urgent pleas to find kids, including a boy."

"When will they learn that I can't find boys?"

"No idea. It's in all the gossip rags. Anyway, you also got fifteen interview requests. Sixteen thousand alerts on your media nicknames. Someone created a Guardian Angel sweatshirt and wants your permission to market it."

"Market it?"

"Yeah, Guardian Angel is your number one nickname. It's even trending on Twitter."

"More like Squawker." I turned the van onto the Interstate access ramp, accelerated to the speed limit, and locked in the cruise control. "I don't care about the sweatshirts. Email me the info on the girls. Do the usual with the interviews."

"You sure? One's for an audience with the Pope. If you can't trust him to keep a secret, then—"

"You can't trust anyone. I know." A sharp pain stabbed through my skull—a migraine ready to pile-drive my brain. "Listen. I have to go. Just send my regrets to all of them. You know the boilerplate."

"No problem. Hey, speaking of plates, don't forget to alter the plate on your rental."

"Already done. Don't be such a worrier."

"What kind of ride did you get?"

"A minivan. Dodge. It's pretty nice. Power back gate and sliding doors."

"Sounds perfect. Do you need anything else from me?"

"Yeah." As the pain spiked, my voice dove into a tailspin. "Roses for Deb and a LEGO set for Tommy. I think I got some decent cash this time, so ..." I closed my eyes tightly. With no one else on the road, I could afford the risk. "Make it special."

"I'll have them there by noon, though Deb'll probably toss the roses again." Keyboard clicks sounded from the speaker. "Take care of yourself. You sound terrible."

"Migraine's coming on." I opened my eyes and massaged a temple. "I have meds with me."

"So you just keep popping those pills." His voice took on a nagging tone. "When's the last time you slept?"

"What's it to you?" I grabbed the bottle from the passenger's seat and flicked off the lid. "You're my manager, not my mother."

"And you're my paycheck. I have to keep you alive."

"Good luck with that." I pushed the terminate button, tossed back two Excedrin, and swallowed them. The caplets slid down without need for water. My throat knew the drill. But no meds could block the nightmares that were sure to come. Migraines were warning beacons. Sleep would dredge up the Halloween horrors. But I had to get at least a couple of hours … for Amy's sake.

The scent of her soul followed the highway. Amy was probably less than ten miles down the road, and my plan had to be executed after dawn. I could afford to get some shut-eye.

After taking an exit off the Interstate and parking in an abandoned lot, I slid my holstered Beretta from under my seat, laid it on the passenger's seat, and covered it with the ski mask. I then opened the bag, took out an envelope of cash, and stuffed it into the glove compartment.

My gaze rested on the off-white bunny in the bag—Beans, they had called him. I pulled him out. Soft, yet worn, he was about the size of a two-liter bottle and carried Amy's now-familiar scent. He would definitely keep my nose on the trail.

Leaving the engine running, I adjusted my seat, leaned back with Beans in my arms, and closed my eyes. Although my head pounded, exhaustion would soon overwhelm the pain. Sleeping in agony was nothing new.

As always, the dream started in bright sunshine—Deb, Tommy, Emily, and me walking hand in hand on a paved path through Timber Park, all dressed in pirate costumes complete with eye patches and foam swords. Deb looked stunning, as usual. The descending sun shone on her shoulder-length auburn hair, and her bright smile drew my gaze to freckles that sprayed from her dimples across her button nose like a shower of sunshine. It was hard to tear my eyes away from her.

I walked with a stuffed parrot perched on my shoulder, pinned there by Emily's careful hands. Decked out in perfectly arranged purple silk and purple barrettes in her satiny brown hair, she was definitely more meticulous than most eleven-year-olds.

"Don't let Rupert fall off," she had warned. "His head is barely attached." Even in the dream the pins felt like bird claws pinching my skin, pain that throbbed in time with the headache's pulses.

As we drew close to the pavilion where the Halloween party would take place, clouds rolled in and darkened the sky. Soon, thunder rumbled in the distance.

Tommy shuddered and pulled close to Deb. Even at the age of fourteen, he didn't shy away from a public display of fear and a need for his mother's touch. Such was the way with his autism.

I slowed our pace and eyed a storm cloud on the horizon. "Looks like we might have to head home."

Deb ran her fingers through Tommy's unruly mop of dark hair. "The invitation said to go to the Russells' house if it rains. I think it's not far past the pavilion."

"We should hustle." I glanced again at the threatening sky. "Nothing's stopping that storm."

Emily reached up and chirped, "Carry me, Daddy."

I smiled. Who could resist those lovely brown eyes? When I scooped her into my arms, she compressed my biceps. "You're so strong."

I gave her my usual response in a throaty growl. "To keep you safe from the wolves."

As she held the parrot in place, we jogged ahead, though in the dream we seemed to be going nowhere—four figures rushing through streaming mist. Cold rain fell. Thunder boomed. Tommy cried out in terror.

With the pavilion in sight, I grabbed Tommy's hand and quickened the pace. Deb held his other hand and hurried with us. We rushed under the shelter and gathered at the center, just out of reach of the windswept rain.

"Looks like we'll be here awhile," I said as I scanned the park, deserted except for a costumed clown, likely another partygoer. Clutching a fistful of Sugar Daddy candy sticks, the clown ducked his head and ran toward us. Water dripped from his saturated green wig and streamed down his smeared makeup. He called, "Make room for the Sugar Daddy."

When he came within a few paces, lightning struck a nearby tree. The clown flew back and slid on his bottom. The tree fell and crashed onto the pavilion roof. A beam slammed against my head and knocked me out.

Pain shot through my body and jerked me awake. Still hugging Beans, I exhaled and glanced from side to side. Emily was gone, just as she had been when the storm's cold rain revived me. Dazed and covered by rubble, neither Deb nor Tommy had seen the clown—Sugar Daddy—take Emily. Like a phantom, she had been spirited away.

An odd aroma remained, though at the time I didn't realize that it was the scent of her soul. I learned of my new gift too late to help her. The memory of her scent stayed with me, even to this day, but I never could find it in the air again.

I raised the back of my seat and pushed Beans into the bag. Dawn's light allowed a view of its purple material. I shifted my gaze to the finger-length wooden cross hanging from the rearview mirror and caressed the purple ribbon tied around the center. "I'm so sorry," I whispered. "I couldn't protect you from the wolves."

I inhaled and again detected Amy's scent. A knock on the head had given me this gift, and it seemed that the recurring headaches renewed the power, though every pang brought a fresh reminder of the moment my own little girl fell prey to the wolven fangs.

A tear found its way to my cheek. I swiped at it and slapped the van into gear. For Amy's sake, and for Emily's, I had to press on.

After I returned to the Interstate and drove about ten miles, the scent weakened. As often happens, I had passed the exit leading to Amy but didn't realize it until the deteriorating scent clued me in. I took the next exit, returned to the previous one, and picked up the trail again.

Within another five minutes, I entered a residential area populated by two-story homes on half-acre lots. I lowered the windows, slowed the van to a crawl, and studied each house. With Amy's scent so strong and pervasive, finding the exact source became more of an exercise in detective work than simply following my nose.

At the ninth house, a green Chevy pickup truck and a blue Mustang sat on the driveway pad, both reflecting the morning sunlight. A breeze pushed swings on a rusted set in the side yard, and pasteboard within the house's lower windows blocked any view of the interior. A light shone from an upstairs room, proof enough that someone was home and likely awake. I wouldn't have to use a picklock like I had so many other times. Still, I would keep the set in my pocket in case I needed it for an inner door.

I accelerated. It didn't take Sherlock Holmes to figure out that this house was the best candidate.

As I returned to the neighborhood's entrance, I spoke to my phone. "Where is the nearest pizza delivery restaurant?"

A map appeared on the screen with a pushpin at the center labeled "Luigi's." A mechanical voice emanated from the speaker. "Four point three miles. Turn left on Evergreen Road."

I glanced at the clock—8:15. The pizza place probably wouldn't be open yet, but someone might be there getting ready for the lunch shift.

After texting Mahoney the address of the suspected house, I hurried toward the pizza restaurant, donning a curly wig, a thick mustache, and a prosthetic nose along the way. When I arrived, I talked the manager into baking a pizza earlier than usual. A couple of twenties helped him decide. The money seemed to open a gate of generosity. He added a reheated calzone, which I ate while the pizza baked, a welcome treat since I hadn't had a bite in at least eighteen hours.

When I returned to the van with the pizza in an insulated bag, I took off the disguise and stowed it in my suitcase—one of two suitcases I kept in the rear section along with a black bag for my stuff and a smaller purple bag filled with items I might need for rescued girls. Since the girls sometimes required medical help, I also carried a well-supplied first-aid kit, having taken a course in treatment of superficial wounds.

I drove back toward the house. A fight likely loomed, and I never felt comfortable fighting while wearing a disguise. In any case, my opponents wouldn't have cameras ready to get a photo of me. I wouldn't need a mask.

When I arrived, I parked behind the pickup. I touched the cross's ribbon again and breathed, "Blessed be the Lord my strength, who teaches my hands to war and my fingers to fight."

I lowered my hand and rolled my fingers into a fist. It was time to go.

After attaching a sound suppressor to the Beretta and tucking it and the ski mask under my coat, I pulled on my gloves, grabbed the pizza, and got out of the van. As I hustled through a frigid breeze toward the front door, I glanced at the room upstairs. The light was still on, but no shadows moved across the glow.

I rang the doorbell. It was time to put on the act.

A gruff voice penetrated the door. "Whaddaya want?"

"Pizza delivery," I shouted. "Better hurry. It's getting cold."

"No one ordered a pizza. Get lost."

"You mean Amy Horowitz doesn't live here? I'm sure I wrote the address—"

The door flew open. A stocky bearded man grabbed my arm, jerked me inside, and slammed the door. Standing at least six-foot-three and filling out his flannel shirt with taut muscles, he gave me a hard shake and let go. "What do you know about Amy Horowitz?"

"So this *is* the right place." I laid the pizza on a bar separating the kitchen from an eating area—unfurnished except for a TV on a small table and an easy chair with ratty upholstery, a baseball bat leaning against it.

I opened the pizza and turned it toward him. "Pepperoni and extra cheese, right?"

The man took a threatening step toward me. "Look, I told you we didn't order—"

"Sure you did." I spotted keys to a Chevy on the arm of the chair. "You mentioned your Mustang. I saw it parked outside."

"That's not my Mustang. Mine's the—"

"So where's Amy?" As I looked around, my gaze swept up a staircase to the second floor. "The guy who ordered said it's her birthday. I have a present for her."

"I'll show you Amy." The man withdrew a switchblade, flicked it open, and set it near my throat. "Tell me how you knew she's here."

I stared cross-eyed at the blade and feigned a frightened stammer. "I … uh … like I said … the guy who ordered—"

"Rubio?" the man shouted toward the stairs. "Did you order a—"

"Shut up." The deep voice from the second floor sounded like a lion's growl. A girl's moan blended in. "You'll get your turn in a minute."

I slapped the blade and punched him in the throat. As he stood stunned, I grabbed the baseball bat and slammed it against his neck. Something cracked, and he collapsed to the floor. Now lying on his back, he stared at me, apparently paralyzed in every limb as he labored for breath.

I reached under my coat, withdrew the Beretta, and knelt next to him. Pressing the end of the silencer against his mouth, I whispered, "If you even squeak, I'll blow your brains out."

His wild, pain-streaked eyes told me he'd cooperate. With the gun drawn and my footfalls quiet, I ran up the carpeted stairs and stopped at a hall with a door on each side and a wall at the far end. A lanky, pale man, bare-chested and wearing khaki pants, walked out of the door on the right, calling, "All right, Jackson. You're up." He turned toward me and stared at my gun. "Who are you?"

I waved the barrel. "Raise your hands, walk backwards, and let me see who's in the bedroom."

His hands at shoulder level, he complied with slow steps. "You a cop?"

"You wish." With the way now clear, I followed the hall to the bedroom and glanced inside. In the light of a floor-standing flood lamp, Amy sat on a bed staring blankly with a sheet covering the lower half of her naked body. Blood smeared the sheet near her thighs, and a small video camera on a tripod aimed its lens at her.

The man whipped out a knife and lunged at me. I fired a muffled shot. A bullet ripped into his chest. As he staggered forward, I dodged. He crashed face first to the floor and writhed on his stomach for a moment before going limp, the knife still in his hand.

I felt for a pulse at his neck and detected a weak, erratic heartbeat. He wasn't going anywhere. I slid the gun to its holster, lunged into the bedroom, and kicked over the camera. As I crouched in front of Amy, I searched her eyes— glassy and wandering. I spoke in a soothing tone. "They drugged you, didn't they?"

I pulled out the ski mask, slid it on, and scanned the room. Next to the tripod, a pair of girls' jeans, a green T-shirt, and ripped pink panties lay on the floor. The shirt would help, but with the injury she likely suffered, the jeans would have to wait until I could get her new panties and a pad.

I helped her put the T-shirt on, then stripped off my coat and sweatshirt. "It's cold outside; you need something warmer." I pulled the sweatshirt down over her head. "I see some blood. Where are you hurt?"

After instinctively pushing her arms through the sleeves, she laid a hand over her sheet-covered crotch and spoke in an almost inaudible voice. "Here."

Although I had already guessed the truth, rage boiled inside. As I clenched my teeth to keep from shouting, I brushed my gloved fingers across her tangled blonde locks and looked into her lovely blue eyes. "That man will never hurt you again. I promise."

A siren wailed in the distance. No one outside the house could have heard the gunshots, though maybe a nosy neighbor was concerned about a pizza delivery taking so long. Not a likely scenario, but I couldn't take any chances.

I threw my coat back on, disconnected the camera from the tripod, and stuffed it into a pocket. After grabbing the jeans, I scooped Amy up in my arms, the sheet around her hips. "Let's go."

CHAPTER TWO

CRADLING AMY, I stepped over the rapist's body and rushed downstairs. Jackson lay on his back with his eyes closed. I set Amy on the chair with the jeans in her lap, withdrew my gun, and checked Jackson's pulse. Dead.

My hands trembled. Before today I had killed one other kidnapper in self defense. Now I added another, maybe two, to the gruesome list. They deserved to die, but killing them still shook me to the core.

Casting off the tremors, I scanned the room again. A phone lay next to the TV. I slid the gun away, grabbed the phone, and stuffed it into my coat pocket with the camera. Any phone had to be checked for a clue to Emily's whereabouts. The chances of finding anything were next to zero, but I couldn't let that stop me from turning every stone.

After picking up Amy again, I dashed outside and hurried with her to the minivan. The siren still seemed distant. Maybe it wasn't coming this way at all, but I couldn't risk slowing down.

I laid her on the back seat and jumped behind the wheel. Trying to calm my racing heart, I eased out of the driveway and drove at a normal speed toward the neighborhood exit.

No other vehicles appeared. A false alarm.

I glanced back. Amy now sat upright. "Who are you?" she asked, her speech slurred.

"A friend." I took off my gloves and set them on the console. "I'm taking you to your parents."

"Where are my pants?"

I measured the quality of her voice. She still seemed only half coherent, but she was coming around. "In your lap. In the back you'll find a purple suitcase with underwear that should fit and some sanitary pads. I don't have shoes for you, though. One fell off when they took you. I guess they ditched the other one."

"Maybe. I don't remember." Moving slowly, Amy reached into the rear compartment and pulled the purple suitcase to her seat. After selecting a pair of panties, she ducked under the sheet and began getting dressed.

I spoke toward my phone, still mounted on the dashboard. "Call Mahoney."

A moment later, his voice piped in. "Did you get her?"

"Yeah. She's drugged. Semi-conscious. Trauma drama hasn't started yet. Since they were shooting a video, they probably didn't want her too wiped out, so she'll clear up soon. And I have the camera. I'll send it to you when I get a chance."

"How many kidnappers?"

"Two. One's dead for sure. Broken neck. Big guy. Had to take a baseball bat to him. The other's probably dead by now. I shot him when he attacked me."

"Sounds like quite a brawl."

"Not really. They weren't together, so I took them out one at a time. I got lucky."

"Lucky works in a pinch." Keyboard clicks blended in with Mahoney's words. "Your text with the address came in a while back. I'll call the police right after I contact Amy's folks. And I got a handoff. I'm sending the address of the meeting place to your phone. She'll expect you there in twenty minutes."

"Perfect." I bent my brow. "No fan girl, right?"

"Sounded pretty down to earth to me."

"Hold on. I have to look at the screen." While something buzzed in the background, maybe Mahoney's electric razor, I transferred the handoff's address to the dashboard GPS, and began following the directions. "Okay. I'm back."

"I'm picturing you driving with your knees."

"No. With my nose."

"The wonders of that nose." He laughed. "Hey, I'm sure you scoured the place for Emily leads."

"Got a phone to analyze. I'll let you know what I find."

"If you need to break into it, give me a call." More keys clicked. "I'm the prince of passwords."

"I don't expect to find much, but I'm curious about their marching orders. Apparently they wanted to shoot a porn video before bringing in other men to …" I glanced at the rearview mirror. Amy was still fumbling around under the sheet. "Well, you get the picture."

Mahoney growled an obscenity. "All too well."

Amy popped out from under the sheet. Tears streamed as she glared at me in the mirror. "Who are you? What did you do to me?"

"Gotta go." I pressed the terminate button and met her hot stare in the reflection. "Amy, have you heard of the Guardian Angel?"

"Who hasn't?" She half closed an eye. "What about him?"

I touched my chest. "I'm the angel, and I just rescued you."

She gasped. With each second, anger faded from her eyes. Then, her mouth dropped open, and she whispered, "Is that why I'm …" She looked down at her lap. Her chin quivered. Then she murmured a faint, "Someone raped me?"

I tightened my grip on the wheel. "Amy, I'm sorry I was too late to stop him. The guy who did it is—"

Amy let out a wail and lay on her side. Sobs poured forth. Her body shook in rhythmic spasms as she wrapped her arms around herself and curled into a fetal position.

I stayed quiet. Crying without interruption always seemed to help the girls settle down.

As her sobs continued, I let out a silent sigh. The poor kid. Nightmares were in her future, and who could tell if they would ever end?

When she quieted, I cleared the front passenger seat and patted it. "You can sit up here with me if you want."

She sniffed and breathed a wispy, "I'd rather not."

"I understand. Of course you're scared. I'd be scared, too, and I don't know how long it would take me to get my courage back." I looked at her again in the mirror. She stared at her hands, folded tightly in her lap. "Just let me know if you change your mind."

She replied with a soft, "Okay."

After a couple of silent minutes, I pulled Beans from the bag and reached him to her. "Your parents sent Beans with me."

She gathered him into her arms and held him close. After a moment of silence, she whispered, "I guess you really are the Guardian Angel."

I nodded. "And I shot the monster who raped you. I'd do anything to protect you."

Silenced ensued again. After a few minutes, she said, "I'm coming to the front." As she climbed forward, I guided her with a hand. When she settled, she kept a tight hold on my hand and gazed out the windshield. "How far is it to my house?"

"Not far, but I'm taking you to a woman who'll drive you home. The police will meet you there. They'll have a lot of questions."

She looked at me with teary eyes. "I remember. The Guardian Angel doesn't want to be seen by anyone. That's why you're wearing a ski mask."

"And the woman we're meeting might be wearing one, too. Sometimes the women try to imitate me, sort of like a fan thing. But it won't last. When warmer weather comes, I'll switch to disguises."

She looked me over as if her gaze could detect a lie. "Why can't you just take me yourself? You can keep your mask on."

"It's complicated. We always phone ahead to let parents know their child is coming home. Some call the media, so I can't show up. Too many questions. Reporters try to follow me. And it's better for girls to be with a woman. We always choose moms who have daughters. She'll be able to help you with stuff I can't handle. She might even take you to the hospital first." I nodded toward her lap. "To check for injury and ..." I cleared my throat and looked straight ahead. "And for whatever else they need to check."

"I understand." She turned her head for a moment before meeting my gaze again. "So when you drop me off, I won't see you anymore."

"Not likely. But I'll watch the news reports. They always show the happy reunion when a kidnap victim is rescued."

A weak smile brightened her face. "I'll be sure to wave at you." She lifted my hand and kissed it. "Thank you for saving my life."

"You're welcome." I drew her hand close and returned the kiss. "Thank you for making my life worth living."

We closed in on the rendezvous point, a span of pavement with faded lines, maybe a former transit park-and-ride lot. A woman wearing a trench coat and ski mask stood near a Ford Explorer and waved at us.

When I pulled into the space to the right of the Ford, Amy began stripping off the sweatshirt.

"No." I grabbed the hem and pulled it back down. "Keep it. Something to remember me by."

She hugged herself. "Thank you. I love the color." She pushed Beans into my hand. "So you'll remember me."

"But I can't—"

"Don't you want to remember me?" Her eyes took on a hurt look.

"Of course I do, but ..." What could I say? That she was just another girl like dozens before her? Of course not. "But I couldn't take something you sleep with."

She touched the sweatshirt. "I have this. I'll wear it to bed every night. I'll feel like my guardian angel is watching me."

I laid Beans on her lap. "Really. You need to keep him."

Her lips tightened as she collected Beans, and she said nothing more.

The handoff tapped on my window, her masked face nearly touching the glass. "Excuse me? Is Amy ready?"

I grabbed my phone, opened the security app, and lowered the window. Cold air blasted in. "Password?"

She rattled off a series of letters and numbers that matched the ones on the screen. Nodding, I said, "We're ready. She's barefoot, though. Watch where she steps."

I closed the window to seal out the frigid air while the handoff hurried around to Amy's side and opened the door. "Want me to carry you, sweetheart?"

"No. I'm fine." As Amy got out, she smiled and whispered, "Bye."

I gave her a nod and watched them pass in front. Amy and I locked gazes, her expression forlorn, yet searching, as she held my sweatshirt's sleeve over her mouth. What was going through her mind? An image of the vile beast who brutally penetrated her? Loss of innocence? Could she ever trust anyone again? Maybe she was hoping for something more than a drive-by hero.

My mantra returned to mind. *Every girl is unique. Every girl is loved. Every girl needs a hero.*

Just as the handoff opened her Ford's front passenger door, I lowered the window and leaned my head out. "Amy?"

She raised her brow. "Yes?"

I gestured with my head. "Come here."

She tiptoed toward me, careful to avoid a shard of glass. When she drew close, I took Beans from her and held him to my chest. "I'll sleep with him every night, and I'll think of you."

A broad smile ran across her face. "And don't forget to watch for my wave."

"I'll watch."

Her gait now lively, she retraced her steps and climbed into the Ford.

When the handoff closed the door, she walked back to my window, set her hands on the frame, and looked me in the eye, though the ski mask blunted the effect. "I just wanted to tell you that I'm your biggest fan, and I want to be your handoff anytime you're in the area."

"Thanks, but choosing handoffs is Mahoney's department. You do a good job with Amy, and you'll be at the top of his list."

"Trust me. I will. I'm a momma bear." She turned to go, then pivoted back. "And I need to say this." Her tone turned serious. "You're a great man. A true hero. I hope my son turns out as brave as you."

"I appreciate the vote of confidence, but ..." I nodded toward Amy. "You should get her home quick. Her parents will probably want to take her to the ER. She's been raped"

Her eyes widened. "Raped? Oh, my God." She rushed around to the driver's side, threw the door open, and leaped in. Seconds later, the Ford squealed out, leaving a skid mark on the pavement.

As their SUV turned onto the road, I caught a glimpse of the woman lifting off her ski mask. Long, dark tresses fell to her shoulders. She looked youngish, maybe early thirties, much like Amy's mom. A good fit. Mahoney had done his job well in spite of the fan-girl display.

Thoughts of Mahoney refreshed a memory—the first time I made contact with him, the day he answered my anonymous want ad. I asked for a computer wizard who could keep a secret. He replied with a note telling me my name, address, phone number, and favorite cereal along with an added suggestion that I needed him to button up my security. I was sold.

I slid my phone from its mount and sent a text to him— *Amy handed off. Heading to Seattle. Update when I get there. FYI, I gave Amy my sweatshirt. Spare me the grief about security. It's plain. Hunter green. No logo.*

After returning the phone to the mount, I sank low in my seat and blew out a sigh. Another job done. Time to take care of the next difficult duty. I faced the phone and said, "Call Deborah."

A ringing trill emanated from the speaker, then another, then two more. As usual, voice mail engaged.

"Hey, this is Deborah Pritchard. I can't come to the phone right now. If you're calling to order from the computer store, press one. Otherwise, leave a message."

A beep followed.

I spoke in a resigned tone. "Deb, it's Mike. Let's see …" I glanced at the clock—9:30 a.m. "It's afternoon there, so I guess you might be with your running group. Or is it weight-training day? Anyway, I was wondering about Tommy's birthday. It's a big one. You know, the adulthood thing, so I thought maybe I could come home for that."

When I imagined Deb's exasperated expression, I sighed. "Look, I know the agreement, but I don't want to miss his special day. When I have to leave again, he'll eventually get over it, but he might never get over me missing his special birthday."

I searched for a poignant ending, but nothing came to mind. I had to say something; the pause was already too long. "Well, I love you, and tell Tommy I love him. Good-bye."

I pressed the End button. Something beeped but not from my phone. It seemed to come from somewhere on my body.

Patting my coat, I searched for the confiscated phone, then pulled it out and unlocked the screen. A message alert flashed. When I brought it up, I read the text. *I saw your handiwork. Great job. Two stupid toads down, a thousand to go. But I'll get you back. Soon. Very soon.*

Another beep followed, and a new message appeared with an attached photo. *This lovely pic is going up on all the best websites. A hundred of my friends are going to stare at it while they entertain themselves. The video of Amy's deflowering is worth a ton of money. No wonder you took it for yourself.*

I withdrew the camera from my coat pocket and set it on the passenger seat. The urge to smash it made my fist shake. I had to send it to Mahoney so he could forward it to the police, but just thinking about anyone, even investigators, viewing that video made my blood boil.

My hand still shaking, I tapped on the message's photo icon. A picture of Amy appeared—nude and lying spread eagle on a bed.

I swiped it off the screen. My teeth clenched until they hurt. But why did it upset me so much? This wasn't the first time I had found one of my rescued girls displayed in porn. And it probably wouldn't be the last. The pain meant the calluses weren't quite tough enough. Yet, did I want them to be that tough?

A third beep sounded. *Don't bother tracking this number. It won't work. I'm using a dead man's phone. I'm disposing of it.*

I cleared the screen and searched the message archives. Nothing.

Next, I brought up the recent phone calls. Again, scrubbed. I then checked the setting for the GPS tracker. Turned off. At least no one could find me that way.

Finally, I brought up the contact list. Besides Rubio's, only one entry appeared. I whispered the name. "Sugar Daddy."

.   .   .   .   .   .

A towel around her neck, Deborah raised a set of keys toward her apartment door, but the ring slipped from her sweat-slickened fingers. She stooped and snatched it from the terrazzo floor. As she rose, she glanced over the railing at the pool where afternoon sunlight glistened off oiled skin on bronzed bodies.

She whipped the towel off and dried her hands, still watching as a bikini-clad swimmer climbed from the water and reclined in a chair near the cabana.

Deborah squinted, trying to focus on this girl. How old might she be? Fourteen? Her hair was dark, the bikini, purple. Her height was the same as Emily's. And her face had a similar structure.

Deborah's heart raced. Could it be? After all these years?

When a chiseled young man walked up to the girl and kissed her, Deborah shook her head. No. Of course she wasn't Emily. How ridiculous. This girl was probably at least eighteen, not fourteen. And Emily's nose was smaller, her chin narrower.

Closing her eyes, Deborah inhaled deeply. *Get a hold of yourself. Emily's gone. Obsessing over her is crippling. Tommy needs you. Focus on here and now.*

Deborah opened her eyes and looked at the pool again. Now the girl looked like any of the several high school seniors who frequented the pool. Yet, the young man who kissed her bore a resemblance to a young version of Mike—the same dark hair, athletic build, and strong chin, though this man lacked Mike's deeply set eyes and thick eyebrows.

As other teens splashed around in the pool, Deborah imagined a dive into the cool water. A swim would feel really good, but since Paula and Tommy were scheduled to come back from the library soon, that pleasure would have to wait. With Tommy's unpredictable behavior, visits to the library could never last more than a half hour. Such was life with an autistic son. *Unpredictable* had to be predicted.

Deborah wiped her face and threw the towel back to her neck. Jogging in this weather was for camels and roadrunners, not for normal humans who were trying to get back into shape. January was turning out to be one of the warmest ever, even by Fort Lauderdale standards.

She unlocked the deadbolt and doorknob and walked in. Tommy and Paula sat cross-legged on the carpet playing with LEGO bricks, both engrossed in building a castle.

Deborah set a hand on her hip. "Didn't you two go to the library?"

"Mom, you're back." Tommy hopped up and gave her a hug, then stepped away, sporting a wide grin.

She ran her fingers through his hair. "Of course I'm back. I never fail, right?"

"Right." He grabbed her upper arm. "Make a muscle."

She raised her arm and flexed. As he followed his routine of squeezing the biceps and letting out a whistle, Deborah cocked her head. "Tommy, it's running day. Remember? Weights are tomorrow."

"Oh, yeah." He grabbed her thigh and squeezed. "So strong."

Paula lifted her diminutive frame from the floor and whispered to Tommy, "Aren't you going to tell her about the surprise?"

"You bet." He scurried to a colorful box near a wall and brought it back. "A new LEGO set." His eyes seemed to dance. "From Dad."

Deborah peered at the floor. The pile of pieces did seem bigger than usual. She mustered a happy tone. "That's great, Tommy."

"Look what I made." Tommy plopped to the floor and began describing his new creation, something about a cross between a castle tower and a rocket ship. The words blurred as he rattled on.

Paula sidled up to Deborah. "And there's more." Wrinkling her freckled pixie nose, she nodded toward the table in the kitchen where at least two dozen gorgeous roses erupted like fiery lava from a green vase.

"From Mike, I suppose," Deborah said, trying not to sound too exasperated.

Paula nodded. "Arrived just after you left."

"When will he learn?" Deborah took a hard step toward the kitchen, but Paula caught her wrist.

"Don't trash them. They'd look great on my table."

"Take them, then." Deborah crossed her arms and glared at the LEGO pieces. "Probably less than an hour till he connects the dots and hits the Dad-panic button."

"Maybe not. He's pretty juiced. And I used them as an incentive. When they showed up, I knew the library wasn't happening, so I said no LEGO play until you finish your math. Worked like a charm." Paula strode to the kitchen and picked up the vase. As she walked back, she gave a blossom a long sniff. "Your loss is my gain."

"Speaking of gain …" Deborah glanced around for her purse. "I need to pay you."

"Already done. I paid myself from the cash box, so we're good till next week."

Deborah winked. "Good thing I trust you, you little pilferer."

As Paula reached for the door, she looked back with a cocky smile. "I figured you could afford it. You got a bunch of orders for the locator app. It's really taking off."

"Well, that's good news." Deborah touched Paula's shoulder. "Can you stay for a little longer? I was hoping to go for a—"

The wall phone chimed from the kitchen. Tommy jumped up, walked stiff legged to the phone, and stared at the caller ID screen. "Blocked," he whispered as it rang again. "Maybe it's Dad."

"Or a spam call. Let voice mail pick it up."

Tommy kept staring through the fourth ring. Mike's voice followed.

"Deb, it's Mike. Let's see … it's afternoon there, so I guess you might be with your running group. Or is it weight training day?"

Tommy bounced in place, his expression anxious.

"Anyway, I was wondering about Tommy's birthday. It's a big one. You know, the adulthood thing, so I thought maybe I could come home for that."

Deborah rolled her eyes. "Here we go again."

Tommy dashed to his bedroom and slammed the door.

"Look," Mike continued, "I know the agreement, but I don't want to miss his special day. When I have to leave again, he'll get over it, but he might never get over me missing his special birthday."

Paula opened the door. "I'd better go. If you want me to come for more hours, I can. Winter break, you know."

"I'll keep it in mind. Thanks."

"See ya." With the vase still in hand, Paula left and closed the door.

Deborah stalked to the phone and glared at it as Mike's tone took on a syrupy flavor. "Well, I love you, and tell Tommy I love him. Good-bye."

"Don't hang up." Deborah grabbed the receiver. "Mike? Are you still there?" A dial tone hummed in her ear. She slammed the phone to its cradle. No way to call him back on his super-secret phone line.

She padded to Tommy's room and listened at the door. No sounds came through. "Tommy?" She tapped on the door. "Everything okay?"

"I'm busy," came the gruff reply.

She touched the knob, then pulled her hand back. "Well … all right. Let me know if you need me."

Keyboard clicks sounded but nothing more.

Her fists tight, Deborah marched back to the kitchen, found her purse on the counter, and dug out her mobile phone. After unlocking it, she brought up the contact list and scrolled to "Mike—Emergency only."

Her finger trembling, she pressed the call icon and held the phone to her ear. She tapped her foot as she crossed an arm over her waist and propped her elbow. A trill sounded once, then a voice.

"Deb? Is that you?"

"Yeah … uh …" Her ears flashed hot. Why would an unfamiliar Bronx-flavored voice answer with her name? "Who is this?"

"Deb, is this an emergency? Just tell me, and I'll call for help."

"Only my husband calls me Deb," she snapped. "Who are you?"

"Calm down, now. Just calm down." His voice took on a soothing tone. "Mike gave you this number in case you need help, and I'm that help. I called you Deb, because that's what I've always heard him call you. Now tell me what your emergency is. A break-in? An accident?"

Deborah took a deep breath and forced her muscles to relax. "I am perfectly calm. Just tell me who you are, and we'll get along fine. Are you the Mahoney person some of the girls' parents have mentioned?"

"Sorry. I can't tell you who I am. Mike's orders."

Deborah firmed her lips. Score. If he wasn't Mahoney, he would have just said so. "Mike's orders? Why is he giving you orders?"

A sigh breathed through the speaker. "Deb, do you have an emergency? What do you need? I'll make sure you get it."

"What do I need?" She kept her voice calm and even. "I'll tell you what I need. I need my husband to come home and stay home." She pressed the End button and dropped the phone back to her purse.

She inhaled deeply and let the air out in a slow stream. For some reason, that *emergency* call felt good. The message would surely get back to Mike. Maybe coming from someone else for a change, the emergency would finally penetrate his brain. A troubled son and a lonely wife needed him home ... for good.

CHAPTER THREE

I STARED AT THE confiscated phone. This clue could be my chance to find Sugar Daddy. When I tapped on the contact entry, a message window asked for a password. Guessing it would probably be impossible.

I barked at my phone mounted on the dashboard. "Call Mahoney."

After a click and a short hum, he answered. "What's up, Mike? Did you sprout wings and fly to Seattle?"

"I wish. I'm still sitting where I passed Amy off." I looked again at Jackson's phone screen. "I need password help. I found a contact on the perp's phone, but it's locked. The entry says Sugar Daddy."

"Sugar Daddy? That's hot. I get the connection."

"Well, prince of passwords, what do we do?"

"Can you overnight it to me? Send it to the office instead of the drop box. I have the tools here to break in."

"Sure, but get this. The creep texted me. Threatened me and sent a nude pic of Amy. Said he'd post it on the net."

Mahoney grumbled something inaudible. "Send every-thing to me. I'll figure out a way to crush that cockroach."

"Can you keep Amy's photo off the net?"

"No way, my friend. The first place he posts it, the pervs will download it to their local drives. It'll be on a thousand sites in under an hour. But if I find one, I can search for the file name and get as many scrubbed as possible."

"Thanks, Mahoney. You're the best."

"Speaking of the best, your wife called."

"Deb called you? What happened?"

"No emergency or I would've texted you right away. I guess she just got upset about something and tried the hotline."

"What did she say?"

"Mostly she tried to find out who I am, but I didn't give an inch. She ended with saying she needed you to come home to stay."

The words drove a familiar dagger into my heart. "Yeah. That sounds like Deb."

"Just thought I'd tell you. She seemed pretty calm when she said that part."

Hot prickles crawled along my skin. I closed my eyes and fought back tears. "I guess because she's said it so many times."

"Or maybe my voice calmed her down. My baritone is legendary."

"Don't break your arm patting yourself on the back." My eyes still closed, I set Jackson's phone on the passenger seat. "Look for the phone and camera in the morning. I'll forward the texts now."

"I'm ready to rumble. Just be careful. You're already trending on Twitter. Apparently Amy's parents are burning up the Internet praising you, and you're at folk-hero status in Spokane."

"Why should I be careful about that?"

"The Seattle chief of police heard about you killing Amy's kidnappers. He's not exactly the head of your fan club. He says no vigilantes on his watch."

"I'm not a vigilante. I killed them in self-defense."

"You and I both know that, but you don't have any witnesses this time. Could be trouble down the line."

"Thanks for the warning." I opened my eyes, terminated the call, and forwarded Sugar Daddy's messages to Mahoney. I then searched the GPS for the location of the closest FedEx office and drove there in a hurry.

When I arrived, I put Jackson's phone and the video camera into the purple bag and walked inside at a casual pace, stealthily checking for security cameras. A small one hung at a corner, its lens aimed at me. I kept my face turned away. I wouldn't give anyone a reason to view the transaction, but dodging all media had become a habit.

Avalon waited on me, an attractive redhead in her early twenties. She set the bag and some bubble wrap inside a box and addressed it to Sunshine Family Dental as I instructed. As she filled out the paperwork on the service counter, a small tattoo peeked out from under her wristband.

"What is that?" I asked, pointing at the tattoo.

"My badge of courage." She pulled the band back a bit, revealing an eagle. "I'm supposed to cover it up while I'm at work."

"Courage, huh? How did you earn it?"

"A year or so ago, a couple of guys jumped out of a car and grabbed me." She nodded toward the door. "Right out there in the parking lot. I fought and screamed. Kicked one in the groin. Clawed the other one's eyes. Some people looked, but no one did anything. Finally, a man riding a motorcycle stopped, pulled a pistol from his saddle pack, and aimed it at them, swearing to everything holy that he'd kill them if they didn't let me go."

"Well, good for him. And good for you, too. Always fight back."

She smiled. "That's exactly what Ernie said."

"Ernie?"

"The guy on the motorcycle."

I extended my hand. When Avalon shook it, I said, "The eagle is a perfect symbol for you. You're a fighter."

"Thanks. I'm just glad Ernie stopped to help. I don't know where I'd be if he hadn't."

"Probably chained to a dirty bed waiting for your next customer."

She cringed. "Well, that's a disturbing image."

"All too real, though." I withdrew my wallet to pay the shipping charge. "Do you have a way to contact Ernie?"

She nodded, her smile widening. "He's my husband now."

"Perfect." I slid out a hundred dollar bill and set it on the counter. "Keep the change. Use it to take him out to dinner."

Without waiting for a reaction, I strode toward the door, again keeping my face turned from the camera. Once outside, I hopped into the minivan and drove away. In a puff of exhaust vapor, I left Spokane in the rearview mirror—another job finished, another girl restored. Yet, one girl still remained missing, my girl. And no trace of her scent lingered anywhere.

What else lay to the east, much too far away for the mirror to show? Home. Deb and Tommy. The end to this never-ending crusade. And peace? Rest?

I shook my head. The circle had been broken. Peace and rest could never visit our home, not until Emily walked safely through the door, or maybe when the clown who snatched her lay in a pool of blood while smoke rose from the barrel of my gun.

Cruising west on Interstate 90 toward Seattle, I settled back in my seat. I had four hours to think, four hours to dwell on this Sugar Daddy. Could he really be the clown who stole Emily? What might he do to get back at me for killing his two lackeys? That is, if he could find me.

I mentally recited my security measures. The publicized route to contact the so-called Guardian Angel went through Mahoney, and that channel passed through multiple layers of anonymous transfers. It would take a genius hacker to follow them all, and since Mahoney switched the layers on a daily basis, the trail would grow cold before the hacker could finish.

The only weak spot was the emergency number I had given Deb, but that wasn't a problem. No one knew of the Guardian Angel's connection to her, so who would guess to snoop in her phone? Not only that, when it came to keeping secrets, Deb was a multi-walled vault, and Tommy was in the dark about my alter ego. Our bases were covered.

My concerns now somewhat alleviated, I turned to the phone. "Bring up the Castillo file."

A photo of a young brunette appeared—flawless skin and beautiful brown eyes that could pierce the hardest of hearts. As Mahoney had said, in many ways she looked like Emily—Latina features exemplified in dark eyes and hair along with skin that seemed forever sun-kissed. Emily had picked up that look from my father, as if the genetic expression skipped over me and anointed her instead. She was a beautiful angel. Truly beautiful.

As tears welled, I swallowed and spoke with as much force as my tightening throat would allow. "Read the file."

The phone's voice, feminine yet mechanical, replied. "Emma Castillo. Age 14. Went missing four days ago. Last known clothing—blue jeans, white athletic shoes, purple polo shirt, and denim jacket."

"Purple," I whispered. "I didn't catch that before."

"Last seen at a party," the phone continued. "Police discovered date-rape drugs at the house where the party took place, but no source could be found. Witnesses say Daniel, an older male teen, gave Emma a lot of attention during the party, but police ruled him out as a suspect."

I huffed. *Yeah, right. They always have an alibi.*

"Meeting arrangements. You are to go to the parents' house at any time, day or night. If they are not home, you will find a key to the back door under a flower pot at the edge of a patio. The bag will be on a table in the living room with the scent source inside."

The Castillo's home address appeared. I punched it into the GPS, then settled back in my seat again and muttered, "Date-rape drugs. More like forever-rape drugs." Yet, their presence meant that she probably wasn't a runaway. Another abduction. And in the same state as Horowitz. Highly unusual.

As the cruise-controlled van took me across the rolling grasslands of central Washington, I planned my trek—make sure I can get through Snoqualmie Pass, stop just outside of Seattle for a few hours of sleep, then get a shower and a bite to eat at a truck stop before arriving unannounced at the Castillos' at about three in the morning.

Although a packed snow layer slowed my progress through the pass, I made good time. I stopped at a Walmart near the highway and parked at the back of the lot. Clutching Beans and reclining my seat, I dropped off to sleep within seconds.

As often happened after a rescue, I dreamed about Deb. We lay together in bed the night after I set up the communications system with Mahoney. Moonlight shone through a window, bathing us in a soft glow. The next morning I would embark on my first quest, so going right to sleep was out of the question.

Deb snuggled close and let out a humming purr—her love sound, a gentle motor that vibrated deep in her bosom. "How long do you think you'll be gone?"

"No idea. Mahoney's looking through the candidates. When he picks one, I'll know how far away the parents live. Then maybe I can guess."

"Well …" She nuzzled my neck. "To find missing girls, you'll go places where hookers hang out, won't you? I mean, I know you won't cheat, but you might need me to … well … relieve the pressure, I suppose."

As her warm breath caressed my skin, I smiled. "Are you saying you want to come with me?"

"You know I can't." She ran tantalizing fingers along my arm. "I just want to show you what you'll be missing while you're gone."

I woke up, as I always did at that point in this recurring dream. Keeping my eyes closed, I tried to go back to sleep, thinking of Deb, hoping to pick up the dream where it left off. Those were better days. Before Tommy's meltdowns. Before the searches for Emily became futile.

Before Deb stopped believing in me.

Yet, the dream never progressed beyond her sultry seduction. Maybe my subconscious mind knew that I couldn't stand a fleeting taste of the bliss that I hadn't enjoyed in so long. In any case, somehow I had to find a way to be the husband she needed, by being at her side, by somehow completing this mad quest, finding Emily, and earning the right to finish that dream, forevermore wrapped in her embrace.

After my nap, I drove to a nearby truck stop for a quick meal. The rotisserie chicken and wilted broccoli tasted like a salt-and-grease delivery system, though they filled my belly. The shower felt heaven-sent—a soaking rain after a ten-year drought. The shampoo and soap aromas bathed my senses in sweet strawberry and luscious lavender. After drying off and getting dressed, I felt more alive than I had in months, as if something in the air invigorated me. Maybe I would soon discover why.

I arrived in the Cedar Park neighborhood at 3:07 a.m. and stopped next to a playground. A few streetlights illuminated the area, providing only a silhouette view of a bird perched at the top of a set of monkey bars, perhaps a small owl.

A rooster weather vane wavered on the roof of a single-story house, one of five homes in view. According to the GPS, the one with the vane belonged to the Castillos. A pickup truck sat in the driveway, a good sign that they were home. An evergreen in the front yard cast a deep shadow over the porch—perfect for a surreptitious rendezvous.

I drove a few blocks away, parked in a dark area, and walked from there with the Beretta tucked in my inner holster. A misty breeze moistened my face. Although the temperature was in the forties, the air felt like a sauna compared to the frigid winds of Spokane.

In spite of the warmer climate, I put on the ski mask—my winter hiding place. It was time for a new chapter in this three-year hero charade.

The number of years sparked a series of thoughts. Of course I knew that Emily and Emma had similar physical features and were the same age, but other similarities didn't fully register until that moment. Their names started with the same two letters. And the purple shirt? Could purple be Emma's favorite color, too?

Nausea churned in my stomach. A cry of despair tried to punch through. Had I subconsciously blocked these similarities? Had I switched to the Spokane job to avoid my own trauma drama?

I shook my head. Maybe Deb was right after all. This crusade might eventually drive me insane.

Swallowing down the turmoil, I pressed on, whispering, "Every girl is unique. Every girl is loved. Every girl needs a hero."

As I neared the house, something moved high in the evergreen. I ducked close to a hedge bordering the walkway and peered at the tree. A man straddled a limb. As he scooted along the bark, a streetlight revealed more details. Something dark coated his face, maybe skin paint. He wore camo pants and a black sweatshirt and held a black object in one hand, the other hand braced on the limb.

I narrowed my eyes and searched every illuminated inch. Could the object be a gun? Was he one of Sugar Daddy's goons? Or maybe it was a video camera, clutched by a media hound looking for a scoop. I reached under my coat and withdrew the Beretta. Either way, I couldn't let him spoil the rescue of an innocent girl.

Watching him while holding the gun low, I crept along the side of the Castillos' yard to the back. After finding the key under the pot, I holstered the gun, unlocked the door, and stepped inside, making sure to pull the door in place without letting it click.

I withdrew my phone, turned on the flashlight app, and swept the beam across the interior—a short corridor that led to a living area. Padding softly, I followed the corridor to its end and found the table with a purple denim bag on top. I peered inside. A pair of dirty gym socks lay inside.

I squinted. Foot odor again? It worked for Amy, probably because she had a strong affinity for her shoes. Perhaps she was a track athlete. But it wouldn't necessarily work for everyone.

After grabbing the bag, I doused the light and retraced my steps. Just before entering the corridor, a new light flashed in my eyes.

"Don't move or you're dead." The voice was masculine, strong, unafraid.

I froze, blinded by the light. "Mr. Castillo?"

"Who wants to know?"

The ski mask jerked away. I lowered my head, but probably not in time to avoid their eyes. "The Guardian Angel. I came to search for Emma."

"Oh, my God, Rick," a woman called. "Turn off the flashlight."

The beam darkened. As shaking hands pushed the mask back over my head, the woman continued. "We thought you'd knock first. We've been kind of jumpy ever since … you know."

"Understandable." I straightened the mask to align the holes. "Someone's watching in the tree out front, so I came in the back way. I hoped to get in and out without disturbing you."

Barely visible in the dimness, Mr. Castillo, a gun in hand, hustled to a window at the front of the house and peeked outside. His shirtless form carved a silhouette that bulged at the waistline. "There he is. Still in the tree. I can't make out his face."

While he continued staring through the window, I turned to Mrs. Castillo. "Have you contacted any media? Talked to anyone about requesting my services?"

She combed back tangled dark hair with her fingers. Now that my eyes were adjusting, I was able to see her face, a near copy of Emma's, just as attractive though more care worn. "We didn't tell anyone." She retied the sash in front of a pink terrycloth bathrobe. "Mr. Mahoney warned us not to. Emma's life depends on it."

Mr. Castillo spoke from the window, still peering out. "Emma should never have gone to that party. I was against it from the start." As he turned toward me, his tone sharpened. "Boys these days. They're dogs sniffing for blood. And the girls? They're all in heat. Every one of them." He returned his gaze to the window and lowered his voice. "Even Emma."

Mrs. Castillo gasped. "Rick, how dare you say that about—" She bit her lip and looked at me. "I'm sorry. It's just that my husband and I don't agree on—"

"He's coming down." Mr. Castillo hissed. "And he's got a gun."

Still holding the bag, I whipped out the Beretta and joined him at the window. The stalker, now at ground level, skulked toward the door, his gun gripped in front with both hands.

"I can handle him." Mr. Castillo waved toward the back. "You get out of here."

"Okay. Be careful." I put the gun away and strode toward the rear-entry corridor, but Mrs. Castillo grabbed my wrist, stopping me.

"Godspeed finding my Emma." She kissed my hand. "Your face is gentle and kind. It's too bad you have to hide it."

"Thanks." I pulled away and rushed outside. As soon as I neared the front yard, a gunshot rang out. A man fled across the street, limping in the glow of streetlights. Seconds later, he vanished in the shadows.

New lights flicked on at nearby houses. I glanced at the Castillos' front door. A dark silhouette stood at the opening, the size and shape of Mr. Castillo. When the form waved a hand, I waved in return and hustled toward my van, the purple bag in tow. In moments, police would arrive, and I didn't want to be anywhere near this neighborhood while they conducted a manhunt for the stalker. I could try to detect Emma's scent in a safer place.

I drove out of the neighborhood, parked at a convenience store with my window down, and peeled off the ski mask. My pounding heart slowed. What did it all mean? How could Sugar Daddy have tracked me down in just a few hours? I grabbed my phone from the dash and searched through a list of warning codes until I came across "Security Compromised." I texted *Code 20* to Mahoney, then settled back in my seat and waited for the sounds of approaching police.

Since Mahoney set up an alarm system for incoming warning codes, he would wake up, but it might take him a while to locate any potential security hole, and he wouldn't get back to me until he was certain of our system's integrity.

I listened to the sounds of early morning—cars in the distance, a buzzing noise from somewhere, but still no sirens. What could be taking so long?

After a few minutes, a siren closed in, then a police cruiser zipped by, then another. Moments after a third one passed, the sounds settled. No cars slowed to give me even a glance. Perfect. Now I could get to work.

I fished Emma's socks from the bag, pressed both against my nose, and inhaled. The odor was strangely subdued—dirt blended with a subtle perfume. Skin lotion? Maybe. Whatever it was, it masked Emma's essence, assuming it was even there. This wouldn't work.

I opened the bag again. Another item lay inside—a diary with a purple cover.

As I withdrew the diary, my hand trembled. A tiny gold key protruded from a lock on the front. I turned it and opened the cover. Pretty handwriting on the first page spelled out, "Emma Castillo – Stuff I Think About."

I pressed the page to my nose and inhaled. Nothing more than a hint of dust. I looked toward the neighborhood. I couldn't go back and ask for a different scent source, not with police prowling everywhere.

Looking again at the diary, I began reading Emma's neat script on the introductory page.

Name: Emma Castillo

Age: 14

Profession: Just a kid who wants to be an actress and a singer.

On the following page, her first entry began.

I'm fourteen today, and I got this diary for my birthday. It's pretty cool. I've been asking for one, and I should've guessed Mom would get a purple one. She knows I like anything purple. More tomorrow.

I flipped to the last page. If there were any clues to her disappearance, they would be recent, though the police had surely already gone through it and photocopied everything.

The top line started with the end of a sentence. I turned to the beginning of the entry three pages back and read again.

So I posted a stupid duck face picture of myself, and Daniel said I was hot. I know he was just trying to kiss up, but then he messaged me a party invitation. I told him no way my dad would let me go. He doesn't trust me to do anything. Daniel said I should lie. Tell him I had to study with a friend. But then I'd have to lie to my mom, and I hate doing that. I want to go to the party, and I'm glad he invited me, but he's like 18. Gigi says he just wants to have sex with any girl who'll give it, even one as young as me. She's probably right. Maybe she knows from personal experience. I'll just tell them the truth and see if they'll let me go. Mom will trust me, so maybe she'll convince Dad. The party's not far away, so who knows?

I closed the diary and clutched it tightly. How could the police dismiss Daniel as a suspect? Could they be secretly tracking him now that he feels off the hook? Maybe.

I reopened the diary to the final page and scanned the entry again. Emma's writing was quite mature for her age—no spelling errors, no chat speak, good communication skills. She definitely got her message across, especially her respect for her parents. Well … at least for her mother. She and her father obviously had a falling out somewhere along the line.

Emma's words didn't reveal any sexual activity of her own, but she was clearly not naïve. Whatever her father's suspicions were, no clues about them appeared in Emma's entry.

I lifted the diary to my nose again and took a deep draw of the final page. This time the aroma of ink entered, and a new sensation joined it—freshness, vibrancy, and … a hint of shame? Maybe regret?

The sensation never failed to amaze me. A scent could stay consistent enough to be tracked yet change based on the mood of the one who left it. The subtleties had taken some time to learn, but now they were easy to detect, like downturned lips reflecting a shift in a person's mood. The face itself wouldn't change. Anyone could identify a friend no matter how emotions altered the friend's features, and anyone could also detect a friend's mood shift. So it was with me and scents.

I let Emma's scent and moods flow across the frayed nerve endings within my wounded heart. The sensation seemed to heal and wash afresh, a cleansing more luxurious than any truck-stop shower could offer.

As I exhaled, I smiled, maybe the first real smile in years. In the midst of a diary's aromas, I had found the scent of Emma's soul, so beautiful, so filled with life.

And the strangest part of all? She smelled like Emily.

I stepped out to the parking lot's pavement and inhaled. The aroma of bacon floated in the air, probably from the waffle restaurant across the main road. As I took successive breaths, I filtered out various odors—exhaust fumes, oil, and something like citrus.

Soon, the essence of children's souls came through. A shudder ran across my body. After so many experiences, the sensations still ignited a sense of wonder and stirred up mystery. I rarely detected happy kids, just the desperate ones, the tortured ones, the lost ones. And try as I might, I couldn't follow a scent without a sample to keep reminding me of its character, to separate my target from all the others. And the scent of a boy's soul always vanished soon after I detected it. Why? I had no idea.

After another minute, Emma's scent, faint and wispy, entered and joined the others. I mentally isolated it, closed my eyes, and concentrated on the flavor—fruity and smooth, like warm apple butter spread across freshly baked bread.

I whispered, "Be brave, Emma. I'm coming."

CHAPTER FOUR

CLUTCHING HER PAJAMA top, Deborah tiptoed out of her bedroom, guided by three dim night-lights stationed around the apartment's living room and kitchen. Earlier, loud noises had throttled her sleep, but exhaustion crooned a lullaby—*the sounds were all part of a dream, ignore them, you need to rest.* Yet, nagging suspicions kept prodding her subconscious mind. How long had she lain there debating with herself? Impossible to know. But motherly instincts finally held sway. The noises had to be investigated.

She walked to the apartment's entry door and tried the knob. The door swung open easily. Dim light revealed splintered wood in the jamb. A desperate call erupted from her gut. "Tommy?"

She rushed to his bedroom, threw open the door, and slapped the light switch. Tommy's bed was empty.

"Tommy?" She spun and turned on the living room light. *I need the app. My purse. Where is it?*

Her scan landed on the sofa near the entry door where her purse lay with its contents spilled. She leaped for it and searched inside. No sign of her phone.

Her heart pounding, she jumped to the wall phone and pressed Paula's speed dial. After three rings, a groggy whisper came through. "Deborah? What's wrong?"

"Tommy's gone. So's my phone." Deborah took a deep breath and forced her voice to settle. "I need you to pull him up on your locator."

"I'm on it. Two seconds."

Deborah tapped her foot. Sweat dampened her neck. Those seconds felt like forever. She glanced at a digital clock on the kitchen counter—5:18 a.m. Dawn was coming. That would help.

"Okay. I got him on the app. I'll be down there in two minutes. Gotta get my pants on."

"Me too. Just hurry." Deborah hung up, then called 911. When the operator answered, Deborah spoke breathlessly, "My son's been abducted—age seventeen, five-foot-nine, dark brown hair, wearing Star Trek pajamas. His name's Tommy Pritchard. Did you get that?"

"Yes, ma'am." The woman's voice was calm. "What is your location?"

Deborah rattled off her address along with Paula's number. "Listen, I can't stay here. I have to look for Tommy. That number is my sitter's mobile phone. GPS should be enabled. Find her, and you'll find us. Don't call unless you have to. We'll be using her phone to find my son. He's wearing a tracking device." She hung up and ran to her bedroom. She stripped off her pajamas, snatched a pair of jeans from a hanger, and pulled them on, then grabbed a T-shirt and yanked it down over her head.

She slid her feet into a pair of gym shoes, rushed back to the entry door, and took the car keys, driver's license, some cash, and a credit card from her purse. After sliding it all into her pocket, she stepped outside. Stooping, she began tying her shoes, but her fingers fumbled with the laces. As the cool early-morning air chilled her moist skin, she whispered, "Calm down, Deborah. For Tommy's sake, calm down."

As she continued tying, the image of her purse came to mind. Why would a kidnapper take a phone but leave the money and cards behind? That didn't make sense.

After fastening both bows, she rose. Footsteps hammered the nearby stairs from above, drawing closer. Paula appeared, scrambling down from the upper floor while looking at her phone. "He's close by. Probably faster on foot." She turned the corner and shot down the next flight of stairs.

Deborah dashed after her. Within seconds, they reached ground level and stopped in the complex's parking lot. Paula stared at the screen for a moment, then pointed toward the street. "That way."

As they ran abreast along an empty sidewalk, Paula called out updates. "He's three blocks away. ... Two blocks. ... One block." She pointed at a McDonald's restaurant at an upcoming corner. "There."

They broke into a sprint. As they ran across the parking lot, Deborah glanced from car to car. "Is he inside?"

Paula halted at the side door and looked through the window. "I see him."

Deborah joined her. Tommy sat at a booth, still wearing his Star Trek pajamas. An employee sat across from him with a phone to his ear.

They ran inside and stopped at the booth. Deborah threw her arms around Tommy and hugged him. "Thank God you're all right."

When she drew back, he smiled, his mouth filled with a biscuit. "Hi, Mom." He turned to Paula. "Hi, Paula."

The employee, a fortyish man wearing a tie with his uniform, pressed a button on his phone, slid out of the booth, and nodded at Deborah. "All's well that ends well."

She extended a hand. "Thank you."

As they shook hands, he smiled. "I'm Brandon, shift manager."

Paula's phone trilled. While she answered, Deborah focused on Brandon. "What happened? Did someone bring Tommy here?"

Brandon shook his head. "He came alone. Said something about chasing a guy who stole your phone. He was too excited to give any details, so I settled him down by asking about his pajamas. Worked like a charm."

"Thank you again." A sense of dizziness swept in, and her legs felt like rubber. "I need to sit."

Brandon helped her slide into the booth next to Tommy. "Breakfast is on the house for all of you."

She waved a hand. "No, thanks. We just need to go home."

"That was the police," Paula said as she ended the call. "They're right outside. They'll be in here in a second."

Deborah exhaled. "Interview time." She looked at Brandon and smiled. "All right. Coffee, please. Hot and black."

"Same here." Paula slid into the booth on the opposite side. "With five sugar packets. I need a boost."

Two police officers came in and spent ten minutes or so interviewing Tommy and Deborah. They ascertained that a man dressed in black entered the apartment around five a.m. The noise woke Tommy, and when he saw the man take his mother's phone and leave, he tried to follow the getaway car. He soon became lost and walked into the McDonald's for help.

After getting a description of the prowler, the police gave the trio a ride home and promised a visit from a CSI unit later. All three returned to Deborah's apartment and gathered at the dining table. While Paula set out cereal bowls and spoons, Deborah sat next to Tommy and spoke tenderly.

"Why did you chase that man instead of waking me up?"

He stared at the table. "So I could be like Dad."

"Like Dad? What do you mean?"

He lifted his head and made eye contact. "I want to be a hero."

"A hero? How is your dad a hero?"

"I'll show you." He got up and disappeared into his bedroom.

Deborah glanced at Paula. "Any ideas?"

As she poured Total cereal into the bowls, she shrugged. "Only that he named a LEGO man Mike and always uses him as the hero."

A moment later, Tommy approached carrying a closed scrapbook, a birthday gift Mike sent last year. Tommy had never mentioned it since that day.

He set the scrapbook next to his bowl and sat down. "Dad gave me this."

"I know." Deborah touched the faux-leather binding. "Did you ever use it?"

He nodded. "I thought about it when he called yesterday."

"And it made you sad, didn't it? That's why you always shut yourself in your room when he calls." She set a hand on his cheek. "Honey, it's good that you think your dad's a hero. I haven't told you everything that's going on about him, but—"

"No." He pushed her hand away. "That's not it."

"What's not it?"

"That's not why I go to my room."

"Then why do you go?"

He looked at Paula as she set a carton of milk and a small bunch of bananas on the table. He whispered, "Not while she's here."

Paula stretched her arms and let out a fake yawn. "I think I'll check the online store for orders. Then I'm hitting the sack."

"Can you dig up a spare phone for me?" Deborah asked. "Most of my contacts are backed up on the net. You know how to find them, right?"

"Sure thing, but why *most*?"

Deborah gazed at her inquisitive stare. This was no time to explain the secret emergency number. "Never mind. Please just do what you can."

"No problem. And I'll call maintenance about your door." Paula smiled and left.

Deborah looked again at Tommy. "Okay. Why do you go to your room when your dad calls?"

"To see what he did." He gestured wildly with his hands. "Every time he calls, a girl gets to go home."

"A girl gets to—" She narrowed her eyes. "What are you talking about?"

"What I've been working on." He opened the scrapbook to the first page. An Internet article unevenly cut from printer paper lay under a plastic sheet. A bold headline ran across the top—Guardian Angel Rescues Local Teen. The accompanying photo showed a girl in her parents' embrace. "See?" he said, pointing at the photo. "This is the first one."

"The first one? That's not the first time the Guardian Angel rescued someone."

"That's not what I mean." His voice stayed animated. "It's the first time I saw it. Every time Dad calls, I go to my room and look for the news."

"News of a rescued girl?"

He nodded. "About an hour after, most of the times. Maybe two hours sometimes."

Deborah pulled in her bottom lip. Should she just tell him or continue asking leading questions? "Well, what do you think it means?"

He gestured with a curled finger. "Come here."

She leaned close. "What?"

"I think …" He lowered his voice to a whisper. "I think Dad is the Guardian Angel."

Deborah copied his quiet tone. "What makes you think that?"

"Don't you see?" He waved his hands again, though he kept his voice low. "When he saves a girl, he thinks about Emily, so he calls home."

Deborah felt her mouth drop open. She snapped it shut. Tommy had scored high on pattern-recognition tests, but he had never combined that skill with family empathy before. "Well, Tommy, that's a plausible theory. Do you have any other evidence?"

"I post a lot on the Guardian Angel stuff. That's where—"

"You do?" A tight knot formed in her throat. "What do you post?"

"Everyone has ideas, so I posted mine."

Deborah gasped. "Oh, no, Tommy. You didn't post our names, did you?"

"Mom." Tommy's face flushed scarlet. "I'm not stupid. I know Dad has to keep his secret identity. Just like Clark Kent."

"Then what *did* you post?"

"That the Guardian Angel might have lost his own girl and never found her, so that's why he looks for other girls." Tommy grinned. "Everyone said my theory was the best."

Deborah stared past Tommy and whispered, "Your posts reveal who we are."

"No, I use a fake name. Everyone does."

She refocused on him. "Is it a message forum?"

"No." His tone turned sour. "I can't get into those."

She nodded. Forums were blocked on his computer, another safety boundary Mike insisted on. "Then where do you post your comments?"

"Places like CNN and Fox."

"I see." She turned the scrapbook to the last page. Under another plastic sheet protector, a printout featured a brief story about Amy Horowitz, a girl in Spokane rescued from sex traffickers yesterday. The color photo showed her standing between her parents, smiling and waving.

Deborah squinted at the girl's sweatshirt—way oversized. It looked like the green one Mike's mother gave him a few years ago. Could he have given it to her?

She scanned to the bottom where the comments section began, but a jagged scissors cut had sliced the entries off. An administrator taking care of the site could read the IP addresses of those who commented. It wouldn't take much detective work to track down a zealous Guardian Angel fan, someone posting in an unusually enthusiastic manner, which would be typical for Tommy.

The Guardian Angel's enemies could lean on the administrator to get that information, track all the big enthusiasts, and crosscheck to look for a missing girl in the family. There couldn't be more than a few. Then, using the IP addresses, they could find the candidates and search for the person who came up with the missing-girl theory.

"Mom? Are you all right?" Tommy prodded her arm. "Why aren't you talking?"

"Because I'm worried."

He grasped her hand. "Did I do something wrong?"

"No, honey. You're fine. I just have to figure out something."

He glanced from side to side as if someone might be watching. "Do you think Dad really is the Guardian Angel?"

She looked him in the eye. "If he is, I think he'd want us to keep it a secret."

"But if it's true, then …" Tommy looked at their clasped hands. "Then he really *is* my hero."

"He's mine, too, Tommy."

He regained eye contact, tears sparkling. "Then you should be with him. Right? I mean, you're married."

"I know." Her own tears welled. "But right now, it's just not possible. We've already talked about this."

His head drooped. "I was hoping at least one of us could be with him."

"You keep hoping. Maybe someday."

Tommy's gaze wandered to the doorway. "I guess we can't go back to bed. We can't lock the door."

Deborah looked at the splintered wood. Whoever wanted to break in had been really forceful. But why the urgency? Had someone pinpointed this apartment as a likely home of the Guardian Angel or his family? If so, why would he steal the phone and nothing else? Maybe to get more evidence before taking violent action? They probably thought the phone would contain contact information that might prove what they suspected. Then they could return later. Yet, no one but Mahoney knew Mike's direct phone number. And no one knew Mahoney's number except—

Heat rushed to her face. Mahoney's number was in her phone. The burglar could track him down.

She jumped from her seat. They had to leave. Right away. But Mahoney needed to know what was going on. How could she get his number?

"Mom? Are you okay? Your face is all red."

Closing her eyes, she mentally pushed Tommy away and concentrated. What did Mike say when he entered that number into her phone? Didn't he give her a memory prompt? What was it?

She clenched her fists. *Think, Deborah. Think.*

A mental image of Mike appeared as he tapped on her phone's screen, and his voice blended in. "It's the four digits of my birth year reversed, then your birth year in the right order. Then the two digits of the year we were married.

Tommy's voice intruded. "I'm pouring the milk, okay?"

"Go ahead." She opened her eyes and grabbed the wall phone. As she whispered the digital clue, she pressed the buttons and held the receiver to her ear. One ring. Two rings. Three. How odd. Mahoney answered right away last time. What good was an emergency number if the responder didn't answer?

After five rings, a click sounded and Mahoney's voice came through. "Please leave a message." A tone followed.

Deborah bit her lip. Should she leave a message? No. Her words might find their way to the wrong ears.

She hung up and began pacing as she recounted the events and her suspicions. The burglar got the phone, and Tommy spooked him. The burglar didn't want to hurt anyone because he wasn't sure of the Guardian Angel connection yet. Then he tracked the number to Mahoney and sent someone to mug him to get info on Mike.

As she took in a cleansing breath, she whispered to herself, "Mike's in trouble."

"Are you okay, Mom?" Tommy spoke while chewing. "Better hurry. Your cereal's getting soggy."

"I can eat it soggy." She grabbed the phone again and pressed Paula's speed dial button. As the phone trilled, a new thought came to light. If the prowler could act so quickly, might he have put a tap on her land line?

After three rings, Paula answered. "What's up?"

"Hey, um, could you come down again?"

"Sure. Why?"

"I'll tell you when you get here. I have to show you something."

"All right, mystery lady. But I haven't had time to call maintenance yet."

"Skip it. I need you now."

"Okay. Be there in five."

"Perfect." Deborah hung up and set a hand on Tommy's shoulder. "Get your suitcase. You and Paula are going to a motel."

"A motel?" He grimaced. "I hate motels."

"I know, honey, but you also hate sleeping without all the doors locked, and I can't get ours fixed right away."

He eyed the broken door for a moment before sighing. "Okay." He walked toward his room with sagging shoulders. "I hope it has a pool."

Deborah smiled. Tommy took that pretty well. His ability to adapt to change had improved, such a contrast to the hours of ceaseless wailing whenever Mike left on another rescue quest. Only sleep interrupted the fits of despair that sometimes lasted a couple of weeks. Most observers would think him childish, immature, emotionally unbalanced. But they would be wrong. They couldn't know how deeply he loved his father and how much pain he suffered at every departure.

Her unspoken words reverberated. Pain. Wailing. Depression. So familiar. Too familiar.

A tear crept down her cheek. Tommy wasn't the only one who suffered, though her own pain stayed quiet, suppressed, festering. For months and months she had sat at home, worrying, wondering, trapped by responsibility. And what had those emotions wrought?

A frigid woman who couldn't even accept a gift of flowers.

Time and time again she had excused her behavior by telling herself that the flowers were just Mike trying to bail out his family's sinking boat using a leaking bucket, that they served only to remind Tommy of him and incite another crying spell.

She shook her head. Her excuses were lies. She had been vindictive. Resentful. Bitter.

And maybe even jealous?

Deborah bit her lip hard. Why hadn't she seen this before? Such blindness. Such foolishness. Far worse than Tommy's innocent despondency. At least now that the mask had melted away she could do something about her stupid self-centeredness.

She clenched a fist. Mike needed help. And she would give it to him.

She picked up Tommy's scrapbook, strode to her bedroom, and opened the safe. After removing the money from the cash box, about a thousand dollars, she sat at the desk in front of her laptop and scrolled through her contact entries looking for Harold the Hacker. She had given him discounts on computer equipment more times than he deserved.

When she found his profile, she printed it out and grabbed the page from the printer. It was time to call in a favor.

CHAPTER FIVE

WITH DAWN STILL two or three hours away, I followed Emma's scent to SeaTac, a city that grew up around the international airport between Seattle and Tacoma. It carried a reputation as a hive for traffickers and their victims. If not for the Castillo case, I could cruise "the track" here, attempt to rescue some girls from their slave masters, then put them up in a local outreach program.

In times past in other cities, I had tried to convince downtrodden girls to leave the streets, but my efforts were often futile. Such was their fear of pimp retribution and their mistrust of men in general.

I drove along that track, a strip of Highway 99, hoping Emma's scent would strengthen, but the aromas of many troubled girls mixed in and confused my senses. It was like trying to extract a single ingredient in a complex stew even as a spoon stirred the pot.

As I cruised past grungy motels advertising hourly rates, I pulled over now and then and spoke to girls on the street, asking if they had heard about a girl named Emma. Some assumed I was a potential John. Most asked if I was a cop. A few cursed like sailors, some spoke with the diction of a grammar teacher, and some could barely put a sentence together, maybe because of drugs.

I met friendly girls, mean girls, apathetic girls, as well as older women who strutted their aging assets like an electric sign with half of its bulbs burned out. The diversity was far from unusual.

One truth I had learned over three years of searching for missing girls in places like this—every girl was unique. Stereotyping them was the hallmark of the ignorant, a way to dismiss them as harlots just doing business to make money and get high.

No. They were troubled human beings who walk the streets because they think they have to. I had yet to meet a girl who enjoyed the streets, loved "the life" as many of them called it. Maybe some would say they did, but it would be a lie or a symptom of insanity. No one could enjoy living at the border of hell.

Although the girls displayed unique qualities, they all expressed sympathy when I told them I was just a dad looking for his little girl, that I loved her no matter what, that I just wanted her to be safe.

Of course, this was all true. I was still looking for Emily. My Amy and Emma quests, along with many others, were sidetracks in a much longer obsessive journey.

I laughed at myself. Sidetracks? What a stupid thought. How could girls' lives be sidetracks? *Every girl is unique. Every girl is loved. Every girl needs a hero.* The words were still true. They had to be true. I couldn't entertain any other option.

Yet dark thoughts kept gnawing at the corners of my mind. *They're all sidetracks. If not for Emily's abduction, you wouldn't be here. Amy and Emma would be lost forever, and you would never know.*

The thoughts plunged like a knife, deep and true. I had no idea how to answer.

During my cruise, a pretty black girl, maybe twenty years old, hopped into my van before I could say a word. Her actress's smile probably fooled a hundred men into thinking she was glad to see them.

"Looking to party, honey?" she asked with a perky bounce.

I put on a weary frown, hoping to appear even sadder and more exhausted than I already was. "I'm afraid you won't like my answer. I'm looking for my daughter. She was kidnapped."

"Oh." She blinked at me. "Then why'd you stop? Obviously *I'm* not your daughter."

"I'm just hoping for information. Maybe she's been trafficked here." I held out a five-dollar-bill. "Just for a minute of your time?"

"Sure." She took the bill. "What's her name?"

"Emma. Emma Castillo."

She rolled her eyes upward and whispered, "Emma … Emma …" Then she looked at me again. "Doesn't ring a bell, but most girls change their names when they hit the streets."

I nodded. "I've heard that."

"How long has she been gone?"

"A few days."

"Oh. Well maybe she hasn't been turned out yet." She opened the door and hopped back to the pavement. Then she gave me an authentic smile. "Hey, good luck with finding her. I mean it."

"I know you do. Thanks." When she closed the door, I drove away.

And so went most of my interviews … until I met Starlight.

A white girl with pink hair to her shoulders strode toward me along the sidewalk, head down, a mobile phone in hand, her stare fixed on the concrete. I stopped at the side of the road and waited for her to draw near.

Short shorts exposed thin, bare legs on a five-foot-nothing frame, boosted by two-inch heels. A tight jacket accentuated a narrow torso and nearly flat chest. She had to be well under eighteen. Maybe she had been recently "turned out" and could give me a lead to pimps who were working with girls that young.

Keeping her head low, she passed right by without a glance. I pulled into the parking lot of a tobacco shop, got out, and jogged after her. "Excuse me," I called.

She stopped and turned. Fear in her eyes gave her the aspect of a pre-teen, but she quickly disguised it with a hand on her hip and a cocky tone. "What do you want?"

"Information." I halted a couple of steps away. "I'm looking for someone."

"I don't talk to cops." She spun and walked faster than before, laboring on her high heels.

"Wait. I'm not a cop." I caught up and kept pace at her side. "I'm looking for my daughter. She was kidnapped by a sex trafficker. I was told she might not have been turned out yet. She's about your age, so maybe you can point me in the right direction, since you're new yourself."

She stopped and faced me, though her eyes failed to make contact. She spoke in a near whisper, barely audible against the sound of a street sweeper droning nearby. "I'm not that new. I've been doing this a few months."

"New enough. Can you tell me anything? I'm desperate. Her name's Emma."

She finally looked me in the eye. Tears glistened in the light of streetlamps as her voice rode the edge of crying. "Listen, Mister, I don't know where your daughter is. I just got done with nine drunk guys at a party. I'm tired, I'm cold, and I want to go to bed. So unless you got money and want to be number ten, leave me alone."

When she turned to leave, I grasped her wrist. "Wait. Just give me one more minute."

Huffing a sigh, she gave me an impatient glare. "What?"

"First, what's your name and how old are you?"

She rolled her eyes before looking at me again. "I'm Starlight, and I'm eighteen."

"Well, Starlight. Unless ten plus two equals eighteen, I think you're lying."

"Go to hell."

She stalked away, but I caught up and kept pace with her again. "Starlight, listen. I know you hate what you're doing. I can get you off the street. Into a shelter. You'll have food, a bed, the option to go home if you want. And you won't have to service drunks or anyone else."

She halted again and glared at me. Her frame still looked twelve, but her face seemed older, worn-out, ravaged. "Look. You got no clue what it's like. If I go to a shelter and my man finds out, I'm dead."

"No, you'll be fine. I can make sure you're protected until—"

"Like you protected your daughter?" She drilled a new stare at me, then turned and marched away once more.

I watched as she faded into the night. What could I say? Her arrow plunged straight to the heart. I hadn't protected Emily. My own daughter. How could I possibly promise to protect a stranger?

My hands deep in my pockets, I strolled toward the minivan. The weight on my legs felt as if I were dragging a ball and chain. Some hero I was. I couldn't even convince an enslaved pre-teen to come with me. She preferred nights of sex with drunks over trusting me to get her to safety.

As I walked, I mentally muttered. If only I hadn't pointed out her lie. Maybe she would've stayed soft toward me. Maybe I should've said my daughter had run away instead of being kidnapped. If I hadn't been so stupid, Starlight might be with me now, searching for a place other than the street to call home, protected from the pimp who kept her in chains.

When I got back into the van and started it up, I lowered the window and kept it open. As I drove, I sniffed the air. Maybe finding Emma's trail would take my mind off this newest failure.

At the southern end of the track, I detected Emma's scent pretty strongly, but it quickly faded, as if she were on the move. I drove north again. The scent didn't return until I drew near the track's northern extremity, as if she was being transported at the same speed I was driving, but maybe imagination or exhaustion skewed my perception, or maybe a strong breeze stirred the stew pot. I just had to concentrate harder.

With renewed focus, I tried again. The scent led me to an off-brand motel where it stayed strong. I parked well away from a lighted sign that was supposed to flash the motel's name. With several bulbs burned out, only "Mote" was discernible.

I glanced at the dashboard clock—5:58. Still no word from Mahoney. By now he should have found a way to contact me. Walking into an ambush here wasn't likely, but I would feel a lot better knowing Mahoney had patched any security breach.

As I turned toward the phone, a thought-phantom shadowed my mind—Amy's traumatized expression. If I had taken action just five minutes sooner, I could have saved her from a hellish attack, and she wouldn't relive those nightmares—

With a shake of the head, I chased the phantom away. *Stop it. Beating yourself up won't do any good.*

I spoke to the phone. "Call Mahoney."

The phone rang again and again. With each repetition, I stared harder at the screen. Finally, voice mail picked up. This was a first.

"Mike, as you know, I take my phone everywhere, so either the battery's dead, or I'm dead. If the former, then I'll move mountains to get another battery, so if I don't call you within an hour, assume the latter. In that case, our whole system is compromised. Act accordingly."

The call disconnected.

I blinked. The breach was real. Sugar Daddy had obtained my schedule and sent a gunman to the Castillos' house. If he could get that information, he might also be able to find my home address.

My heart thumping, I cleared my throat and said, "Call Deborah."

The phone rang once, twice, three times. I imagined the kitchen and eating area filling with the sound. Of course, Deb wouldn't answer. I had to leave a message, but I couldn't just blurt out an announcement about the danger or even give her a return number to call.

When the answering machine kicked in, I spoke with a steady voice. "Deb, it's Mike. I got a call from my grandmother. She has a present for me. Can you pick it up? Thanks."

I disconnected. Since my grandmother died years ago, the cryptic message should clue her in that something was wrong. But how long would it take for her to get the message? Should I call her mobile phone?

I inhaled deeply and tried to settle my nerves. Emma's scent flowed in. New urgency to save her welled up. I couldn't dwell on problems that were out of my reach. I had to save Emma.

From my suitcase, I grabbed the same disguise I used at the pizza shop and applied the items. I had to be ready for anything, including an ambush.

With gloves on and my silenced Beretta holstered under my coat, I walked into the lobby and up to an unattended service desk. I tapped on a silver bell perched on the counter. From a back room, a dark-skinned man, perhaps Indian or Pakistani, shuffled into view. His eyes seemed curious as he blinked at me. "Yes?"

I smiled. "A work associate of mine checked in here recently. I called him on his cell phone and invited him and his daughter to go out to breakfast, but I forgot to get his room number. I tried calling him back, but there's no answer. Do you happen to remember a man and a girl traveling together?"

The clerk shifted to a computer on the desk. "What's the last name?"

"I just know him as Raphael. Like I said, he's an associate at work. Not really a friend. You'd probably remember the girl. About fourteen. Dark hair just past her shoulders."

He nodded. "I know who you're talking about. She didn't come inside, but I saw her. Looked like she was sleeping in the passenger seat. Leaning against the truck's window."

I took a guess. "Ah. Raphael's pickup. He's been complaining about it. Lots of engine trouble."

"Looked new to me." He pointed at the computer. "I found the room, but I can't tell you the number."

"Why not?" I leaned to try to get a view of the screen.

"He said for no one to disturb him." The clerk turned the monitor. "If you had seen him, you'd know why I'm doing exactly what he said."

"He is an intimidating fellow." I took another shot in the dark. "That beard makes him look pretty menacing."

"No beard. Just a mustache." The clerk squinted. "Are you a cop?"

"What makes you think that?"

"You're guessing. You don't really know this guy."

I raised a hand in surrender. "All right. You got me. I'm a cop."

"Thought so." The clerk looked at his computer monitor. "The guy's name is Stewart. Drove a black F-one-fifty. He's in room number …" He turned to me again, his eyes suspicious. "Wait. Let me see your badge."

"I don't carry one when I'm undercover."

"Makes sense, but I can't give you his room number unless you prove you're a cop."

"Yeah. I get that." I looked out the window at a swirl of windblown leaves. "All right if I hang around outside?"

"Go ahead. But watch out. A storm's coming." He nodded toward the back room. "Saw it on the weather report. Could hit at any minute."

"Fair warning. Thanks." I strode out to the parking lot. Above, the moon illuminated a line of dark clouds to the southwest. As I watched it roll this way, a stiff breeze buffeted me and made my coat flap.

I reboarded the minivan and drove it slowly around the motel's rectangular building, headlights on to look for the truck. I glanced between the exterior room entrances and the vehicles parked in front of the doors as well those on the opposite side of the lot. I passed by several pickups, some new and some black, but none that were both.

When I reached the back, I spotted a black F-150 parked on the motel-side of the lot. In the glow of a floodlight, water droplets shimmered on the freshly waxed surface.

Although a pair of empty spaces bordered the truck, I parked on the opposite side to keep my lights from shining into the windows. I hopped out, gently closed the door, and looked past the truck at the closest rooms—123, 125, and 127, with 125 immediately in front, the most likely candidate.

Keeping the truck between me and the rooms, I skulked closer. Since the kidnapper rented a room in the back, he likely wanted to stay as far from highway traffic as possible, not to sleep, but to listen for sounds of approach so he could wake up at the slightest provocation.

Wind whipped through the lot with a loud whoosh. Huge raindrops fell and splattered on the pavement. As a downpour commenced, I held a palm out and smiled. Noise. Just what I needed.

I gathered a handful of pebbles and hid behind the truck. Rain soaked my wig and made the prosthetic nose peel. I ripped the disguise off and slung it to the ground. It wouldn't do any good now. I just had to make sure no one could get a photo of me.

I tossed a pebble at room 125's door. It struck sharply and bounced away. No one responded. After a few seconds, I tossed one at room 123 with the same result.

As rain seeped into my clothes, the wind brought a shiver. I couldn't keep this up for long. I tossed another pebble at 125, harder this time. It clicked against the door, loud enough to reach my ears even over the drumming rain.

A light flicked on inside. The door swung open. A bulky shirtless man stalked out and looked around, a thick mustache easily visible. He had to be Stewart. Barefoot and wearing jeans, he frowned at the swirling rain and muttered something unintelligible.

I drew my Beretta. The moment Stewart turned and headed toward the door, I rushed him and cracked the gun butt against his head while bulldozing him into the room. When he toppled to the carpet, I fell, slid over him, and rolled past two beds to a wall.

Breathless, I looked across the dim room at his motionless body. Good. I didn't have to fire a shot.

Someone grabbed my hair and jerked me upward. A meaty hand slapped the gun away, sending it flying toward the closer bed. It landed on a blanket next to a sleeping form.

A fist slammed into my chin. I collapsed to the floor and looked up. A bearded man nearly as big as Stewart stalked toward me, a knife in hand. "Who are you?"

"Dale Rivers." I climbed to a crouch and forced a hard shiver and a plaintive tone. "I thought … this was my wife's room. I thought she was … having an affair, so I followed her—"

"Liar."

He launched a leaping kick. His toes crashed into my chin. My head snapped back, and I fell on top of Stewart.

He stood over me and pointed the knife. "You get one more chance. Are you a cop?"

"Okay. Okay." Now splayed over Stewart, I held up a blocking hand and gasped for breath. "I'm not a cop. I'm an enforcer from the car dealer. Stewart didn't make his payment on the Ford, so I came to get it back. I slipped in the rain and fell over him." I gave him a scared-puppy look. "I'm really sorry."

"He didn't buy it from a dealer. He bought it from me." He clenched the knife in a fist, ready to strike. "Now you're dead."

As he thrust, I knocked the blade with one fist and punched him in the face with the other. Something popped. His body dropped on me, and the blade plunged into my shoulder. Pain tore down my arm. I clawed at his face, but he didn't move.

Wincing, I pushed his hefty body to the side. As he rolled, the knife jerked out, still clutched in his fist. New pain racked my body, but I managed to climb to a standing position. Blood oozed from the searing hot wound in my shoulder.

I looked at the bed. Emma sat there with the gun poised to shoot. Smoke curled from the end of the barrel's sound suppressor.

I lifted a gloved hand. "Emma. Don't shoot. I'm here to rescue you."

Topless and covered from the waist down by the blanket, she stared at me as if in a stupor. "How do ..." Her speech slurred as her lips labored to spit out the words. "You know ... my name?"

"Emma Castillo." I forced a calm voice in spite of the pain. "Your mom and dad sent me. They gave me your diary. It's purple. Your favorite color."

She set the gun down and pulled the blanket up over her chest with a jittery hand. "Can … can I go home now?"

"Very soon." With a palm pressed against my shoulder, I staggered to the door and closed it. The storm noise faded. Cold air brought a hard shiver that sent new peals of pain through my body. The blade hadn't pierced more than an inch, but it must have hit a nerve. At least it was my left shoulder. I could manage.

After peeling off my wet coat and laying it on the unoccupied bed, I turned the heater on and scanned the room. Two empty pizza boxes and three paper drink cups with protruding straws lay scattered next to the bathroom, and a pile of wrinkled clothes sat in front of a closet alcove.

As I shuffled to the clothes, I looked at Emma. Now clutching the blanket tightly around herself, she seemed more lucid. "Do you know where your clothes are, Emma?"

She shook her head. "They hid them from me … so I wouldn't try to get away."

I picked through the pile of clothes—men's shirts, pants, and underwear. "Do you know how long you've been here?"

"Maybe three days. I'm not sure. I've been so dizzy."

I visually searched the room for pill bottles or other signs of drugs. "Did they give you pills?"

She nodded. "Last night before bed. Not since."

"Then maybe your head will clear soon." I wasn't sure how to ask the next question, but since her diary indicated her knowledge of the issue, I just blurted it out. "Did they bring men here to have sex with you? To rape you, I mean?"

Her face slowly twisted into a mournful mask. She clenched her eyes shut and nodded again, tears seeping through.

I found a duffle bag at the bottom of the pile. Emma's jeans lay inside along with a bra but no panties, shirt, or shoes. "Do you know how many men?"

Her voice quivered through spasms. "I think … maybe ten? But not all of them raped me. Maybe six of them. Some didn't want to … because I'm having my period."

"Did these two rape you?" I gestured toward the bodies on the floor.

Emma nodded.

I lifted the jeans and bra and set them on the bed. "Are you bleeding now?"

"I'm not sure." She reached under the blanket and pulled out a T-shirt covered with blood. She squinted at the shirt as if confused. "I think … the bleeding stopped. But I'm a mess. They … they didn't have any pads for me. So I stuffed my shirt in—"

"I get the picture." A growl erupted from my gut, but I squelched it. "I need to get you to a hospital."

"Can I get cleaned up first? I'm all bloody and sticky."

"You'd better not. If their penetration tore anything, soap and water might burn, and the police will want to collect evidence."

Her mournful face returned. She tried to speak through an emerging sob. "I still smell them. It's awful. It makes me want to throw up."

I gazed into her sad eyes. Of course I wanted the police to catch the other rapists, and DNA evidence might be the only way to convict them, but how could I tell a weeping, violated little girl that she had to carry the scums' filthy semen until someone could examine her? "I understand." I picked up the gun and slid it into its holster. "I'll help you get to the bathroom."

Something grabbed my ankle and jerked my feet out from under me. When I fell to the floor, Stewart lunged for my gun. We both grabbed the butt at the same time. As we fought for control, it slid from the holster. I thrust my knee into his groin. The moment he flinched, I pressed the barrel against his chest and pulled the trigger.

The gun popped, muffled by the silencer and his body. He grunted, then clawed at my face. I fired again. A second bullet thumped into his chest. He stared at me for a moment, then closed his eyes. His arms fell limp.

I peeled his hand away from the gun and checked his pulse. A slight tremor weakened, then stopped. Still on the floor, I looked up at Emma. She stared, wide-eyed and pale, and whispered, "Is he dead?"

"He is." I rose to my feet, my legs shaking. "I had to shoot him."

"I know." She licked her quivering lips. "I … I shot the other one, didn't I?"

I nodded. "But it's all right. You did it to save my life."

She looked down at her lap and cried. Her head bobbed in time with her spasms.

Trying to hold back my own tears, I helped her wrap the blanket around herself, slid my arms under her, and carried her to the bathroom. When I leaned over to set her in the tub, pain spiked anew in my shoulder. I concealed a grimace with a tight smile.

Still wearing gloves to avoid leaving fingerprints, I turned on the light, plucked a towel from a rack above the toilet, and gathered the soap and shampoo from the sink counter. I laid them all on the toilet lid within her reach and gazed again at her sad brown eyes. "Can you manage by yourself now?"

She inhaled a halting breath. "I think so."

"Okay. The water should wake you up pretty quick. When you're alert, check your privates to see if there's any injury. And take your time. You'll feel better if you get as clean as you can. I'll bring your clothes in a minute."

"Thank you."

I grabbed another towel, exited, and closed the door. After tossing the towel onto the bed, I took off my gloves and looked at the two bodies on the floor. Stewart was dead, but what about the knife-wielding man?

I leaned over and checked his neck pulse. No heartbeat. Blood covered his chest and drained to the floor. Apparently Emma's shot pierced his back and exited on the other side. By the grace of God the bullet missed me.

While the sound of running water emanated from the bathroom, I holstered my gun, sat on Emma's bed, and stared at a framed picture on the wall, a watercolor rendition of a farm scene—log fences, cornstalks, a tractor, and parents and children wearing straw hats and shucking ears of corn over a wicker basket.

Letting my thoughts wander, I placed myself in the scene. What would it be like to spend peaceful years plowing fields, sowing seeds, and harvesting produce? To relish the joys of getting dirty, sweating through manual labors, and walking into the house to grateful smiles and welcoming arms, far, far removed from this madness?

With what I knew now, I could never go there. Cries of agony would always call me back. The scent of tormented souls would never let me rest.

CHAPTER SIX

I tore myself away from the reverie and looked at the bathroom. Emma would be a while yet. I put the coat and gloves on again and left the room, taking care to keep the door from latching. I jogged to the minivan through steady rain. After collecting the two suitcases and the first-aid kit, I hurried back, set the door's locking bolt, and laid the suitcases on the bed.

Water continued running in the bathroom, so I stripped down, dried off with the towel, and put on a fresh set of underwear, pants, and socks. I stood in front of the mirror and examined the shoulder wound. Blood oozed from a one-inch vertical slice—not gruesome, but painful enough to stiffen the joint.

Staying shirtless to give the wound some air, I sifted through the girls' items in the purple suitcase and found a black T-shirt, a sanitary pad, and white panties that looked Emma's size, but no shoes. It seemed that kidnappers often tossed shoes away to discourage their victims from running.

When the water shut off, I took the new items along with her jeans and bra and tapped on the door. "I'm going to open the door a crack and set your clothes on the floor."

"Okay. Thank you again."

I did so and closed the door, then wiped the knob with a shirt I found on the floor. Emma's voice sounded crisper, more alert. The drugs were wearing off. Would she suffer the usual trauma drama? Time would tell.

I found a gauze pad and a bandage in the first-aid kit and sat on the bed closer to the exit door. With one hand, I tried to press the pad against the wound while wrapping the bandage, but with my left arm barely moveable, my efforts failed miserably.

Soon, the bathroom door opened. Emma poked her head out. Her piercing gaze found its way to me. She smiled and said, "Hi."

I smiled in return. It felt so strange being undisguised and facing someone who knew about my profession. Yet, this girl seemed special, a trusting soul who displayed an unusual level of confidence. "Hello, Emma. How are you feeling?"

"Kind of weak."

"Same here. One of those guys stabbed me." I tried again to maneuver the bandage, but it slipped from my hand and fell to the floor.

"Here. Let me." Her hair wrapped in a towel and her feet bare, Emma stepped out of the bathroom. The jeans fit perfectly, of course, but the T-shirt was too small. The hem didn't quite reach her pants. She tiptoed around the corpses, grimacing as she passed them.

She sat to my left on the bed. Narrowing her eyes, she studied the wound. "Let's see what we can do with this." She rummaged through the first-aid kit and withdrew a tube of ointment, a spool of white tape, and a small pair of scissors. "This is an antibiotic," she said, showing me the tube. "I have to rub it over the wound. It'll probably hurt."

"Go ahead." I smiled at her manner—speaking to me as if I were a child. "And thank you."

"You're welcome." She squeezed out a dab and massaged it into the cut. As I winced, she kept her stare on her work. The tiny smile reappeared. "I help at a nursing home. I've watched the nurses do stuff like this lots of times."

When she made eye contact, I gave her an appreciative nod. "I'm glad to have a skilled nurse."

Her little smile grew. "It's not hard." She laid a gauze pad on the wound. "Hold this." While I held it, she cut strips of tape and applied them to the pad's edges. She then wrapped an ace bandage around my shoulder and under my armpit multiple times until she ran out of material. Using a metal clip from the kit, she hooked the end of the bandage in place. "Try it out."

As I rotated my shoulder, she studied her work with a furrowed brow. "It looks like it'll hold."

"I think so." Still sitting, I turned to my suitcase and withdrew a dry polo shirt. As I raised my arms to slip it over my head, I grimaced. The pain was pretty intense but not excruciating.

Emma grabbed the hem and helped. When she pulled it down to my waist, she folded her hands in her lap and whispered, "Thank you for saving me. I'm sorry you got hurt."

I copied her low tone. "I would risk a thousand stabs to save a wonderful girl like you."

"Well … thank you again." She intertwined her fingers, staring at them as if gathering the courage to say something. Then she looked at me and whispered, "Are you the Guardian Angel?"

I held my breath. Such an admission seemed impossible only a few hours ago, but with my cover likely blown to pieces, did it really matter? Bringing comfort to Emma mattered more than anything. "Yes. I am."

"That explains a lot." She shifted her gaze to the bodies and shuddered. "I'm glad you just got a cut. Those guys could have killed you."

"But they didn't, thanks to you." I focused on her hands, still fidgeting in her lap. "Were you hurt at all?"

She kept her stare on the bodies. "I'm fine."

I angled my head to look at her eyes. Tears sparkled in each one. "I'm not trying to get too personal. I'm just asking because men like those might have been rough, and younger girls can get injured and bleed, especially virgins."

She swallowed so hard, the sound reached my ears. "Um … they weren't the first."

I tensed in spite of my efforts to stay cool. "Oh. … I see."

She looked at me, her eyes wide. "It's not like that. I never wanted to. He made me do it." Traces of grief lined her face as her body quivered ever so slightly.

"Your father?"

A tear fell to her cheek. She firmed her lips and nodded.

"Did he threaten you if you told anyone?"

Again she nodded, her entire face taut.

More questions begged to be asked, but they felt like added abuse. Maybe it was time to let her be. "You don't have to say another word, Emma. You're amazingly brave and strong. I've met a lot of sexually abused girls, and most of them are withdrawn, inward, trusting no one, especially men. But you're outgoing and eloquent. You go to nursing homes. You help the elderly—"

"It's all an act." Emma burst into tears and covered her face with her hands. "It's all just an act."

I set my hand just above her back. I ached to touch her, hold her, comfort her, but what would physical contact mean to her right now? I withdrew my hand. "Emma, take your time. Cry all you want. I understand."

"No, you don't." She lowered her hands and looked at me, her eyes red and wet. "He said he'd kill me. He said he'd kill my mom." She drew in a convulsive gasp. "If I even … even gave a hint." She swallowed, steadying her voice. "So I pretended. I put on an act. Going to the nursing home was part of it. I mean, I liked helping them and all that, but I did it to … to take my mind off it. And it made people think I was normal. Nobody could guess what was going on. It was the only way to make sure my mom and I would be safe."

I nodded. Her diary. She wanted to be an actress, and she was already living life on a hellish stage. "So why are you telling me now?"

She sniffed hard. "So you'll understand why I'm not hurt. My father was rough sometimes, and I guess I got used to it." She ran a finger along the bedspread and followed the path with her eyes. "And because I think maybe you're … well … different, I guess."

"That I'll protect you if your father finds out you told someone?"

As new tears coursed down her cheeks, she kept her gaze on the bedspread. "Well … I was hoping."

"Of course I'll protect you." Again my arms begged to embrace her, but I couldn't. Not without her permission. At least she had opened up a bit. Maybe I could risk another question. "How did you keep from getting pregnant? That is, if you did avoid it."

"He made me take birth-control pills." She continued tracing. "He keeps them hidden somewhere."

The scoundrel's words returned to mind. *Dogs sniffing for blood. They're all in heat. Every one of them.* The urge to crush his throat tightened my fingers.

Emma looked at the bodies again. "What are you going to do about them?"

"I'll let the police deal with them."

Emma slid off the bed and stood in front of me. After brushing away tears with a sleeve, she lifted her brow. "Are you going to take me home now?"

"After I scrounge around a bit for clues. I want to find out who their contacts are. If they have phones or a computer, we can get them and leave."

"Stewart had a phone." Emma walked to the night table between the two beds and lifted a castoff shirt, revealing a mobile phone. "Here it is."

"That'll do. Let's go."

I slid the phone into my pocket, put on my gloves, and grabbed my suitcase and coat while Emma carried the smaller suitcase and first-aid kit. We stepped out to the covered sidewalk, leaving the door unlatched. Rain poured on the parking lot, and water streamed down from the edge of the protective overhang.

"Oh. I forgot." Emma took the towel from her hair and tossed it back into the room. "Ready." Wet hair draped her shoulders and painted spots on her T-shirt, nothing compared to the drenching that downpour would deliver.

I hung a "Do Not Disturb" sign on the knob and closed the door. "I'll take our things to the van, then I'll come back and carry you."

Emma blinked. "Carry me?"

"Right. It's raining so I thought maybe you'd want …" I let my words trail off. They sounded bizarre, like babbling nonsense from a demented old man. "Sorry. I don't know where I was going with that. Just wait here while I pull the van in close."

"Sure. No problem."

I draped the coat over my head and shoulders and ran across the parking lot with my suitcase in hand. After boarding the minivan and stowing the suitcase, I drove to the building, stopped parallel to the walk, and pressed the button that opened the sliding side door.

Emma dashed into the rain, her head low and her bare feet raising splashes on the wet pavement. Still carrying the smaller suitcase and the first-aid kit, she jumped in. When she settled on the back bench, I pushed the button again and drove around the motel toward the front of the lot.

I resisted the temptation to look back. I had now killed four men in the past twenty-four hours. Of course they deserved far worse than death, but delivering the penalty wasn't my mission. I just wanted to rescue girls from those monsters' filthy paws.

When we pulled onto the road, I set the GPS to return to the Castillos' house and looked back at Emma as she sat on the bench, hugging herself and shivering.

"Scared?" I asked.

"Just cold."

I turned the heater up a notch and took off my gloves while watching her in the rearview mirror. "It should get warmer in a few minutes."

Her brow arched up. "Do you mind if I sit up front?"

"To get closer to the warm air?"

"That's one reason." Without waiting for a reply, she crawled to the front, sat down, and buckled her seatbelt, the first-aid kit in her lap.

I glanced at her through the corner of my eye. Her trust in me felt good. I had to respond in kind. This beautiful girl, this abused angel, needed real love, someone who would give and not take, someone who would live for her … sacrifice for her … die for her. I had to find the scoundrels who initiated her torture. "So tell me what happened at the party. Who kidnapped you and how?"

"Oh. Well, I don't remember much." She looked at her lap. "I danced a little, but the music was too loud, and I got a headache. So I went to the dining room where the food and punch were. The chaperones took turns hanging out there because it wasn't so noisy."

A siren wailed to the rear. I turned off the main road into a residential area. The GPS recalculated, giving me a route that stayed off the main roads.

"So you had chaperones?"

She nodded. "My father wouldn't have let me go otherwise. A man and a woman. My mom knew the woman, so she thought it would be all right."

"Okay. Go on."

She ran a finger along the red cross on the first-aid kit's lid. "While I was drinking some punch, a guy I know came off the dance floor, kind of sweating, so he got some punch, and he started talking to me, saying how pretty he thinks I am."

"Did his compliments make you feel good?"

She kept her eyes averted. "Well … yeah. Shouldn't they?"

"Of course. I'm just trying to follow the emotions as well as the story." I nodded. "Go on. I'll stop interrupting so much."

"Well, the guy was facing away from the chaperone … the woman chaperone … and he unbuttoned the top of his shirt and whispered something about how hot it was. He said it was cooler outside, and he wanted me to go out there with him. I thought that would be all right, so I went."

"Wait. Were you still holding your punch?"

She rolled her eyes upward for a moment before looking at me again. "No, he carried it for me."

"I see. And did you drink it after he gave it back to you?"

"I think so."

"Go on."

"The last thing I remember was getting real dizzy. The guy called the chaperone, and then I guess I passed out. I woke up riding in Stewart's truck with my hands and feet tied."

"So Daniel and the chaperone were the last to see you at the party."

"How did you know his name?"

"I read it in your diary. You were pretty groggy when I told you your parents gave it to me."

"I guess I was. I don't remember that at all."

"I just read a couple of pages. Mostly the last entry."

"Okay." Her face flushed red. "Anyway, yeah, as far as I know, they were the last to see me, but I don't think Daniel was involved. The chaperone is his mother, so—"

"Never mind. I figured it out. Daniel and his mother worked together. He spiked your punch while she called for Stewart who hauled you out before anyone knew what happened."

Emma's voice rose. "I don't believe it. She's a woman. A mother."

"Trust me. Lots of women are involved in trafficking. Even mothers."

"But why?"

"For the money they can get from selling a sex slave. To please their men." I shrugged. "Maybe to please her son. Who knows?"

Emma gasped. "While I was unconscious, do you think Daniel—"

"Not a chance." I shook my head hard even though I wasn't sure. "He's a kid. He would have been grossed out. You know. The blood."

"I guess so." She stared straight ahead and whispered, "A mother."

While she contemplated, I concentrated on our surroundings. We were closing in our Emma's neighborhood. I had to be watchful for police or media.

Ahead and to the right, a police helicopter hovered just above the tree line, maybe two miles away. I decelerated and looked at the GPS map. That area was pretty close to the Castillo house. Something was up.

I pulled over to the side of the residential road and parked, my eyes fixed on the chopper.

"Why did we stop?" Emma asked.

"Just a second." I turned the radio on and pressed the seek button until the frequency stopped at a news channel. After a weather report and traffic update, a news sequence began.

"A manhunt is on for the killer of a Seattle couple. Residents in and around Cedar Park are warned to stay indoors—"

"Cedar Park is *my* neighborhood," Emma said.

I nodded, trying to listen through the interruption.

"In a prepared statement, the police department said that investigators have obtained an eyewitness account that has turned them toward a suspect who is not yet in custody. The department declined to elaborate beyond their original account that the male murder victim shot and wounded an intruder and reported the incident to a nine-one-one dispatcher, but before police could arrive, the intruder apparently returned and killed the husband and wife."

Emma murmured, "That's so sad."

My heart racing again, I turned off the radio. The poor girl was an orphan now. How could I possibly break the news to her?

Staring straight ahead, I battled to keep my composure. "Since it's dangerous in Cedar Park, maybe we should go somewhere else. Do you have any relatives in another neighborhood? I can take you there."

She shook her head. "Not in Seattle. I have grandparents in Dallas, and an aunt in Houston. We moved here from Texas three months ago so my dad could take a job at Microsoft. We don't know many people yet. It's hard to make friends."

"Emma …" I slid my hand into hers. "Emma, I have bad news."

"What? What could be worse than …" She gestured with her head toward the rear, apparently indicating the motel. "Than that?"

"Just let me make sure." I took my phone from the dashboard mount and called up the Internet browser. After locating a Seattle news site, I found the murder story in the headlines. The second paragraph revealed the tragic truth. I leaned toward Emma and read out loud while she looked on. "The victims' names have now been released. Rick and Angela Castillo died of multiple gunshot wounds—"

Emma gasped. "Mama? Daddy?" She stared at me for a moment as if trying to process an avalanche of thoughts. Then she covered her face and sobbed.

I reached and rubbed her back, but she shrugged my hand away and shot a searing glare at me as she spoke through spasms. "Did you kill … kill them? You were there. You read my … my diary. You must have been there."

"Of course I didn't kill them." My words blurted out unleashed, unguarded. Her automatic reaction to assume the worst was understandable. Why should she trust any man?

I took a deep breath and continued in a calm tone. "I was there to get what I needed to track your scent, but I left when the murderer came the first time. Your father shot him. I thought he and your mother were safe, so I left."

She half closed an eye. "How do I know … you're telling the truth?"

"I risked my life to save you. I took a knife to the shoulder."

Without looking at me, she dropped the first-aid kit to the floorboard, crawled to the back bench, and sat with her feet up, her arms hugging her legs.

"Emma." I reached for her hand, but she jerked it away. "Emma, you can trust me. I—"

"Why should I?" A tear dripped to her chest as she spat out her words. "Maybe you wanted … a … a sex slave for yourself. Maybe you're … you're just like my dad after all."

Pain stabbed my heart. I tightened my jaw and fought back the urge to shout my credentials, recount the number of girls I'd rescued. Savage grief had scrambled this poor girl's thoughts. After being drugged and then raped multiple times, it was no wonder she was becoming hysterical.

"Okay. All right." Breathing deeply to stay calm, I got out of the van, reentered through the side door, and sat next to her on the bench seat.

She kept her head low, but her eyes followed my every move.

"Now that we're both here …" I tapped on my phone's screen and looked for a police report. "Let's find some evidence."

She locked her stare downward as I browsed. After a minute or so, I found the murderer's description, provided by Mr. Castillo while on the phone with the dispatcher—short, stocky, and bearded. I turned the phone toward her. "This is how your father described the gunman."

She brushed a tear and read the screen, her eyes darting back and forth. When she finished, she looked up at me. New tears streamed as she whispered, "I'm sorry."

"You have nothing to be sorry about, Emma." I set the phone down and opened my arms.

With a cry of grief, she slid over and climbed into my lap. We wept in each other's embrace. Warmth flowed across my skin—the magical touch, my reason for living. The scent of her soul billowed and caressed my senses. She was so much like Emily … so much like my beloved baby girl. And this precious girl needed a daddy.

Each time a sob shook her body, I whispered a soothing phrase.

"I love you, Emma."

"I'll take care of you."

"You're safe with me."

When her spasms settled, I kissed her cheek and helped her off my lap and back to her seat. I retrieved the phone and brought up the dialer. "I can contact your grandparents or your aunt. Put you on a flight and—"

She shook her head. "No."

"No? But you said you have grand—"

"*You* said you'd take care of me." She pushed a finger into my thigh. "I want to stay with you."

"But your relatives will want you to come be with them."

Spasms still throttled her words. "No ... no they won't. They quit speaking to my mother and me when we ... started going to church. I don't want to be with people like that." She wiped away another tear. "Besides, I'm ... I'm missing. They'll just think I'm dead. So you can keep me."

An adrenaline rush made my heart thump. A new daughter? If only it could be true. But keeping her would be illegal. Unethical. Immoral. Wouldn't it? "Listen. We'll think about it. Right now I have some calls to make to check on my own family."

Her shoulders sagged. "I never thought about your family. I'm sorry."

"Don't worry about it." I punched the speed dial for the home phone. After getting voice mail, I hung up and dialed Deb's mobile phone.

A man answered. "Hello."

I tightened my grip on the phone. "Who is this?"

"Are you Mike?"

"Who wants to know?"

"Don't play games. I saw the blocked ID message, so you must be Mike. Hang on, I need to get my boss on three-way. He's in a different town."

Emma slid closer, hip to hip. She could probably hear every word.

A few seconds later, a new voice came on. "Mike Pritchard, so good of you to call."

"Who are you?" I growled. "Why do you have my wife's phone?"

Emma let out a little gasp. She then folded her hands and bowed her head, her lips moving silently.

"The gentleman who has your wife's phone procured it during an early morning visit to your apartment. So much for your meticulous security."

I seethed. He had to be Sugar Daddy. "What do you want?"

"Let's just say the tables have turned. I am now the pursuer, and you are the pursued." He laughed. "Yes, the Guardian Angel has lost a few feathers in his wings and will soon be grounded."

"Cut the crap. You sound like a villain from a bad movie. Just tell me what you want."

"The answer is simple. I want you. You see, you have retrieved quite a number of girls, though they are now a bit worse for the wear. Yet you retrieved them nonetheless. You're a true hero and celebrated nationwide. Your success, however, is easy to explain. Up until now you have been dealing with penny-ante ruffians who have no idea how to do battle with a man of your admittedly stellar abilities. But now you have stepped into my territory and trampled on the wrong toes. Simply put, I will destroy you."

"Destroy me?" I added a disdainful huff. "Your first assassin in Seattle couldn't. What makes you think the next one will do any better?"

"Oh, I don't need to destroy you personally. I have your wife, Deborah, your son, Tommy, and your … what do you call him … rescue manager? Mahoney, I think his name is."

My throat narrowed. "Prove it. Let me talk to my wife."

"She is not with my associate right now, but perhaps Mr. Mahoney will be able to provide sufficient proof. My associate will put him on."

While I waited through the pause, my hands grew jittery. I glanced at Emma again. Still in a prayer posture, she twisted her intertwined fingers. I whispered a prayer of my own. "Give me wisdom. Give me strength. Give me victory over my enemies."

"Mike? It's Mahoney." His voice and accent were unmistakable. "Are you all right?"

"Yeah. I'm fine. What's going on? Have you heard from Deb and Tommy?"

"This … uh … gentleman says he has them. He let me call your apartment complex's manager so I could ask him to check your unit. The door jamb was busted, and no one was home. And since he has her phone … well. You add it up."

"Have you seen Deb with him?"

"I'm blindfolded, so I can't see anything. I haven't heard anyone else, but if I give you any more info, I think he might break another one of my fingers."

"*Another* one?"

"Yeah, he was trying to persuade me to give him your mobile number, but I told him I didn't know it, that you always called me, and I never called you. But don't worry. It's just a pinky. It'll heal. Anyway, they got your Seattle assignment from my phone. They're satisfied for now."

"Sorry this is happening, Mahon—"

"So, Mike," Sugar Daddy said, "I will be happy to free your family and your manager in exchange for your surrender. As you noted, I sent an assassin who failed, but since you no longer have an accessible schedule, I have no way to try again. That's why I have to resort to this method."

My muscles tensed. I could barely move my taut lips. "Just spit it out. What are the terms?"

"They're quite simple. I noticed on your alternate missions list a certain suspected stable in Spokane. I am in that city now. I will meet you there at … let's say … sunrise tomorrow. Come unarmed. Come alone."

"What do you plan—"

"And by the way, I also have Emily. She's been a popular treat with my customers for quite a while. When you come, I'll tell you more about her living nightmare."

The call terminated.

I stared at the screen. My fingers locked. My mind went blank. My tightening chest forced me to gasp for breath.

A cool hand slid into mine. "Mike?"

I forced my head to turn toward … a girl? Who was she? Where were we?

"Are you all right?" The girl caressed my hand. "I heard him call you Mike. I don't know what else to call you other than Guardian Angel."

I whispered the name. "Guardian Angel." As if shouted from heaven, the words broke through and blew away a cloud of fog. Still feeling stiff, I whispered, "He said he has Emily."

"Who's Emily?" Emma tilted her head. "I heard you mention Deb and Tommy. Who are they?"

"Deb's my wife. Tommy's my son. And Emily ..." I swallowed hard. "Emily's my daughter. She was kidnapped by ..." I couldn't say it.

"Kidnapped? How long ago?"

"Three years."

Emma's mouth dropped open. For a long moment we both stayed silent, just staring at each other. Finally, she caressed my knuckles with her thumb and spoke softly. "Is that how long you've been rescuing girls? You've been looking for Emily at the same time?"

I nodded, barely able to keep my voice in check. "Something like that." I let out an odd laugh that sounded insane even to my own ears. "You know, you're a lot like Emily. If you two were together, I'm not sure I could tell one of you from the other."

A tear fell to her cheek. "You miss your daughter a lot, don't you?"

I nodded again. I couldn't breathe another word. My own tears dripped. Then, like a dam bursting, sobs poured forth. I cried like a baby, gasping and heaving.

Emma climbed back into my lap and embraced me. As I continued weeping bitterly, she rubbed my shoulder and whispered, "I love you, Mike. I'll take care of you. You're safe with me."

CHAPTER SEVEN

DEBORAH SAT IN a booth at the McDonald's, a canvas bag at her side as she spun a new mobile on the table. With Tommy and Paula safely checked in at a nearby motel, the freedom to do something to help Mike felt good, like being released from a locked room.

Harold the Hacker sat on the opposite bench with his laptop open. Dressed in baggy jeans and a torn black T-shirt and sporting shaggy gray hair and beard, he didn't look much like the stereotypical buttoned-down geek, but he knew his line of work.

As he stared at his screen, he typed at a blurring rate. Every few seconds, he stopped and grabbed a fry from a box, stuffed it into his mouth, and continued typing.

After a couple of minutes, he stroked his beard. "That phone number is a strange bird. It's registered to a dead lady here in Fort Lauderdale."

"So Mahoney's here." She tapped a finger on the table. "Right here in this town?"

"Well, it's registered here. That doesn't mean Mahoney's here. A mobile phone can be anywhere. I just have to find her address so we'll have a place to start looking."

"But how can it be in Fort Lauderdale? The number doesn't have a local area code."

"That's a toll-free prefix, not an area code."

Deborah's cheeks warmed. "Now I feel really stupid."

"Don't. It's a fairly new prefix." He typed for several seconds, then touched his screen. "Bingo. Got it." He turned the laptop toward Deborah. "See the pushpin? That's the registration address. But it doesn't mean he's there, like I said before."

She studied the red pushpin's location and typed the address into a map on her phone. "That's about six miles away."

"Ah. You're handy with maps. I should have known." Harold turned the laptop his way. "Anything else I can do for you?"

Deborah withdrew Tommy's scrapbook from her bag, set it on the table facing Harold, and turned page after page. "These are articles about the Guardian Angel's accomplishments."

"Cool. I love this guy." He pressed a finger on an article, stopping Deborah's turning. "I remember this one. He rescued twenty sex slaves in Miami and busted their pimps. That was all over the news. The guy's amazing."

"Yes, he is." She closed the book, looked Harold in the eye, and whispered, "He's my husband."

"Your husband?" His near shout brought several pairs of eyes looking their way.

"Shhh."

"Sorry." Harold glanced around before whispering, "You're married to the biggest hero on the planet, and you never told me?"

"I'm telling you now, because I need more help. I hoped maybe if you knew why, you'd be willing."

"I'm willing." He crossed his arms. "But you did say you'd pay me to find that address."

"Okay." Deborah put on her negotiator's expression, stern and immovable. "A gaming headset with surround sound."

He let out a huff. "Get real. What gamer doesn't already have one?"

"All right. What's your offer?"

"A Logitech G nine-twenty racing wheel. The real thing. No cheap knockoff."

"You got it."

His brow shot upward. "Really? I should have asked for more."

"Yep. You're too easy."

"How do I know you'll do it?"

"I'm a woman of my word." Bag in hand, Deborah rose and scooted out of the booth. "I'll get Paula to set up your payment tonight. Bring the book."

Harold stuffed the final fry into his mouth, packed up his laptop, and rose, the scrapbook tucked under his arm. They walked together to the parking lot and stopped near the street. As she programmed the route on her phone, Harold looked on. "Are you going to that place?"

"Of course." She studied the directions. In current traffic, it would take about thirty minutes. "And you're coming with me. I might need your help."

"But that wasn't part of the bargain."

"Then I'll add to the freebies." She gestured with her head and strode toward her Ford Focus parked nearby. "Let's go."

He followed her to the car and stopped at the passenger door. "Well, then I want a new laptop with double the memory of what I have now. No. Triple. And five times the disk space."

"Is that it? Are you sure?" She unlocked the doors with a fob and got in the driver's side, setting the bag on the center console.

As she laid the phone on a dashboard mount, Harold climbed into the passenger's seat, set the scrapbook and the laptop on the backseat, and closed the door. "If I asked for a channel on a communications satellite would you give it to me?"

Deborah started the engine. "No."

"Okay. Then I guess that's it."

"Done." She backed out of her space and drove toward the road. "Send the details to Paula and tell her I said it's okay."

"Cool." Harold rubbed his hands together. "This is better than working for the Geek Squad."

As she followed the phone's directions, she glanced at Harold. "It might be a lot more dangerous than the Geek Squad. That's why I'm giving you so much."

He swallowed. "Like, *fatal* dangerous?"

"No idea. If you want to back out, do it now. I can take you home."

Harold firmed his jaw. "Hey, if you're up for it, so am I. I have to protect the lady, right?"

Deborah opened her bag and gave him a peek inside at a loaded handgun resting at the bottom.

His eyes shot wide open. "Okay. So the lady's going to protect me. I can deal with it."

"This lady has had a lot of training. Mike made sure of that."

Harold sat in silence for a moment, shifting uneasily, as if getting up the nerve to say something. Finally, he blurted out, "So why did you and Mike split up?" He cleared his throat. "That is, if you don't mind me asking."

"It's all right." She took in a deep breath. "You know we lost our daughter Emily to a kidnapper, a guy at a Halloween party dressed as a clown."

Harold nodded. "I've heard that much."

"Well, as you might have heard from stories about the Guardian Angel, Mike has a special gift that helps him track down lost girls. He's been on a crusade ever since. At first, he came home after every rescue, but when he leaves again, our son is devastated. He cries and won't eat for days. Twice I had to take him to the hospital. That doesn't happen when I have to leave, but it does with Mike. So I finally told him if he must go on these rescue missions, just stay away. Or come home and stay home. Tommy can't handle the good-byes."

"Tommy has autism, right?"

Deborah nodded. "And a couple of other issues."

"That's a tough spot you're in."

"And Mike, too. When he gets contacted to find a girl, he can't say no. He thinks he's the only person in the world who can find her. He keeps saying, 'every girl needs a hero.' How can he possibly refuse?" She looked at the rearview mirror's frame. A handmade star with Emily's photo at the center hung from a purple string. The star swayed with the car's motion, like a pendulum on a ticking clock. "I can't blame Mike for believing that. He probably *is* their only hope."

Harold touched the star. "Is this Emily?"

A rush of grief welled from Deborah's gut. She firmed her lips and nodded. A single word would probably make the dam burst.

Harold ran a finger along the string. "So he's like the only lifeline for a drowning girl. If he said no, he'd be cutting the rope and letting her fall. The parents would be crushed. And maybe he thinks turning his back on a girl would be bad karma. You know. What goes around comes around. He'd be turning his back on Emily."

Her lips still tight, Deborah nodded again. When the eruption quelled, she cleared her throat and forced an even tone. "Another motivation keeps him on the road. He blames himself for Emily's kidnapping. He won't admit it, but I think he hopes that rescuing these girls will make up for how we lost her."

"Why? What happened? I never heard the story."

Deborah brushed tears from both cheeks.

Harold waved a hand. "If it's too painful, you don't have to—"

"No. No. It's all right." She took in another deep breath. "Halloween three years ago. We were all walking to a party in the park. Mike, Tommy, Emily, and me, dressed as pirates. A storm threatened, so we hurried to the pavilion where the party was supposed to be. We were early, as usual. Mike's always been obsessed with punctuality, so it didn't seem odd that no one was there yet.

"Just as the rain started, a man in a clown costume ran up and joined us under the shelter. Called himself Sugar Daddy. He said the party location was changed because of the storm, and the hostess asked him to come to the park to redirect everyone.

"Well, Mike couldn't find the address on his phone's map, so the clown offered to take us to the place as long as someone stayed to do his redirecting job. He said it wasn't far, so we wouldn't get soaked. I volunteered to stay with Tommy because he has a phobia about being out in the rain. So Mike and Emily went, and the clown directed them to a secluded part of the park—no path and lots of trees. Mike said he felt suspicious, but he didn't act on it. Then, when Mike's back was turned, the clown hit him in the head with something and knocked him out."

Harold winced but said nothing.

"Then the hostess showed up at the pavilion and told me she didn't send a clown. I tried to call Mike but got no answer. Then I called the police. They found him, still unconscious. Emily was gone. He woke up two days later. About a month after that, he discovered his gift, but it was too late to find Emily. To this day he hopes he'll pick up her scent again, but since he hasn't been able to, I think she's probably dead."

Harold stared, his mouth hanging open. "No wonder Mike feels guilty. I mean, I don't blame him, of course, but I would be counting all the reasons I shouldn't have trusted that clown and kicking myself in the butt every day till doomsday."

"That's exactly how Mike felt. He was a police detective back then, so he thinks he should've been more suspicious. And ever since that day, he gets terrible migraines, probably from getting whacked by the clown, and then he dreams about losing Emily. He would wake up crying and tell me about the dream. The story changed slightly every time, but I didn't say anything. After all, it was just a dream. But every change removed him further and further from responsibility."

"Responsibility?"

She nodded. "Mike didn't want to go to the party at all, so he was in a grumpy mood. Not mean, just kind of aloof. Passive aggressive, I suppose. He wouldn't carry Emily when she asked to be picked up or hold Tommy's hand when the storm scared him, but he did both in recent dreams. In fact, the last I heard, a tree fell on the pavilion and knocked us all out, and that's when the clown took Emily. What I didn't realize until about a year after it all happened is that the dreams took the place of his actual memory, and he believes the dream account instead of reality."

Harold whistled. "That's an unusual coping mechanism."

"Unusual is an understatement." Deborah sighed. "I'm worried that he's on the brink of insanity."

"Why? What does he do?"

"Every girl is like a surrogate Emily. He hugs them. Talks to them like they're his daughters. And one day at the mall, a girl tripped and fell down a couple of steps. She scraped her knee and limped a bit, but she was fine." Deborah looked at Harold. "Mike offered to carry her to a nearby bench. A teenager."

Harold fidgeted. "Uh … yeah. That's not cool."

"Not only that, he doesn't sleep or eat right. Just pops Excedrin to deal with his horrific headaches. Then he tries to get rid of his guilt by sending me flowers, but every time I look at them, my heart breaks. I love him, but I can't join him."

"Why can't you?"

Deborah firmed her tone. "Because Mike needs to come home. Rest. See a doctor. Convalesce and deal with his guilt feelings instead of trying to smother them with quest after quest after quest. He'll never run out of girls to rescue. Never. This crusade is going to kill him."

"And if you join him, you're helping him kill himself. You'd be saying everything's fine, and there'd be no reason to stop."

"Something like that. And then there's Tommy. I can't leave him with Paula for more than a few days." She brushed a new tear. "Anyway, that's the situation. Thank you for listening."

"No problem, but mind if I add a bit of advice?"

"Not at all. Fire away."

Harold looked Deborah straight in the eye. "Everyone needs a hero sometimes, not just girls."

She took in his sincere stare. His words were profound and true. Mike needed her. Now more than ever. "Thanks, Harold. You're right."

They remained quiet for the rest of the drive.

When they arrived at the pushpin location, Deborah parked in a vacant lot and studied the building—a dental office, apparently closed for the day. Her bag in hand, she walked to the door and pulled the handle. Locked.

Harold followed, the scrapbook and his laptop in tow. "This is the right address. Not a dead lady's home, though."

"We have to get inside." She walked toward the rear of the building and looked back. Harold stayed put, one hand in a pocket. "Aren't you coming?"

"Breaking and entering wasn't part of the deal. And an alarm will go off. We'll get caught."

"Not likely. Whoever stopped Mahoney's contact system probably already broke in and disabled the security." She marched to a door in the back, pulled her gun from the bag, and broke a glass panel with the butt. Reaching in through the jagged hole, she turned the deadbolt and opened the door. As expected, no alarm sounded.

She slid the gun away, walked in, and hurried past a series of exam rooms and a reception area, void of furniture or any sign that this office building might still be in use. When she reached the front door, she unlocked and opened it. Harold stood fidgeting outside as he glanced around, looking like a reluctant burglar.

She hissed, "Let's go."

Once he had entered, they checked each room until they came upon an office with a huge desk and three wide-screen monitors on top. A refrigerator, stove, and sink aligned one wall, and an open door led to a small bathroom with a shower stall. A fully dressed mattress lay against another wall along with an open package of water bottles.

Deborah let out a low whistle. "He must have lived here."

"Check this out." Harold set the scrapbook and laptop down on the desk and picked up an open Dr. Pepper can along with a napkin around its base. "Still wet and almost full."

"Someone's coming back soon."

"Let's get this done and scram out of here." Harold circled the desk, set the can down, and sat in a high-backed swivel chair. He studied the screens and their program windows—maps with dozens of pins, spreadsheets with lists of names and schedules, and contact directories. "Looks like a communications center, but the streams are static. I'm guessing they're dummy windows." He slid a mouse controller on the desk. A message appeared on all three screens—Enter Password. "Yep. It's all window dressing."

"Can you guess it?" Deborah asked as she set her bag on the desk.

"No way. Even if we got lucky, it could lead to a second password screen, then a third. And if we guess wrong, it might lock us out or even wipe the system. Our chances are practically zero."

"We might as well try."

"All right. But I think it's useless. Just keep a lookout for our soda-drinking friend." He cracked his knuckles and spoke as he typed. "Password. ... Nope. Too obvious. ... Admin ... Nope. ... Operator ... Nope." He pointed at the screen. "There it is. We're already locked out. No telling when it'll give us another chance."

"And we can't afford to wait."

The sound of a slamming vehicle door penetrated the room.

Harold flinched. Deborah's heart thumped. She pointed at the bathroom. "In there."

Just as they rose, a knock sounded at the front door. A muffled call followed. "FedEx."

Deborah looked at Harold. The expression on his face reflected her thoughts. A delivery? To a vacant office?

"I'll check on it." She hurried to the lobby, turned the front door's lock, and opened the door. A uniformed young woman stood outside holding a small box. Eyes weary and dark hair disheveled under a FedEx cap, she raised her brow. "Oh. You surprised me. I was expecting the guy who usually answers the door."

"My first day here." Deborah extended a hand. "I can take the package."

"New hire, huh?" The woman gave her the box and held out a tracking device and stylus. "Sign, please."

With the box tucked under one arm, Deborah took the stylus. She couldn't sign her own name. Maybe Grandma Stokley's name would work. She scribbled Beth Stokley and handed back the stylus. "So, what's your impression of my new boss? Is he nice? Does he ever talk to you?"

A hint of pink coloring her cheeks, she shrugged. "He's nice. Always smiles. I remember that because his teeth are so white against his dark skin. He always seems to be in a rush, though. Never could figure that out 'cause the place is always deserted."

"It takes a while to set up a new practice." Deborah smiled and nodded. "Thank you."

"Have a good day." The delivery woman turned and walked toward a FedEx van in the parking lot.

Deborah scanned the area outside. No sign of another vehicle, but the Dr. Pepper owner still might come back at any moment.

After closing the door and relocking it, she strode back to Mahoney's office while reading the package's return address—Northwest Dental Supply in Spokane, Washington. She split the sealing tape with a fingernail and opened the box. Inside lay a purple bag with a yellow sticky note attached that said *Horowitz*. She spread open the top, revealing a mobile phone and a miniature video camera. Interesting.

She slid the items onto the desk next to Harold. "Care to hack a phone?"

"Sure." He picked it up and turned it on. As he manipulated the screen icons, he talked her through his findings. "Let's check recent calls. ... Nope. History is wiped. ... Next, recent text messages. ... Ah. One thread." He tapped on the entry and squinted at the text. "First message is incoming.

'I saw your handiwork. Great job. Two stupid toads down, a thousand to go. But I'll get you back. Soon. Very soon.'"

Deborah eyed the Dr. Pepper. A slight sizzle from within sounded like a burning fuse. They had to hurry.

Harold's eyes scanned down. "No reply. Then another incoming. 'This lovely pic is going up on all the best websites. A hundred of my friends are going to stare at it while they entertain themselves. The video of ...'" Harold gulped. "'Of Amy's deflowering is worth a ton of money. No wonder you took it for yourself.'"

Deborah looked at the screen. "Amy's the name of the girl Mike rescued in Spokane yesterday morning. Amy Horowitz."

"The deflowering sounds ominous." Harold looked at Deborah. "Um ... I'd rather not pull up the photo, if you don't mind."

"No need. Anything else?"

He tapped on the screen a few more times. "This is interesting. Only two contact entries. One for a guy named Rubio and one for Sugar Daddy."

Dizziness washed through Deborah's head. "Sugar Daddy?"

"The clown who took Emily, right?" He turned toward her. "Ooh. You look pale. Do you feel faint?"

Deborah leaned against the desk and closed her eyes. "Just dizzy. I'll be all right."

"Okay. Let's see what else we can find out." He tapped on Sugar Daddy's contact list entry. "Locked. Password protected."

Another vehicle door slammed outside.

"Let's haul." Deborah picked up the purple bag, slid the phone and camera back inside, and snatched her own bag. Harold grabbed his laptop and the scrapbook. Together they rushed to the lobby.

Just as they turned toward the rear exit, the front lock clicked. They dashed out the back and hurried around to the front. At the entrance, the door stood open, revealing a man heading toward Mahoney's office.

Deborah and Harold ran to her car and jumped in. The moment they closed the doors, she started the engine and sped away, careful to keep the tires from squealing.

When they were safely out of sight, she exhaled. "That was too close."

"Tell me about it." Harold set his computer on his lap with the scrapbook on top and mopped his brow with a hand. "I'm a mild-mannered geek, not Indiana Jones."

"Well, I think we got everything we could, so mission accomplished."

"I'm just glad you didn't have to use that gun."

"Same here." Deborah let the newly gained information tumble through her mind—the phone, the ominous note about Amy's mistreatment, the photo that likely showed her in some form of undress. Yet, Mike had rescued her. She was safe at home by now. Her parents had to be sky high with joy, probably more than happy to help Mike in any way they could. That might be the lead they needed.

"Harold, check the last page of the scrapbook. There's an article about Amy's rescue. Let's see if we can get in touch with her parents."

"Gotcha." He opened the scrapbook and scanned the article. "Let's see. Amy's a runner on her school's track team. Mom's a nurse at the air force base. Dad's a training specialist there. Police say Amy wasn't a typical target for sex traffickers. They usually go after runaways or street kids. They speculate the kidnappers were new at this.

Sometimes it's easier to just grab someone than to take the time to lure."

"Is that enough info to dig up their contact information?"

"Probably." Harold withdrew his mobile phone and tapped on the screen. "Searching for trending Guardian Angel news."

Deborah retraced the course toward their starting point. "Tell me everything you see."

"This is interesting. The parents of missing teenager Emma Castillo were found shot to death in their home early this morning. Although there were no eyewitnesses to the murders, an anonymous caller reported seeing a man wearing a ski mask sneaking toward the Castillo home before dawn. Investigators say that Rick Castillo shot and wounded a prowler and reported the incident to police, but the intruder apparently returned and killed Castillo and his wife. Castillo described the prowler as short and stocky with a full beard."

A tight knot formed in Deborah's throat. "What's that got to do with Mike?"

"The article was tagged as a Guardian Angel story. The comments at the end mention him." Harold's eyes darted up and down as he scrolled the screen. "Check this one out. The Guardian Angel wears a ski mask. Maybe he killed the rents so he could find Emma and keep her for himself. Rumors say he lost a daughter of his own. The description Castillo gave of the killer is bogus. It was dark. The Guardian Angel is an angel of death."

Deborah huffed. "The fool."

"If he's a fool, then there's a whole brigade of them. His comment got more than a thousand thumbs ups, and people are chiming in to agree. Quite a few are coming to

Mike's defense, but the meaner ones are taking over." He sat back in his seat. "It's going viral. People like to bring down a hero. It's human nature."

"It's stupid nature." Deborah's cheeks warmed. "If Mike rescued Emma, he probably knows about the murders by now, but does he know he might soon be the prime suspect?"

"Impossible to guess."

"He can't call Mahoney, and my phone's in the burglar's hands." Deborah ran her fingers through her hair. "I have to contact him, but how?"

"By figuring out where he is." Harold raised a finger. "Let's say he has Emma. He can't take her home. Where would he go with her?"

"Good question." Deborah imagined Mike driving a vehicle with a young girl sitting in the passenger's seat. He would want to drop her off somewhere safe, with someone he could trust, but if he knew he was a suspect, he would also want to get out of town. She whispered, "Of course. Amy's parents."

"So we're back to trying to find their number." Harold looked at his phone again. "That might take a while."

She touched the purple bag at her side. "There was a sticky note attached. Maybe Mike wrote something on the back. I don't remember what happened to it."

"I think it fell off." Harold opened the top and peered inside. "Hello there." He withdrew a business card and peered at it. "Well, will you look at that? Phone numbers and email addresses for Fred and Maria Horowitz."

"Perfect. Just what we need." Deborah inhaled deeply. Finally a breakthrough. "Let's go somewhere safe and get to work. While you hack the phone Mike sent, I'll make some calls."

CHAPTER EIGHT

I DROVE EAST ON Interstate 90, making sure to stay just under the speed limit. Getting pulled over now would ruin everything.

To my right, Emma slept in the reclined front seat, a pillow supporting her head and a blanket covering her curled body. A quick trip to Walmart yielded the bedding, some toiletries, and more clothes and a coat for Emma. A later stop at Wendy's provided welcome fuel for our hungry bellies. At some point, I needed to get her to a doctor to check for an STD. For now, that would have to wait.

After getting through the snowy mountain pass, we made a final stop at a rest area for some sleep. Emma dropped off immediately, finally able to enjoy a drug-free snooze, while I, with Beans in my grasp, luxuriated in a three-hour nap, void of headaches and nightmares. When I woke up at seven p.m., I continued our eastward trek, glad for evening's shade. Since I felt like I was kidnapping a helpless orphan, and a recently raped one at that, any cover worked to ease my paranoia.

As I glanced between the darkening highway and Emma, she stirred, still holding her mostly empty drink cup. When I took it away, she opened her eyes, looked at me, and smiled. Staying reclined, she breathed a relieved sigh. "It wasn't a dream. You really did rescue me." After a few moments, her smile vanished, and her lip quivered. "Are my parents really dead?"

I laid my hand on her blanket-covered arm. "I'm afraid they are, sweetheart. I'm sorry."

She sank lower and covered her head with the blanket. Her muffled voice came through, shaky and forlorn. "Are you going to find who killed them?"

"I hope so." I glanced at Stewart's phone resting on the console between us. "Want to help?"

"If I can."

"Are you good with electronics? Like checking the history on a mobile phone?"

"Pretty good." When she raised the seat, the blanket slid down, revealing a black rhinestone-studded sweater over a purple tunic. Wetness sparkling in her eyes, she resnapped twin purple barrettes that held her hair back. "Stewart's phone?"

I nodded. "I doubt that he has a direct link to your parents' killers, but we might find a clue."

Emma picked up the phone and began manipulating the screen with a finger. "What should I look for?"

"Maybe someone in the contact list he called or texted frequently."

"Okay." While she searched, she hummed a melody, her voice sweet though melancholy. "Lots of texts with someone named Pete, but they're about fishing. Quite a few from Meg. Looks like that's his mother. He doesn't answer her much."

"He probably erases incriminating texts and call history. Check the contact list."

She slid her finger across the screen. "What am I looking for?"

"Any name that rings a bell. Maybe someone he mentioned while you were with him."

She grimaced. "Bill Sanders. The first guy who raped me. He smelled like vomit."

"Okay. Keep going."

Her brow furrowed. "This is strange. G Man?"

"Sounds promising." I reached for the phone. "Let me see."

She handed it over. I pressed the call button and held the phone to my ear. A click sounded, then a gruff voice. "I told you to stop calling me. This had better be good."

I coughed and added a rasp to my own voice. "It is. I have something special."

"You got a cold?" G Man asked.

"Yeah. Too much fishing in the rain."

"All right tell me about your something special."

"A hot Latina. Just got her a couple of days ago. Sweet stuff."

Emma sank low again and covered her head with the blanket.

"How old is she?"

"Fourteen, but just barely."

"What's so special about her?"

"She's the daughter of the murder victims. You know, the Cedar Park couple."

"I just got assigned to that case. How did you get her?"

I winced. Since he was probably aware of the details of the kidnapping, it would be tough to fool him. "That's not your concern."

"Well, *you'd* better be concerned. Some are saying the Guardian Angel killed that couple. You'd better watch yourself. He might be on your tail."

"I heard the murder rumor. What's the scoop on this guy?"

"They say he's psycho. Wanted to replace his own daughter, so he killed the girl's parents."

"Do you believe that?"

"Doesn't matter. He's a suspect, so I need to bring him in and put him through the ringer."

"Makes sense." I wasn't sure where to take the conversation, so I circled back to the start. "Do you want the girl or not?"

"Definitely. I can use her as bait. They say this guy can track a girl almost anywhere."

"Where should I bring her?"

"I'm in Spokane. That's where his trail starts."

"All the way to Spokane? That's gonna cost you."

"Cost me? You're holding a kidnapped orphan hostage, probably with a crazy bloodhound on your tail, and you think you can get a premium for her? You'll be lucky to unload her without getting your head blown off. Just get her here, and I'll take her off your hands."

"All right. All right. But what about the Guardian Angel?"

"Once I get the girl, he'll be on my tail, not yours. I can handle him."

"Where should I meet you in Spokane?"

"I'm staying at the Davenport Hotel, but call me when you get into town. We'll arrange a meeting." He paused to the sound of sipping. "Where are you now?"

"Already on my way. I had to head eastbound to pick up something."

"Good. Talk to you soon."

He sounded ready to end the call, but I needed another piece of information, and he was probably the perfect man to give it to me. "Any news on Sugar Daddy?"

"Sugar Daddy?" His tone turned sharper. "Why are you bringing him up?"

"I heard he might be in town, so I was wondering. He shakes things up wherever he goes."

After a few seconds of silence, he said, "Stay out of Sugar Daddy's business, and we'll both be better off."

"Yeah. Sure. Just keep him out of my territory."

"Don't make me laugh. Your territory runs from the refrigerator to the toilet. You're smaller than small time." He let out a huff. "Just get here as fast as you can, and I'll put out a welcome mat for the Guardian Angel."

"You got it." I terminated the call and set the phone down. "*G Man* means he's an FBI agent. He's up to his neck in this. Wants to buy you to trap me."

Emma pulled the blanket down a notch, revealing only her hair and eyes. "What are you going to do?"

"Expose him … somehow. But first I have to get to Spokane under the radar. He said he'd put out a welcome mat for me, so I have to be careful. They might blockade the highway."

"This highway?"

"Most likely this and every other route." I looked at her socked feet and her new all-weather boots sitting nearby on the floorboard. "If we see a blockade ahead, we might have to park and hike around it. We'll see."

"Why don't we just talk to them? They won't know you're the Guardian Angel. Just say you're my father. I can play the daughter role."

I smiled. "I saw in your diary that you're an aspiring actress."

"I'm hoping. Maybe someday. I've been in a few plays."

"It could work. I might not look like it, but my father was born in Guatemala. My mother is Norwegian. The combination produced fair-skinned me, but my daughter Emily picked up my dad's genes. Like I said before, you and she look a lot alike."

"So you'd tell the police all that?"

"Kind of clumsy, isn't it?"

"Way clumsy."

"Well, we could park somewhere and hitch a ride, maybe cover up in a backseat, tell the driver that you're an escaped sex slave who's trying to avoid detection. Someone in the police force is trying to get you back into the trade, so you need to sneak past them undetected. I'll be your father who rescued you."

"That's not pretending. It's all true." Her expression drooped. "Well, not all of it is true."

"No. Not all of it." I firmed my lips to quell an erupting spasm. When it backed off, I whispered, "I wish I could be your father."

She gazed at me with those beautiful brown eyes. "Me, too."

I slid my hand into hers. She received it gratefully. While we held hands, she hummed that same tune, a haunting melody that carried a kaleidoscope of emotions. It altered her expression from happy, to sad, to angry, and back to happy again.

Soon, she slid away, curled to the side, and dozed off. Heavy respiration filled the van, a sound almost as lovely as her humming voice.

I drove through the darkness, eastward along the lonely highway. On the road ahead, I mentally painted a human silhouette and labeled it Sugar Daddy. Soon maybe he would be roadkill under my wheels.

. . . . . .

Deborah rubbed her tired eyes. "What time is it now, Harold?"

"Two minutes past midnight. Welcome to tomorrow." Harold sat across the table at a Steak 'N Shake restaurant, tapping away at his laptop. A thin cable led from a port to the phone Mike had sent. "The barriers are pretty strong, but they're coming down."

"I'll bet someone like you designed the security."

"True. He was probably a genius." He tapped a key with finality. "Got the number. Sugar Daddy's wrapper is now off."

Deborah withdrew her phone from her pocket. "Let's see it."

He spun the laptop toward her. While she entered the number into her contact list, Harold let out a long yawn. "Can I go to bed now? I'm no night owl."

"One more thing." She turned the laptop back toward him. "Can you track down where he is?"

"Are you kidding me? You mean like track down the location of the phone itself?"

"Right. That's exactly what I mean."

"But it's probably mobile. I found Mahoney's registration address, not the phone itself. That's a lot easier."

Deborah lifted her brow. "And your point is?"

"The phone moves from place to place. A sex trafficker isn't going to have a GPS chip or any locator apps running. I'd have to get access to tower data and find it with triangulation during a call." Harold crossed his arms. "I'm not ready to be fitted for an orange jumpsuit. Not even for you."

"Can you at least tell me where the account was set up?"

"Uh … sure. The area code will tell us that. Not that it means anything for where it is now." He typed in a few keystrokes. "Well, whaddaya know? Spokane, Washington."

Deborah nodded. "Sex trafficking central."

"I doubt it. I'll bet Seattle's a lot worse, and I heard Atlanta—"

"No." Deborah pointed at herself and Harold. "I mean for us. For our purposes. That's where Mike was when he sent the package. That's where he rescued Amy."

"Any word from her parents?"

"Not yet. They've probably been bombarded with messages."

"Then we'll have to keep waiting."

"Not necessarily." Deborah punched in Sugar Daddy's number and held the phone to her ear. What name should she use? The first one that came to mind was Paula's. Maybe a slight alteration. She bit her lip, hoping some pain would drive away the nerves.

After a few rings, a recording picked up. "Leave a message." The voice was male—calm and smooth. "If it's important enough, I'll call you back." The tone followed.

Deborah spoke with a sultry purr. "This is Miss Paulette in sunny Florida. I just picked up some luscious felines, and I heard from a friend that you're the man I should contact. I need to, shall we say, move some pussycats into a new marketplace, but ever since the Guardian Angel came, too many dogs have been chasing my kitties away. So if you want some of the prettiest pets around, give me a call." She rattled off her number. "Bye now."

She pressed the End button and exhaled. "How'd I do?"

Harold's mouth hung open. "Uh … Great. That was … great."

"Good. I hope he—"

Her phone chimed, still in her hand. She stared at the screen. A blocked number was calling. It chimed again.

Harold nodded at the phone. "Aren't you going to answer?"

"Sure." After clearing her throat, she put on the sultry voice again. "I'm so glad you returned my—"

"Cut the act, Miss Paulette. Let's get straight to the point. I'm not worried about cops listening in, so don't bother with phony code words. Your number indicates that you're in Fort Lauderdale. I'm in Spokane. How do you propose to get the girls here?"

Deborah gave Harold a thumbs up. "Why there? Don't you have any operations in my area?"

"Like you said, too many dogs around. I'm concentrating on the Northwest. Spokane's clean. A new market. A feeder for Seattle customers. Cute country girls for my boys on the coast."

Deborah's heart thumped. Now the risky question. "Aren't you worried about the Guardian Angel? I heard he rescued a girl in Spokane recently."

"He did. Killed two of my suppliers. Don't worry. I'll take care of him."

"Oh? Is he in Spokane?"

"On his way. I have a special welcome planned for him."

Deborah ached to ask for more information, but just bringing up the topic probably already raised too many suspicions. "My operations are all in the Southeast. I don't have connections all the way to Spokane, but maybe you can help me."

"What do you have and how many?"

"I have …" She grabbed the first number that came to mind. "Forty-two. They're all under eighteen."

"Forty-two kids? What are you doing? Drugging the water supply at the schools there?"

"They're from all over south Florida, collected over the past year. Like I said, we're getting squeezed, so we want to move them out and get some cash."

"How old is the youngest?"

Deborah took a shot at a reasonable number. "Fourteen."

"Okay. Send me a photo of her. If I like what I see, we'll work out a price, and I'll have her shipped up here. Maybe I can find a place in Atlanta for the older girls and get you some cash for them. We can talk about that later."

"Sounds good. I'll send the photo as soon as I can."

"And Miss Paulette …"

"Yes?"

"Don't call me again. I'll call you."

A click and beep followed. Deborah set the phone down and jerked her hand away. For some reason, it seemed contaminated.

Harold clapped his hands. "That was a magnificent performance."

"Maybe." Deborah shuddered. "But I feel like I need a shower."

"So what did you learn?"

"He's in Spokane setting up a new market."

"Do you think Mike knows that?"

"He said Mike's on his way to Spokane now. Walking right into a trap."

"What's your next move?"

She tapped a finger on his laptop lid. "Look up flights to Spokane."

"You're not worried about the insanity thing anymore?"

"My husband needs me. That's all that matters."

"I'm cool with that." He set his fingers on the keyboard. "Coming right up."

"I probably can't get a flight till morning, and it'll take …" She raised her brow. "How many hours to get there?"

Harold squinted at the screen. "At least nine with a non-stop, but there aren't any available. More like thirteen including layovers. I'll keep looking."

She picked up a straw from the table and twisted it. "Too much time. Way too much."

Harold touched his screen. "Five a.m. is the earliest departure. Arrives at twelve thirty-seven p.m. Pacific time. You can't get there any earlier."

After tying the straw into a knot, she tossed it back to the table. "Book that flight and email the itinerary to Amy's parents. Tell them everything that's going on and give them my phone number. Maybe they can figure out a way to get word to Mike about the trap. I'm going to be helpless to do anything for more than nine hours."

"Can do. Booking the flight right now." Harold yawned again. "I hope you don't need a ride to the airport in the morning. I'm sleeping till noon."

"No ride, but I do need you at the computer store at ten. My manager's going on vacation tomorrow. I was going to fill in myself. I could ask Paula, but she's got her hands full with Tommy."

"Me? A store manager? I don't know squat about that."

"Not a manager. Just be a gopher for Mindy. She can run the store until I get back. You know the merchandise well enough to answer questions, and you can figure out how to ring up purchases at the register."

Harold crossed his arms. "I suppose so, but I'd have to steal hours from my programming project. This'll cost you big time."

"Name it. I'll see what I can do."

"How about a role in the next Star Trek movie?"

* * * * * *

As light snow began to fall, I gazed into the distance. Blue flashes appeared on the horizon with red lights streaming back, like a train of scarlet eyes. A blockade.

I slowed the minivan and prodded Emma. "It's show time."

She sat up straight and rubbed her eyes. "It's snowing?"

"It's not sticking yet. We should be all right."

She stared straight ahead. With each passing second her features turned more and more downward. A tear tracked toward her chin. "I don't feel all right."

I gazed at her sad profile. "You're a very brave girl, especially after all you've been through." I massaged her shoulder. "I need you to be brave a little while longer. Can you do that?"

She sniffed and brushed away the tear. "I'll try."

"Good girl." I released her and refocused on the road. "Now to see if there's a way to get around the roadblock." I tapped on the GPS screen, querying for alternative routes. The airport appeared on the map, to the west of where two highways intersected just outside of Spokane.

I pointed at the intersection. "The police are probably there. Perfect place to set up a blockade. They'd pick up two major routes at once. But there's an exit to the airport between here and there. We could get off and catch a shuttle, maybe a bus with a lot of people on board."

"Better than walking." Emma put on her boots and began tying them. "But I'm up for it if we have to."

I glanced at the van's thermometer. Twenty-two degrees. "Let's hope we don't have to."

Just before we reached the closest taillight in the backup, I turned onto the airport exit ramp. Although it was getting late, now around eleven p.m., quite a few cars traveled this access road. Maybe they hoped to get around the blockade, but the police surely had every route covered. Still, a more remote road might have a shorter backup.

A stop sign loomed ahead at an intersection along with a line of four cars waiting their turns to proceed. A man bundled in a coat stood at the corner under a streetlight, looking into every car as it passed. Snow fell through the light and collected on his hood as well as the grass, though not yet on the pavement.

I focused on him. He seemed familiar ... very familiar.

"He doesn't look like a police officer," Emily said.

"No. I think I know him from somewhere." When we reached the intersection, the man squinted at Emma, then at me. Waving his arms, he stepped in front of us and hurried toward my window.

I lowered the glass. As he drew close, his face became clear. Amy's father?

"Are you Mike?" he asked.

That did it. No use hiding. "Mr. Horowitz?"

"Fred Horowitz." He glanced behind my van as another car approached. "Let me in. It's an emergency."

I pressed the side-door button. As soon as he jumped in and sat, he lowered his hood and pointed ahead. "Go around to the other side of the airport. Maria's parked at the cell phone lot. Amy's with her."

After closing the door, I accelerated while glancing at him in the rearview mirror. His clean-shaven face, closely cropped hair, and intense features made him look like a drill sergeant. I hadn't taken note of that when we first met. "What's up?"

"Deborah called us." He shook snow from his coat, took off a pair of gloves, and rubbed his hands together. "She says Sugar Daddy set a trap for you."

I let out a sigh of relief. Deb was all right. "Is Tommy okay?"

"Fine. He and his sitter are staying at a motel in Fort Lauderdale. It's not safe at home."

I nodded. Sugar Daddy lied. Obviously he wasn't lying about Mahoney, but it proved that his every word was suspect, including his claim about having Emily. "I guessed Sugar Daddy might be setting a trap, but I know how to avoid people like him."

Fred withdrew a phone from his coat pocket and began texting with his thumbs. "With Emma along? Not likely." When he finished, he looked up. "Just letting Maria know I found you. I should put our numbers in your phone so you can contact us."

I handed him my phone. "How do you know Emma's name?"

"Deborah figured out a lot." He began tapping on my phone's screen. "Her phone was stolen. I'm putting her new number in here, too."

I smiled. Deb was always on the ball. "Okay. Do you have a plan?"

"It's still formulating." He glanced around. "Anything in this vehicle that'll give you away at the blockade?"

"Quite a bit. Disguises in my suitcase. Girls' clothes in the other. Amy's stuffed rabbit. A ski mask. The cash you gave me. My Beretta and quite a bit of ammo." I nodded toward Emma. "And her, of course. I also have a first-aid kit, but that shouldn't raise any alarms."

He handed me my phone and looked at the minivan's back compartment. "We'll have to ditch the disguises." He picked up a coat. "Emma's, I assume."

"Right."

He handed it to her. "Emma will take the girls' clothes and Beans and go with Maria. She'll be Amy's best friend who flew in to visit. I'll drive this van. You and I will be ski enthusiasts. You flew in from Florida to ski Mount Spokane with me. I'm local, and I rented this van so we could pick up our skis later and carry them to the slope. That way, our driver's licenses will match our story and the fact that this is a rental van. I guess we'll just have to hide the gun and ammo."

I ran the deception through my mind. My driver's license wouldn't be a problem. I borrowed it from a friend who no longer drives and put my photo on it, but Fred's license might cause a stir. "When you show them your license, won't they recognize your name? It might sound strange that you're taking off on a ski excursion so soon after Amy got home."

"Good thought." Fred drummed his fingers on the back of my seat for a moment. "Then you'll be Maria's brother, and we're all going on a family outing to get away from the media circus."

"That might work." I again tried to poke holes in the plan, but no problems came to mind. Fred seemed like a bright, clever guy. "By the way, how did you know I would take the airport exit and avoid the blockade?"

"Because you're not stupid. Deborah figured out that you're a suspect in a murder in Seattle, and she guessed that you knew it too. You'd be a fool to try to get through the blockade with Emma on board."

"What's Deb doing now?"

"Getting ready to fly to Spokane." Fred pointed at the road. "Turn here."

I made the turn. The roads were wet, though still not snow covered. "Fly to Spokane? Why?"

"She didn't give any details. I assume she wants to be with you."

I didn't bother to affirm or deny his assumption. I could think of a few reasons she wouldn't want to be with me. "Do you know when her flight leaves Fort Lauderdale?"

"Five Eastern time. It's a little after two there now."

"So she'll probably start out for the airport in about an hour. I'll call her then."

When we pulled into the cell phone lot, Fred directed me to a parking space to the right of a Toyota 4Runner, a good snow vehicle.

The moment I pulled in, I handed Fred the cash envelope from the glove compartment, keeping a few hundred for myself. He then began transferring the potentially suspicious items to his Toyota.

Amy climbed out and looked through my window. Her blonde locks protruded from under a pull-over woolen cap and draped a fuzzy collar on her thick coat. She breathed on the glass, fogging it.

I picked up Beans from the console and lifted him. Amy laughed. Her smile was electric.

"That's Amy," I said to Emma as I shut off the engine. "I rescued her yesterday."

Emma slid an arm through her coat's sleeve. "She looks happy."

"She is now. You wouldn't have wanted to see her when I found her."

I opened the door. Amy hugged me and squeed.

The magical touch returned, along with Amy's lovely scent. Goose bumps sent a spray of tingles from head to toe. I patted her on the back and whispered, "I'm glad to see you."

"I'm glad to see you, too."

I looked over her shoulder at Maria as she took items from Fred and stowed them in their vehicle. Bundled in a heavy coat, only her face was visible, though that was enough to reveal a resemblance to Amy. Her blonde hair, shorter than Amy's, framed a loving, serious face.

When Amy and I pulled apart, she grinned and waved at Emma. "I'm Amy Horowitz."

Emma fastened her coat. "Emma Castillo."

Amy circled the van and opened Emma's door. "Come on." Amy held out a hand. "You're my new best friend, so we have a lot to talk about."

"Okay." Emma gave me a smile. "Be careful. I'll see you soon." She picked up Beans and joined Amy.

Within a few minutes, we completed the transfers and hid my gun and ammo under a floor hatch in the back. Fred sat in the minivan's driver's seat while I buckled in at the passenger's. As Maria drove away with Emma and Amy, it seemed that half of my heart went with them.

"They'll go through a different blockade, and we'll meet up at our house." Fred started the engine and pulled out of the lot. Snow had left a thin skim on the pavement, and more flakes joined those. "Now that we're alone, I can ask some questions."

I pulled my seatbelt tight. "Fire away."

"Do you know there's a nationwide APB out on you? You're suspected of four recent murders, including Emma's parents."

"Four? Are they saying I murdered the perps in SeaTac?"

"They say you were selling Emma to the perps, and the deal went bad, like maybe they tried to steal her, so you killed them."

"That's nonsense. I found Emma with them. We fought. They died. I took Emma with me. End of story."

Fred shrugged. "Just letting you know what you're up against. They got a composite sketch from a motel clerk. We're going to have to pray for police blindness."

"I wore a disguise. Wig, mustache, and a prosthetic nose. We'll be fine."

"Let's hope so. Rumor has it that state officers are asking about the guys who took Amy. Apparently the report from the Spokane police isn't satisfying them. Maybe two more murders will get tacked on."

"So I'm not safe in Spokane either?"

Fred shook his head. "Actually, you're a hero here. That's why the FBI called in the state patrol. The Spokane chief is playing coy. Apparently he thinks catching a hero is less important than investigating barking-dog complaints. His officers are very busy, if you know what I mean."

I exhaled. "That's good news. At least I have some friends here."

"Yep." Fred pointed forward. "The alternate exit has a blockade. We're up soon."

"Wait."

He stopped. "What?"

I jumped out, ran to the rear of the minivan, and peeled off a couple of strips of tape from the license plate. When I returned, I wadded the tape and stowed it under my seat. "In case the police call in the plate number. I altered it."

"Good thinking." Fred gripped the wheel tightly and exhaled. "We're on deck."

When we stopped at the checkpoint, Fred lowered his window and handed his license and the rental's registration to a parka-wearing officer. Three other officers sat in two patrol cars on the shoulder just ahead of us. Because of the bad weather, maybe they were taking turns checking the stream of vehicles.

The officer squinted at the license. "Horowitz? Are you related to the girl the Guardian Angel rescued?"

Fred nodded. "Amy's my daughter."

"I hope she's all right." The officer gave the license back to Fred and nodded at me. "May I see your identification, please?"

I studied his eyes. This wasn't protocol. He was already suspicious of me. When I gave him my license, he studied it for a moment and handed it back. "What brings you all the way from Florida?"

"Skiing. Fred and I are going to Mount Spokane. He's my brother-in-law. Picked me up at the airport just now."

The officer looked at Fred. "If you're local, why are you driving a rental?"

Fred laughed. "My car's too small to get my whole family and our skis up the mountain, so I picked this van up when I got to the airport."

After looking us both over again, the officer pointed toward the shoulder just beyond the parked police cars. "Pull over there, please."

"Sure thing, officer." Fred closed his window and regripped the wheel. "We're busted, Mike. It's your call. I'm with you all the way." He drove slowly toward the shoulder.

I looked ahead. The road was clear. "How well do you know Spokane?"

"Better than almost anyone, including the cab drivers."

"And probably better than state troopers. Let's go."

Fred stomped on the pedal. The tires spun in the snow for a moment, then we peeled out and shot into the darkness.

CHAPTER NINE

FRED TOOK A hard left onto a side road. The tires slid before catching pavement. As we zoomed on, sirens blared in the distance. I looked back. No visible pursuit so far. We had the element of surprise, but that wouldn't last.

"Let's go dark." Fred flicked off the headlights. "They'll probably deploy a chopper, but they'll have to call the county in to do that, and the weather's bad, so we have a little time."

I squinted through the windshield. The road ahead was barely visible in the glow of occasional streetlamps and porch lights. "How far is it to your place?"

"It's across the Interstate, and the police will be watching our neighborhood. Can't go there."

"There's another option." I pulled out my phone and called up my mission list. When I found the address where I was supposed to meet Sugar Daddy at sunrise, I showed it to Fred. "Do you know where this is?"

He eyed the screen. "Yeah. Two miles, max. But it's over the river. We have to cross one of the bridges. We'll be out in the open. Easily spotted if a chopper's hunting for us."

I looked back again. Blue strobe lights flashed in the distance. "I can walk that far. Just drop me off and lead the police away."

"I'll set you close to the Meenach Bridge. You can cross on foot while I start the wild goose chase. Get ready."

"Give me two seconds." I climbed to the back, retrieved the Beretta and ammo, and returned to my seat. To the rear, the police lights drew closer. Time was running out. I snapped a magazine into the gun and slid it under my coat. After a left turn off the main road, we rounded a corner that brought the bridge into view, illuminated by streetlamps lining a parallel walkway on each side. It looked as though snow lay thicker on the overpass, but the angle made it hard to be sure.

Just before the bridge, police lights flashed from a parking pad to the right. Fred pointed. "Spokane police."

"Let me out." I ducked low. "First open your door to turn the light on."

He stopped about fifty feet from the bridge and opened his door. The moment the interior light flashed on, I grabbed my phone, opened my door just enough to slide out, and squeezed through the opening. Staying low, I closed the door and crept up an embankment to the right and into the woods.

As sirens drew closer, I walked along the crest toward the bridge, constantly glancing back. A pair of officers from the blockade walked slowly toward the van. Fred turned on the headlights, wheeled around, and drove away. Just as he turned onto the main road and accelerated, the pursuing patrol cars flew past the intersection, giving chase. A helicopter buzzed by in pursuit with a spotlight trained on the road.

Since the Spokane officers stood well away from their blockade, now was my chance. Keeping my footfalls quiet, I hurried toward the bridge while staying hidden in the woods. What story would Fred tell when the police caught up? Maybe he would say that I had gotten out of the car quite a ways back. Even if they didn't believe the story, he was buying me a lot more time.

When I arrived at the bridge and sneaked behind the officers, I jogged with my back bent, following the walk-way. After a minute or so, two motionless vehicles came into view on the road. They had collided and now blocked the way. I straightened and looked back. The Spokane officers weren't here looking for me. They were turning people from the accident while waiting for a wrecker to haul the cars away.

I spun toward the other side. Another set of police lights flashed ahead, a warning blockade from the opposite direction. I jogged on and drew near to an officer at the end. He shone a flashlight beam in my eyes. I lifted a hand, deflecting the light.

"Pretty bad weather to be out for a walk," he called.

I stopped within a few steps of him and took note of his nametag—Alan Petrie. "My car got stuck in the snow back there. Trying to get home."

"Strange coincidence." He lowered the beam, giving me a look at his thirty-something face, bordered by a lined hood. "Just got a call to watch for a man on foot. Supposedly he's the Guardian Angel. FBI wants him for questioning."

I caught a sly stealth in his voice. He knew exactly who I was. "How do they know he's on foot?"

"State Patrol just caught his getaway driver. Alone. The Angel must have jumped out somewhere."

"I can't say I hope they find him."

The officer looked across the bridge. "If he doesn't go into hiding soon, they will."

"What's going to happen to the driver?"

"They'll probably take him to the FBI for a grill session. Maybe book him on charges related to the chase."

I blew out a long stream of vapor. "I'd better get going."

Just as I spun and took a step, he grabbed my sleeve and turned me toward him. "Listen. I'm a father. I have two daughters of my own." Letting out a sigh, he released me. "I'll do what I can to run interference. Just be careful."

"Thanks. I will." I jogged into another tree-populated area to the right of the road. Again hidden, I stopped and brought up the mapping app on my phone, plugged in the address, and oriented myself. The suspected stable was only a half mile in the direction I had been going, easy during good weather, but paralyzing in the cold.

I walked on, alternately glancing at the map and the snowy terrain ahead. Cold air crept through my coat. White vapor rode my breaths. A shiver ran across my back and down both arms. From the cold? Partly. But maybe more from the unknown. I had rescued many newly kidnapped girls who had loving parents and decent homes. Their scents were fresh and easy to follow, and the number of victims kept me busy.

But stable girls? I had only read about them, heard stories about them—without hope, damaged consciences, zero self-worth, and broken hearts. The scents of their souls might be scattered in the wind.

When I arrived at the address, I stayed hidden behind a tree and studied the scene. A thin coat of snow lay undisturbed on a pothole-scarred driveway that led from the road to a small one-story motel. A dark cargo van sat in a space near the main entrance. Since no tire lines marred the snow, it had been here for at least an hour. Otherwise, the place appeared to be abandoned.

I glanced back toward the bridge. No police lights or sirens approached. Fred knew where I wanted to go, but he wouldn't tell anyone, and Sugar Daddy expected me at sunrise. Maybe I had time to check the place out.

After grabbing a fallen evergreen bough, I walked parallel to the edge of the parking lot and circled to the rear of the complex. When I reached an area that lay out of view of the road, I walked across the lot, using the bough's needles to brush the snow behind me. It left a trail, but a shallow one that the falling snow would soon cover.

When I found the back door to the main access hall, I dropped the branch and tried the knob. Locked. I withdrew my set of picklocks from my pocket and went to work. Fortunately, I had done this enough times to make the process easy. This lock, old and fairly loose, disengaged without a problem.

I returned the set to my pocket and pulled the door open. Inside, all was quiet. I stepped in, followed a short corridor, and stopped at an intersection with a motel lobby on the right and an interior corridor to the left that led to the motel's rooms. Other than doors on each side, nothing interrupted the peeling walls—no paintings, no photographs, no windows.

Shedding my coat as I walked, I ventured into the lobby and peered over the service desk—void of computers, files, or papers. I withdrew my gun from its holster and slid it behind my waistband in back. I then unfastened the holster, reached over the desk, and hid it in an alcove.

After putting my coat back on, I reversed course and walked along the corridor, glancing at the rooms on both sides. At one room, a metal bracket joined the door to the jamb, a padlock securing the conjunction. The other doors had no locks. Some didn't even have a knob and stood ajar, though most had brackets that could be fastened by a padlock if needed.

As I walked, I sniffed the air. Faint scents filtered in. Girls were inside some of the rooms. Sad girls. Despondent girls. Hopeless girls. Were they prisoners? If so, my job was to find the warden.

At the end of the hall, the door to the last room stood closed. Like many of the others, it had a bracket but no padlock. The surrounding air carried the scent of a woman. She seemed troubled, though forcing confidence, as if wearing a mask.

I grasped the knob and, careful to be quiet, tried to turn it. It wouldn't budge. I peeked into the peephole but couldn't see anything. I knocked on the door and stepped back. After several seconds, a woman called, "What do you want?"

I shifted from foot to foot. "Um … I saw an ad on the Internet. I called, and the guy told me to come here."

"How did you get in? We're locked down for the night. Only a fool would come out in a snowstorm like this."

"He said to use the back door." I shrugged. "I guess you're not as locked down as you thought."

"Are you a cop?"

"No." I spread open my coat, hoping that the absence of the holster would be enough to satisfy her. "Look. No gun." I bundled my coat and shivered. "It's cold outside. I heard this is a good place to get warm."

"Depends on the kind of warm you looking for."

I wrung my hands. "Look. Maybe you've got a secret code I'm supposed to say, but I've never done this kind of thing before, so I don't know what it is. My girlfriend broke up with me, and it's been nearly a month. I'm desperate."

"It's all right, honey. I'm just making sure you're not a cop."

"Oh … well … back to your question. How many ways of getting warm do you have? Do I have a choice?"

"We have eight right now, but I ain't waking 'em all up so you can go shopping."

I withdrew several twenties and flashed the bills where she could see them. "How much?"

The door opened, revealing a tall black woman dressed in sweat pants and a faded football jersey. "That'll do." She snatched the money and walked down the corridor with a swagger that she probably thought was attractive. "Come this way."

I followed. Although my heart raced like a galloping horse, I managed to keep my body from shaking.

She stopped at the padlocked door and pulled a key ring from her sweatpants pocket. As she slid the individual keys around the ring, her tone altered to a sultry purr. "These two girls will keep you warm. You can count on that."

"Two?"

"You said you're desperate." She chose a key and smiled. "Besides, you paid enough for two."

I gave her a smile in return, though I couldn't be sure if it looked excited or idiotic. "Sounds perfect."

"These girls won't have their makeup on, 'cause we thought no one was coming tonight, but I can get them dolled up if you want."

"I don't need that. I like the natural look."

"That's cool." She pushed the key into the padlock, unlocked it, and opened the door. The glow from the hallway illuminated a small round table and two metal chairs near the entry. An open door at the far wall led to a small bathroom.

We both stepped in. Stale smoke permeated the air, apparently originating from crushed cigarette butts in an ashtray on the floor near the back. At either side of the main room, maybe three paces apart, a girl lay on a thin mattress that abutted a wall.

When the woman flipped on a switch, a bare bulb dangling from the ceiling flashed to life. The girls rose to a sitting position and rubbed their eyes. The one on the left, a black girl with dreadlocks, moaned. "You said no one was coming tonight."

The other girl, a white brunette who looked to be fifteen or so, hissed. "Chock. Watch your mouth."

The warden stomped to Chock and slapped her savagely across the face.

I flinched, then quickly steeled myself.

"Don't get sassy," the warden shouted. "You're lucky Papa didn't hear you say that."

"Yes, Mama." Chock held a hand against her cheek. Her pout, along with her thin frame, made her appear to be no more than twelve years old.

"Mama" pivoted toward me. "She's new. Needs to learn some manners."

I gave her a nod, begging for this nightmare to end. If Mama would just leave, I could try to get these slaves out of here.

She turned again to the girls. "This gentleman paid for two, so both of you show him a good time. If he comes out smiling, you're gold. If he complains, Papa will hear about it in the morning, and it'll be the strap for you." As she passed me, she whispered, "I'll be back in an hour."

After she shut the door, the sound of a closing padlock passed through. I steeled my body once more. Why would she lock me in? I hoped to find the key to the cargo van parked outside, escape with these girls hunkered inside, and locate a shelter somewhere. Now that plan had been shattered.

The white girl patted her mattress. "Come on over. I'll make you smile."

I studied her face—narrow with shallow dimples that, along with her smallish nose, gave her a pixie appearance— really cute, though she looked tired and worn out.

"Let's hope we'll all leave here smiling." Since the room was plenty warm, I took off my coat and draped it over the table, then slid one of the chairs between the two beds and sat down. "What are your names? I heard someone say Chock."

The white girl winked. "So you like to talk first. I'm cool with that."

Chock just stared at her mattress, her expression forlorn.

"Chock," the white girl said with a warning tone, "be nice."

Breathing a sigh of her own, Chock looked at me and smiled, though the attempt looked tortured. She whispered, "Hi."

I nodded. "Hello, Chock."

The white girl touched the front of her gray bare-midriff T-shirt. "I'm Puddin." She pointed at Chock. "Her name's short for Chocolate. So together we'll give you some chocolate puddin."

Chock kept her stiff smile in place. "We're sweet."

"Real sweet." Puddin climbed to her feet and stretched her arms. Her T-shirt rode higher, exposing ribs within her too-thin frame. When she lowered her arms, she smiled mechanically. "How do you like to do it? I'm game for anything." Her attempt at sincerity failed badly.

Chock rose. "Same here." Wearing a surgical-scrubs top and roomy shorts that covered her legs to her knees, she ran her hands up and down her own scant sides, looking more awkward than erotic. She, too, had a thin face, though no dimples.

I motioned for them both to sit. They glanced at each other, then Puddin shrugged. "More talk, I guess." And they sat cross-legged on their mattresses.

"Listen ..." My voice rasped. I was as nervous as a cat. After clearing my throat, I continued. "Chock. Puddin. My name's Mike. I didn't come here for sex. I came to help you escape."

Chock's eyes flashed with hope, but Puddin scowled. "What makes you think we want to escape?"

"The padlock was my first hint. Normally people who want to stay somewhere aren't locked in."

Puddin snorted. "You're so freaking clueless."

I kept my face slack. "Why do you say that?"

She swept a hand toward the walls. "This is my home. I go to school every day. I could ditch this place anytime I want."

"So why don't you?"

"Where would I go? The last I saw my mom, she was on crack all the time. My dad's a drunk, and he rapes me every chance he gets. Here I get food, a bed, and a warm room. And the men who come here don't puke on me like my dad does."

I hid a tight swallow. Was her life really that bad, or had she embellished it for shock value? "There are other options, shelters or churches that would be glad to—"

"Yeah, right. Churches." Puddin glowered. "A pastor comes here twice a week, and he always asks for me." Her face twisted in revulsion. "He's so fat and disgusting. He literally drools on my face. He's a pig."

Anger fumed within. I had to force my body not to shake. "Then why not a shelter?"

"Same difference. I've been to a couple. They didn't work out."

"Why not?"

She cast her gaze on the floor and stared for a moment before muttering, "It's complicated."

"All right, then." I gestured with my head toward the door. "If you're allowed to leave, why the lock?"

She regained eye contact. "Because Chock's new. I'm kind of training her until she gets used to the idea that she's staying. She's pretty stubborn. In a good way, I mean. She's like me, 'cause she won't do drugs. But they'll break her. Maybe threaten her family or something."

"What broke you?"

She scowled. "I'm not broken."

"Well, you stay here. You do what they tell you. You can't really enjoy servicing men all the time."

"It's called survival. I got no place else to go." She looked me in the eye and punctuated each word. "I'm. Not. Broken."

"Well, you certainly don't act broken." That statement was true enough. Her willingness to talk was unusual. Many of the girls I ran into over the years were far quieter. In any case, it was best to move the spotlight from her. "Mama said there are eight girls here. Do the other six want to stay as well?"

"Want to stay?" Puddin laughed under her breath. "If only you knew."

"What do you mean?"

Puddin glanced at Chock before answering. "Look, we all got dirt in our lives, so I'm not trying to badmouth anyone. It's just that a couple of the girls think Papa's in love with them, so they want to stay with him. Even after he whips them, they still don't want to leave because he's all they got, so … " She stared at me for a moment, then looked down at her lap. "I guess you probably think that's really stupid."

"That's not for me to say. I'm not in their shoes." With her head down, I couldn't get a look at her eyes. Maybe that was the answer. She, too, had an attachment of some kind, but whether her chains were forged in the fires of terror or misguided love wasn't quite clear. "Where's Papa now?"

"I heard he got snowed in somewhere. That's one reason Mama decided to close up." She kept her stare low. "She gets nervous when he's not around."

I let the thought sink in. With no one but females here, that made sense, especially considering the character of the clientele and the ages of the girls. "How old are you, Puddin?"

"Sixteen."

"How long have you been here?"

"In this place?" She made eye contact again. "About five months. Papa brought me here from Oakland. Me and two other girls. We were supposed to go to Seattle for some big football game, but he decided to come here instead. Something about setting up a new business in Spokane."

"How long were you in Oakland?"

"I was born and raised there."

"I mean, how long have you been ..." I searched for the right word but nothing came to mind.

"In the life?" She glanced upward for a moment. "About five years."

I barely restrained a gasp. Five years?

"What's the matter? Can't believe an eleven-year-old can turn tricks on the street?" A sly grin bent her lips. "One time my pimp had five men waiting in line for me. They like the young ones."

I studied her cocky air. She was pulling out all the stops to shock me, maybe some kind of power play. "How did you get on the street?"

Her smile slowly wilted as her gaze drifted to another place, another time. "I just kind of snapped. I came home from school and found both my mom and dad out cold, sleeping off whatever they were on, so I took as much money as I could find and walked out. I went to the bus station thinking I'd go to Los Angeles." Her voice took on a faux dreamy tone. "Thought I'd be an actress or something amazingly cool."

"How far did you get?"

She huffed. "Nowhere. While I was waiting for the bus, this guy came up to me. Sweet talked me. Bought me a hot pretzel and a Coke. I don't remember what all he said, but his voice made me float on a cloud. No one had ever been so nice to me. He said we'd go to an expensive restaurant, then out to a movie. Just him and me, hand in hand. Before I knew it, I was in his car and on my way to his place."

Her expression turned sour. "But it was all a lie. The nice restaurant became a drive-through stop at McDonald's, the movie was a porn flick at his apartment, and just him and me turned into him and six other guys raping me. They forced me to smoke crack, I got hooked, and a few days later, I was hustling on the streets, and my new—" She drew quote marks in the air "—boyfriend stole every penny except enough to keep me going with cold cheeseburgers and crack. I tried to get away, but all that got me was a black eye. So I gave up." She shrugged. "Like I said before, where am I gonna go?"

"But you're not hooked on crack now. How did you break the habit?"

"When Papa took over as my pimp, I told him I wanted to get clean. I didn't want to end up like my mom. He told me that was cool and he'd help me as long as I was a good girl for him. So I just smoked cigarettes. That helped a lot." She shrugged again. "I guess he thinks I've been a good girl. Most of the time, anyway. He whipped me pretty good both times I went to the shelter and he found out. I'm not letting that happen again. I have to survive."

I nodded. The attachment was becoming clear. Terror was the key. "So no drugs at all now?"

"Mostly. They like to keep us hooked on something, so they give us pills at night to help us sleep. Chock and I usually don't take them unless we had a busy night. They knock out the pain." She gestured toward Chock with a thumb. "Especially for her. She's not used to getting banged so many times. And oral makes her sick."

The ease with which she spoke about sexual abuse turned my own stomach. How could they survive this torture?

I shifted to Chock. "How old are you?"

Her smile now gone, she glanced at Puddin, who gave her a quick nod. "I'll be thirteen in a couple of weeks."

"If you could get out of here, do you have a home you could go to?"

She shrugged, lifting her shoulders into her dreadlocks. "Sort of. My mom's dead, and my dad's in jail, so my older brother takes care of me and my little sister. He sells drugs, mostly weed, so we do eat. I didn't have it as bad as Puddin did."

"How did you end up here?"

"I didn't come from another city. I live in Spokane."

"I mean in this place. This building. What's your story?"

She looked at the floor. "Well, I always rode the city bus to school, and Papa … he called himself Willy then. He started sitting by me. You know, sweet talking me, like that guy did to Puddin. He's like twenty-five, so I figured I knew what he wanted, but every day when I got to school, he'd just tell me to study hard so I wouldn't end up like him."

"Like him?"

Chock nodded. "A dropout. He swept the floors at a factory. Said if he stayed in school, maybe he could be the manager. So I thought he just wanted someone to talk to. He never asked me to do anything. Then one day when I got out of school, he met me at the bus stop driving an Escalade. Said he got a new job and wanted to give me a ride home. So I got in, and he said he wanted me to meet his boss. Maybe he could give me a part-time job. Papa knew I needed money. So I said all right. Then he took me to an old house, like a shack. It was stupid, but I went in with him. Two other men were there, and they ..."

She pulled in her bottom lip. Her chin quivered.

"They raped her," Puddin said, her tone sharper. "Then they drugged her and took her to a party where ten more men raped her until she was so bruised she couldn't walk for three days."

With every word Puddin spoke, Chock winced, as if lashed by a whip.

"Then Papa brought her here a couple of weeks ago, just like he planned to all along. And soon he'll probably be back on that bus sweet talking another girl until she's done with her rape party and ready to join us."

Anger burned again. This Papa character was their worst nightmare—a devil with a whipping strap. Somehow I had to conquer their fears. "Listen ..." I gave them the most confident expression I could muster. "You can trust me. I'll find a safe place for you. I promise. No one will get the strap."

Puddin rolled her eyes. "Oh, God. How many times have I heard that? I'm standing in hell, and some guy promises me heaven, but then he just takes me to a deeper hellhole."

"But I'm not—"

"Just shut up. I don't buy your damn, do-gooder act. I don't know what your angle is, but you want something. You're all alike." She flopped back on her mattress and closed her eyes. "You paid for us. Do whatever you want to me. I'm done talking."

I gazed at her pitiful form, resigned to getting abused once again. Did she really think I'd do that after all I said?

Chock stood and sidled up to me. She whispered, "I want to leave."

I kept my voice low as well. "Do you know if any other girls might want to join us?"

"I don't see the others much. Maybe Shortcake, an Asian girl next door, but I'm not sure."

"We have to be sure they want to. We can't risk anyone staying who knows what we're doing."

"What about Puddin?"

"Not much we can do about her. She already knows."

Chock shook her head. "I don't think she'll tell anyone."

"Okay, then. It's just you and me for now." I leaned closer to her. "When we get you to a shelter, I'll call a police officer I met and see about getting them to raid this place. Then everyone will have to leave."

"Papa knows a cop that tells him when a raid's coming. We had to leave a few days ago, and then we came right back."

I glanced at Puddin. She looked at me through a slit in her eyelids, maybe unaware that I noticed. This might be a good time to apply a bit of pressure.

I raised my voice. "When we leave, I'll call the police. Since Papa's snowed in somewhere, he won't be able to do anything about a raid."

"A raid?" Puddin sat up in bed. "Where will they take us?"

I stroked my chin. "Hard to say. Maybe to a shelter, but some prosecutors charge the girls with prostitution and lock them up in jail. You never know."

She half closed an eye, apparently skeptical. I decided it was best to let the information stew for a while.

I rose from the chair. "Chock, do you have any warmer clothes?"

"The only dress I have is real short. It's for when customers come. Papa won't give me back my own clothes until he's sure I won't run."

Puddin pointed at a shallow closet. "She can wear my jeans and sweater. They should fit her."

"What'll you wear?" I asked.

"I have a skirt and a coat. And maybe you could bring my stuff back later."

"Can do." I wasn't sure I could comply, but I couldn't miss this opportunity. "When I get Chock to a shelter, once they give her warm clothes and a hot breakfast, I can come back with your jeans and sweater."

"Yeah." Puddin kept her skeptical stare on me. "That'll work."

"Unless they raid the place first. Then I might not be able to find you."

Puddin stayed quiet.

"Okay," Chock said as she took a pair of jeans and a sweater from hangers in a shallow closet. "If you're sure."

Puddin stared straight at me. "Go ahead. And you can wear my shoes, too. There won't be any school today. I'll be fine until I get them back."

I met her stare. She seemed to be using confidence as a weapon, as if daring me to instigate a raid.

Chock slid the jeans over her shorts, fastened them, and pulled a pair of athletic shoes from the closet. When she sat on her mattress and began putting them on, she looked at me. "How're we going to get out? Mama locked the door."

"She'll be back to unlock it soon." I withdrew my phone from my coat pocket and took a photo of each of the girls. Puddin tried to shield her face with a hand while Chock sat stoically. In Puddin's picture, her cringe and rising hand made her look needier than if she hadn't made the attempt.

"These pictures will help me convince the police to come. A girl in trouble is a great hot button. They'll get here in a hurry." I began a new text message, adding address-ees—the number Fred entered for Deb as well as Maria's. Since Fred's phone was probably in the hands of the police, I skipped it. "You girls are welcome to see what I'm texting. Just so you'll believe I'm legit."

Chock finished tying her shoes, jumped to her feet, and looked around my arm. Puddin got up and watched from my other side as I began typing with my thumbs—*Trying to help trafficked girls escape in Spokane. Could be dangerous, but they are worth it. Might need some backup. I also need info on shelters in Spokane.* I included the motel's address, attached the photos, and sent the message. I texted a second message to Deb. *I love you, dearest one. I heard you are coming here. Looking forward to seeing you.*

Chock smiled. Puddin stared at the screen, her expression blank.

I looked at the clock on my phone—3:15 a.m. Since Sugar Daddy said to meet at sunrise, his thugs could arrive at any minute to set a trap for me.

"How long do you think I've been here?" I asked as I focused on the girls. "I forgot to check the time when I arrived."

Chock and Puddin looked at each other. "Thirty minutes, you think?" Chock asked.

"About that." Puddin walked to the closet and pulled her coat off a hanger. "I'm coming with you. Chock can still wear my stuff. Since we're supposed to get clothes at the shelter, this coat will be enough till we get there."

I drew my head back. "What changed your mind?"

"If I'm going to a shelter anyway, I'd rather not go with a cop. And I damn sure don't want to go to jail." She pointed a finger at me. "But you'd better not screw me over like all the others."

"Never." I set my palm gently on her cheek. She flinched slightly, then met my gaze with unblinking brown eyes, hard and fiery. "What's your real name?"

Her expression softened along with her voice. "Jessica."

"Jessica, I would rather die than let you down."

"Okay." Her stony face returned, and she backed away from my touch. "I guess we'll see, won't we?"

Chock buttoned the sweater. "I'm Tiana."

"All right. Jessica. Tiana." I sat on the chair again and leaned toward them. "We have a few minutes. Let me tell you my story."

CHAPTER TEN

I spread out my hands. "So that's the story."

Jessica and Tiana sat cross-legged on the floor, Jessica wearing her coat and Tiana the borrowed sweater.

Jessica gave me her now-familiar skeptical stare. "You're telling me that just because you got knocked on the head, you can detect a girl's scent for miles?"

"Sometimes many miles. I'm not sure what my limit is. But it's her soul I smell, not her body."

She snorted. "Sounds like a fairy tale to me."

"Believe what you want, but if you're coming with me, let's get into position. It's been almost an hour."

The girls returned to their mattresses and pulled their sheets up to their chins. I put my coat on and retrieved a towel from the bathroom.

Keys rattled at the door. I hurried to the front of the room and turned toward the mattresses, keeping my coat open, ready to reach back for my Beretta. My gun hand trembled. I had physically hurt a woman only once before, but I could do it again if I had to.

When the door opened, Mama walked in. "Did the girls show you a good time?"

"Wonderful." I closed the door and set a hand on her shoulder, faking the motions and voice of a half-drunk man. "In fact, I tipped them both and sang them to sleep."

She looked at me like I was crazy. "Sang them to sleep?"

"See?" I gestured toward the girls. "They're sound asleep."

"What did you give them? I swear if you—"

"Shhh. You'll wake them."

"Don't you shush me." She stalked toward the girls, knelt next to Tiana, and patted her cheek. "Chock, wake up."

I lunged at Mama and wrapped the towel around her face. As I dragged her back toward the chair, she kicked and clawed while letting out a muffled scream, but I held on.

Jessica and Tiana leaped up and ran to me with their sheets in tow. They helped me force Mama down to the chair. While I held her in place, the girls tied her arms and legs to the chair's frame.

When they finished, I tried to fasten her gag in the back, but with her constant thrashing, it wouldn't stay in place. "Sorry, girls." Holding the towel with one hand, I drew my gun and whacked her across the temple with the butt. She slumped in the chair and dropped the keys on the floor.

Tiana gasped. "Is she dead?"

I set a finger against her throat. Her pulse thrummed. "Just unconscious."

After stowing the gun and tightening the knots in the sheets, I tried again with the gag, but the towel was too short to tie a good knot. I got another one from the bathroom and joined them together.

While I worked, Jessica stood with her arms crossed, her eyes darting as she tapped her bare foot on the floor.

She said nothing, but her bent brow told me everything I needed to know. She was scared to death that she was hitching a ride with the wrong guy … again.

When I finished, I picked up the key ring and found a key that might be for the van. "Let's go. Quiet now."

When we exited the room, I dragged "Mama" and the chair into her room and locked her inside with the padlock.

As we padded toward the lobby, the girls trailing me, my phone vibrated. I pulled it out and read a message from Maria Horowitz—*Fred's not home. Can't contact him. I'm coming to your address. I'll take as many girls as my house will hold. List of shelters to follow in a second.*

I put the phone away and continued the furtive march. My phone vibrated again, probably Maria's shelter information. I could look at it after I was sure we were safely away.

When we reached the end of the hall, I stopped and peered into the lobby. The motel's main entrance stood to the left and the service desk to the right. "Looks clear."

We walked to the entrance—two pairs of glass doors with a small anteroom between them. Outside, a single streetlight illuminated the lot. The van sat parked a mere five steps to the right of the outer set of doors, the passenger side facing me.

"Wait here while I check the van. If I can't start it, we have a getaway car coming." I strode to the desk, retrieved the holster, and fastened the straps over my shoulders. After shifting the gun from my waistband to the holster, I hurried back to the entry doors and gave them a push, but a deadbolt kept them in place.

I withdrew Mama's key ring and tried keys. The third one fit. I unlocked the door and pushed it open, then crossed the anteroom and pushed the outer door—unlocked. I stepped outside and looked around, blinking at the falling snow. All was quiet. I jogged the few steps to the van, unlocked the driver's side door, and opened it. An interior light came on, not great for a stealthy escape, but it would turn off soon.

When I jumped in, the stench of beer, cigarette smoke, and a blend of other odors assaulted my nose. This van had probably been the site of a few too many parties.

The engine started without a problem. I turned the heater on and hit the unlock button. Leaving the van running, I hopped out, ran around to the passenger side, and opened the sliding door, then hustled back and rejoined the girls. I whispered, "Jessica, you're barefoot. Maybe I should carry you."

"Carry me?" She squinted. "It's like ten steps to the van."

I shook my head. There I went again with wanting to carry someone. What was I thinking? "Sorry. You're right."

We walked outside. The moment Jessica's bare feet touched the snow, she gasped, then ran the rest of the way to the van and jumped through the side doorway. Tiana joined her and quietly closed the door while I jogged around the van and climbed into the driver's seat.

When I closed my door, I looked back to the cargo area. Jessica wrinkled her nose. "It's worse than ever in here."

"How many times have you—" A light flashed through the window in the rear door. Far away, a pair of headlights approached slowly on the road leading to the motel. The car was apparently battling the snow.

"Someone's out there." I shut off the engine. From the dimness of the rear compartment, two sets of eyes stared at me. "I saw a car. I don't know if it's coming here, but I'm not taking any chances. If it goes on by, then we'll leave. If it stops here and it's not our getaway car, then we'll hunker down out of sight and wait for whoever it is to go inside. Then we'll make a run for it."

The van fell silent. The air grew cold. Shivers followed, along with chattering teeth. I took off my coat and climbed into the cargo area with the girls. Crouching, I covered Tiana with the coat and spread out my arms. "Huddle close."

I laid an arm over Jessica's shoulder. She flinched but let it stay in place. I did the same to Tiana. She shifted even closer.

I angled my head so I could see the road through the back window. A black Chevy Suburban turned into the parking lot. I whispered, "Stay low and quiet."

The girls ducked their heads while I kept an eye on the lot. The Suburban's tires slipped as it rolled up to the main entry. While the engine continued running, a trim white man wearing a dark trench coat stepped out of the left rear door, and an equally fit black man in a white hoodie exited from the other side, brandishing an assault rifle at his hip. The driver backed the SUV out and eased it toward the rear of the motel.

When the pair of men converged on the entry, I slowly rose and inched toward the driver's seat while reaching for my own gun and whispering to the men, though they couldn't hear me. "Just keep your eyes straight ahead and walk inside."

Jessica hissed. "You didn't lock the door. We always lock it at night. Customers come in the back way."

I cringed. She was right, but maybe they wouldn't notice. "We'll take off as soon as I'm sure they're well inside."

I climbed into the driver's seat. The white man halted and pointed at the ground. Three sets of fresh footprints led from the door to the van.

"We're busted. Hang on." I started the engine and slammed the stick into reverse. When I hit the brakes and turned the wheel, the van slid and spun until it faced the road.

As I shifted to forward, the black man aimed his rifle and fired a barrage of bullets. Pops ripped through the air. Tiana screamed. The van's two left tires exploded. I applied the brakes, and we slid to a halt.

The white man shoved the rifle down and shouted, "You idiot. He has passengers in the back."

I lowered my window and glared at them. As the white man walked toward the van, he withdrew a wallet from inside his coat and flashed a badge, barely visible in the dimness. "FBI."

I scowled. "So now the FBI's shooting first and asking questions later?"

"Sorry about that. Topper isn't FBI. He's kind of nervous." He stopped several steps away and nodded toward the back of the van. "Are your passengers all right? I saw some smaller footprints. I'm guessing two girls."

At this point it didn't make sense to lie. "They're fine."

"A couple of the sex workers from this place?"

"Sex slaves, you mean. I'm rescuing them. Taking them to a shelter."

"Then we're on the same side. I'm here to shut down this operation." He gestured for me to come out. "Let's talk about it. I need to interview the girls for evidence."

I studied the agent, trying to detect a hint of deceit. If he was G Man, I couldn't surrender the girls to him. "If you're really on my side, you'll let us go. You can interview the girls at the shelter."

He shook his head. "You won't get very far with two flat tires."

"I'll give it my best shot."

He spread his arms. "Be reasonable. Just let me conduct the interviews. Then you'll be free to go. I'll take them to the shelters myself."

"Just a second." I whispered to the girls. "Have a look. Do you recognize either of these men?"

Jessica leaned forward and peeked out my window. "I've seen the black guy before. His name's Topper. A friend of Papa's."

"That's all I need to know." I pressed the gas pedal, but the drive wheel just spun on the snow-covered pavement. The van wouldn't budge.

"I'd say you're stuck." The agent pushed his hands into his coat pockets and walked toward me with a casual attitude. A few snowflakes collected on his dark hair, but he didn't bother to brush them away. "I think I figured out who you are. Am I really seeing the Guardian Angel unmasked?" His laugh seemed almost genial. "An early morning escape with girls in a stolen van isn't exactly your MO, is it?"

I huffed through my open window, spewing a stream of vapor. "I don't know what you're talking about. I'm just a father who's trying to spring some sex slaves. The cops couldn't do it, so I stepped in."

The agent stopped within a couple of paces. "A father? These girls aren't your daughters."

"They're someone's daughters." I stealthily slid my hand around my gun's holster. I could easily take out this crooked agent, but hitting Topper from here would be far more difficult, especially with the subsonic rounds I was using. I had to bide my time and look for another way to escape. "So why are you here?"

He gestured with his head toward the other man. "My associate is well connected with the growing sex trade here in Spokane, and he informed me that this place was finally ripe for picking. We came here to bust it open, and we need every witness we can get to throw the proprietors in prison for good."

"I heard about your associate. He's a friend of the pimp who runs this place."

"He poses as a trafficker. I've done it myself from time to time so I can track down the head honchos." He shrugged. "We don't actually buy or sell girls. It's just a door into the game. Learn who the players are."

I suppressed an urge to shout. "So you play along while innocent girls are getting raped?"

"I'm not here to defend our methods." He averted his eyes for a moment before focusing on me again. "Look. It's dark. It's cold. You're stuck. Let's just go inside and talk. We're expecting the head of the network to show up here in under an hour. When we arrest him, we'll take these girls' testimonies and get them the help they need."

Jessica whispered from the back. "That's bullshit. He's playing you."

I glanced at her from the corner of my eye and whispered in return. "I know he's dirty. But what do you want me to do? We can't go anywhere."

"Shoot him and Topper both. We can walk if we have to."

I peeked at the agent. He tilted his head as if trying to listen. "Jessica, I can't risk you girls getting shot."

"*You* can't risk it? It's not *your* ass getting the strap. I'd rather die than get whipped again."

"I'm not going to shoot at someone who's got an assault rifle. We all might get shot."

She crossed her arms and said no more.

"I see you have a gun," the agent said, extending a hand as he stepped closer. "Let's make this easy."

I withdrew it from the holster and gave it to him butt first. He slid it behind his waistband. When his suit coat lifted, handcuffs jingled at his belt.

He waved toward the motel door. "Come on. We have a lot to talk about."

I jerked the keys out and slid them into my pocket, then opened my door and jumped down to the snow. When I slid the side door open, the streetlight shone on four eyes—Tiana's and Jessica's, one pair disappointed, the other furious.

Taking Tiana's hand, I guided her down to ground level. When I offered a hand to Jessica, she glared at me, kept her arms crossed over her coat, and hopped down. Without a word, the two girls hustled to the entrance, Tiana still wearing my coat.

I cringed at the sight. By this time, we should have been far away from this place. Yet now they marched back to their prison, my promises shattered. I had nearly managed to break their chains, but now the manacles were snapping back in place. I couldn't let that happen.

When the motel door closed, Topper stationed himself in front of it, poised with the rifle as he looked at the street.

"He'll be watching for the head honcho," the agent said as he walked with me in the girls' trail, keeping the pace slow. "Name's Spencer. Special Agent Reese Spencer." He glanced at me through the curtain of falling flakes. "Yours?"

Now that I was without a coat, cold knifed through my shirt. I pushed my hands into my pockets and resisted a shiver. "I'll keep that to myself."

"Right. The ultimate secret." He focused on the footprints ahead. "Once we spring these girls and take down the Spokane network, I was hoping you'd work with me to destroy the Seattle operation. I even went so far as offering to pay for a girl to come here from Seattle to lure you into town. That's how I guessed your identity, though I was surprised at how quick you got here."

I nodded. So this *was* the same agent I talked to on the phone. It might give me some leverage if I let on that I was aware of his game. "You offered to buy Emma Castillo."

He halted. "How did you know?"

"I posed as the seller. I had Emma with me while I talked to you."

"Where is she now?"

"Safe. That's all you need to know."

"Maybe I need to know more. Like I mentioned on the phone, her parents are dead. Some people think you killed them."

I lifted my brow. "What do *you* think?"

"Not a chance. I've seen frame-ups before, and this isn't even a good one." As he resumed a slow walk toward the motel, I followed. "I checked the ballistics report. The bullets used in the Castillo shooting don't match the ammo you used in Spokane."

"Who do you think's behind it?"

"The same guy who's behind this establishment."

As we drew close to the motel, Topper opened the door for us. When we entered, Spencer opened the next door and ushered me in. The girls were nowhere in sight, probably back in their room getting warm.

Standing at the middle of the lobby, Spencer brushed snow from his clothes while I did the same to mine. "So do you know the honcho's name?" I asked.

He shook his head as he swept his fingers through his short dark hair. "Just a couple of street names. You asked about him on the phone. Sugar Daddy. I guess you were fishing for info. I assume he's why you came to Spokane."

I brushed the last of the snow from my shoulders. "Actually, he told me to meet him here at sunrise. He said he has my daughter. But she's been missing for three years, so he might be lying."

"He's blowing smoke to draw you here. Wants to take you out. You've been putting the pinch on his supply."

I shrugged. "I don't get it. I've rescued maybe eighty girls over the years. The police and private agencies rescue a lot more than I do. I'm just a flea biting an elephant's butt."

Spencer laughed. "He must think you have sharp teeth."

"Maybe, but it's not like I take his long-termers. I focus on abducted girls. They're the small minority of the thousands of kids who go missing. The ones I rescue usually aren't in his clutches yet."

Topper walked in, a hand raised. "Someone's coming. No headlights, but I heard the motor."

"We'd better get ready." He extended my Beretta to me. "Partners?"

"Temporarily." I took my gun and held it at my hip. "Got a plan?"

"Care to stand out in the open while we hide? It's dangerous."

"As if I've never faced danger."

"Touché." Spencer nodded toward the reception desk. "I'll hide there. Topper will be in the hallway, and my driver's waiting out back in case we need to leave in a hurry. Take off your holster, stow your gun out of sight, and stand facing the door."

I slid the Beretta behind my belt in back, took off the holster, and extended it to him. I didn't trust Spencer. Not for one second. But at least now I had my gun. I could play along. "What's your plan?"

"Well, what were *you* planning to do when he arrived?"

"No plans. My first priority was to rescue some girls, but barring that, I imagined a standoff. I can't kill him until I find out if he's lying about my daughter. I was just going to play it by ear."

"Fair enough." He slid a phone partway out of his suit coat. "Get him to talk about his role. I'll record the conversation. When we get enough evidence, we'll come out and arrest him."

"I can do that."

Spencer circled the desk and disappeared behind it while Topper walked to the hall and crouched out of sight.

I faced the double glass doors. With two untrustworthy men watching me, guns in hand, I felt like a target at a shooting range. But I had to stay. Running now would be like turning my back on Emily and losing her. Again.

My heart pounded. Sweat moistened my armpits. After seeing Sugar Daddy's painted grin in countless nightmares, I would finally face the monster who stole my Emily. And one of us was bound to die.

CHAPTER ELEVEN

Deborah braced herself for landing in Charlotte. Fortunately, an aisle seat was still available when Harold reserved the ticket, meaning she could get off the plane quickly.

The big airbus thumped down with a screech of tires, and a whoosh of air followed. Deborah withdrew her cell phone from her purse and turned it on. The moment it received a signal, the message indicator chimed twice—two texts from a blocked number.

Holding her breath, she pulled up the first one. *Trying to help trafficked girls escape in Spokane. Could be dangerous, but they are worth it. Might need some backup. I also need info on shelters in Spokane.* The rest of the note contained an unfamiliar address, and an icon indicated a photo attachment.

She tapped the icon. A photo appeared of a young black girl with dreadlocks. Her eyes, sad and withdrawn, pierced to the heart. She seemed resigned, defeated, lost.

Deborah pulled up a second photo. A white brunette with a bent brow and flashing eyes sat on a disheveled mattress that lay on a dirty floor. A hand, blurred by motion, appeared to be rising to try to hide her face.

Deborah looked away from the screen. Tingles crawled along her skin. Mike was in that dingy room with those girls trying to help them, to save them from torture. And how could he not? To see their travail and then turn away and do nothing would be the height of self-serving apathy.

She exhaled. And for so long she had stayed at home, often resenting Mike's quests, thinking him to be the selfish one, when he was doggedly following an inner call he could never ignore. Of course he had to answer it. Of course he had to save these girls.

She tapped on the next message icon and read the note. *I love you, dearest one. I heard you are coming here. Looking forward to seeing you.*

She let a smile break through. Reading those first three words was like waking up on Christmas morning. Joy awaited. They would be together soon. And she could finally express the love and admiration she had denied him for far too long.

As the plane taxied toward the gate, she thumbed through her contact list and stopped at Maria's number. She tapped the call icon and raised the phone to her ear.

"Hello?" The voice sounded tired.

"Maria, it's Deborah. I got a text from Mike. He's in Spokane. Have you heard from him?"

"Yes. He texted me, too. He wanted information about shelters. He also sent the address where he is. I can probably find it, but Fred's the directional genius, and he's been detained by the state police."

Deborah furrowed her brow. "Detained? Why?"

"Something about aiding and abetting Mike. He only had a couple of minutes to talk. I haven't heard from him since, but I got our lawyer on the case. He's with Fred now, and he hopes they'll process out in the next couple of hours."

"What are you doing in the meantime?"

"Trying to help Mike. I sent him info on a couple of shelters, and now I'm getting Amy and Emma ready to go. I figured I should drive to the address. Since you think he's walking into a trap, I hope to be a getaway driver or something."

Deborah whisper-shouted, "You're taking the girls?"

"Just as far as my mom's. I can't leave them alone. It's snowing pretty hard, but I'm sure my SUV can make it. My nerves are about shot, though."

"Okay. Glad you're playing it safe with the girls."

"Emma doesn't want to play it safe. She's dead set on going with me. She really loves Mike. She thinks she can use her acting skills to help."

"Her acting? How?"

"Actually, she has some good ideas, but it's not going to happen. It's way too dangerous."

When the plane stopped at the gate, the seatbelt sign flicked off. Passengers unbuckled and got up, including a man in the window seat, who now stood hunched over waiting for Deborah to move.

"Okay. Hang on a second." She unbuckled, grabbed her laptop from under the seat in front of her, and rose to her feet. As she inched her way into the aisle, she lowered her voice. "Listen, Maria. My next flight has Wi-Fi, so I'll be online the entire time. I'll text you my email address so you can keep me up to date. By the time I get to Spokane we'll have a better idea of what's going on."

"Sounds good. I'll update you whenever I can."

"I'll see you in a few hours. Thank you for being there for us."

"It's a pleasure. Thank *you* for letting Mike come. If not for him, my Amy would be …" A pause ensued, then a stifled sob broke through.

"Don't try, Maria. I understand. Hug those girls for me." The line began moving. Deborah ended the call and slipped the phone into her purse.

As she followed the other passengers toward the exit, her mind wandered to Mike—where he was, what he was doing. Decisions made in the next couple of hours might mean the difference between life and death for him, and she could only read about it from thirty thousand feet in the air.

When she walked into the terminal building, she joined the moving mass of people—lines of ants scurrying to their assigned destinations. For now, she had to set the fears aside and focus on the task ahead—just get to Spokane and save her husband. Nothing else mattered.

．　．　．　．　．　．

Maria stared through the windshield at the falling snow. Whiteness blanketed the road ahead, making the middle line and the pavement edges impossible to see. The GPS had said to turn left at the next intersection, but finding where the two roads joined had become a daunting task.

The GPS called out, "Make a U-turn."

Maria stopped and squinted at the screen. "What did I do wrong?"

"You must have missed the turn."

Maria blinked. What in the world? The voice came from the back. She looked in the rearview mirror. A girl's face popped into view, smiling. "Hello."

Maria flipped on the interior light. "Emma? How did you get here?"

Emma held both hands up. "Please don't get mad. Amy told your mom that I came with you, so that part's cool. I wouldn't be able to sleep there anyway knowing Mike needs me."

Maria set an elbow on the back of her seat. "We've been over this, Emma. It's too dangerous."

"I don't care about dangerous. If not for Mike, I'd be a sex slave. I can help him."

"Oh. Right. The bait plan." Maria shook her head. "Emma, do you have a death wish?"

"No. The plan will work. I even borrowed a costume and makeup from Amy that—"

"Emma, this isn't role playing. This is for real. You know, real bad guys with real guns and knives. You could get yourself killed."

Emma's voice altered to that of a sophisticated lady. "My life is on borrowed time now. Whatever moments I have to live will be poured out for the man who saved me."

"Oh, give me a break," Maria groaned. "You're a stubborn one, aren't you?"

Emma crossed her arms. "I'm determined."

"Whatever." Maria looked into Emma's dead-serious eyes. Taking her back to Mom's might result in her hitchhiking her way to Mike. Probably nothing would stop her. "Well, I guess you have to stay with me now." She shifted into reverse. "But I'm not giving in. When we get there, you're not budging from your seat."

Emma sat back and kept her arms crossed over her coat. Her lips firm, she said nothing.

"Did you hear me?" Maria asked.

"I heard you."

"Then it's settled."

"If you say so."

"Good." Maria drove backwards until the GPS recalculated again and told her to turn left. She shifted to Drive and made the turn. As the wheels stayed on solid pavement, she breathed a sigh of relief. Just two miles to go and one more turn. She could do this. But driving might be the least of the dangers that lay ahead. And with Emma as a passenger, the potential body count had increased by one.

. . . . . .

I peered through the motel's glass double doors. A black Hummer drove under the glow of the streetlight and eased closer, its headlights dark. Whoever was in there would realize that something was amiss as soon as they noticed the crippled van.

Taking slow backwards steps, I drifted into the shadows. I felt for the Beretta tucked behind my belt. Of course it was still there, but the touch kept my jitters in check.

Four men exited the Hummer, one from each door. The driver was a mountain of a man—black, bearded, and wearing a topcoat. The other front-seat passenger appeared to be white, maybe in his fifties. Dressed in an immaculate dark suit, he was a potential candidate for the devil clown.

Two men behind them, one white and one black, carried assault rifles. Both wore close-fitting pullover sweaters that accentuated their battle-ready physiques.

They slammed the doors and left the Hummer in the light, apparently no longer concerned that someone might notice their arrival. But why would that be?

I glanced at Topper. Still crouching in the hall, he was texting on his phone, his rifle now on the floor at his feet. Had he betrayed us? Only one way to find out.

I reached for my Beretta and grabbed it. "Spencer," I whispered.

"What?" He kept his head out of sight.

"We've been sold out."

He peeked over the desk at the armed men, then at Topper, who now held his gun at the ready, apparently unaware of my discovery. "Make a run for it," Spencer said. "I'll cover."

"You go first. Call in reinforcements."

"Right." Spencer leaped from behind the desk. Topper rose to shoot. I fired at him. He sprawled backwards and toppled to the floor while Spencer ran toward the rear exit and disappeared from sight.

The doors in front burst open. The two armed men stood abreast and took aim at me. The white gunman barked, "Put your gun down."

I bent over and set it on the floor. What else could I do? I was cooked.

"Hands up."

I raised them.

The two gunmen parted, revealing the dark-suited man. As he brushed snow from his sleeves, the driver stationed himself at the door and crossed his arms, looking like an insurmountable stone wall.

As the dark-suited man walked toward me, he straightened his lapels, as if trying to appear dapper. His rounded cheeks matched his paunch, somewhat larger than typical for a middle-aged man, and his aquiline nose seemed more hooked than others of its kind. Although he was considerably heavier than the day he stole Emily, he had to be Sugar Daddy.

He picked up my Beretta and studied my face, as if searching for something. His expression turned sympathetic. "You have aged a bit more than one might expect in three years."

Every fiber of my being screamed to strangle this monster, but I would be dead before I could lay a finger on him. I had to bide my time. "Searching for a missing daughter does that to a man."

"I'm sure it does." He walked behind me and began patting me down. "Just stay calm and don't try to escape. You wouldn't get far. Evans and Goose are excellent marksmen."

I looked at the two bodyguards. Because of his long neck, the black man was likely Goose.

Sugar Daddy withdrew my phone and Mama's ring of keys and slid them into his pocket. Fortunately, without my voice commands or passwords, he wouldn't be able to access anything confidential.

He walked around and faced me again. "You know me as Sugar Daddy, but my business associates call me Vega." He nodded at the driver. "Get a rope."

While the driver went outside, I glanced at Topper. Vega hadn't mentioned his fallen accomplice, as if he didn't care that he could be dying.

Vega pulled a vinyl-covered Carver chair from a sitting area and placed it at the center of the lobby. "Sit. Make yourself comfortable."

I stood my ground. My muscles tensing into knots, I growled, "Where. Is. Emily?"

"All in good time."

The driver returned with a coil of rope and a serrated knife. He set both on the floor a couple of steps from the chair.

Vega gestured toward the padded seat. "If you cooperate, we won't have to bind you."

Gripping the armrests, I lowered myself to the seat. Insults blazed through my mind like an inferno, but it was best to keep my tongue in check. "What's next?"

"That depends on you. My first thought was to kill you and put an end to your grand rescue crusade, but I thought of a way you could provide a greater benefit, a business proposition of sorts. If you cooperate, I won't kill you. If you decline my offer, I will. It's as simple as that."

I riveted my eyes on him. I couldn't show even a hint that I might be intimidated. "I get the impression that this offer of yours will be worse than death."

"To some men, perhaps. But a smart businessman will see the benefits. I suppose we will soon find out what kind of man you are." He nodded toward Topper. "Goose, check on him."

While the black bodyguard obeyed, Vega locked his stare on me. "Topper texted me that an FBI agent was here. I assume he ran and you shot Topper to protect his escape." He tilted his head in an oddly curious way. "Tell me, why didn't you run? You had to know you were outnumbered."

I met his piercing eyes. "What are you, a TV reporter?"

"He's dead," Goose called. "Looks like a bullet to the heart."

My cheeks burned. I had added a fifth man to my personal body count.

"Put him in the trunk." While Goose dragged Topper by his ankles, Vega curled a hand and looked at his fingernails.

"I'll tell you why you didn't run. You are feverishly passionate and will do anything to exact revenge. You see me as an insane clown who stole your daughter for his own sexual pleasure, so you hope to gun me down like a rabid animal."

I kept my tone calm. "That evaluation sounds accurate."

"Of you, yes. But your evaluation of me is skewed. I am not insane, and I did not steal your daughter for my pleasure. I procured her for my inventory. I don't get involved in the sex side of the business. In fact, I have very little to do with this establishment. The easier money is in the buying and selling whether for sex or for labor. Simply put, taking your daughter was part of a business transaction."

Rage erupted in a wild scream. "Business? You call stealing innocent girls business? You call dozens of men raping them business?" I lunged for him, but something crashed against my head. I fell and sprawled across the carpet. My skull throbbed. Blackness pulsed in my vision. In the midst of the pulses, Evans stood close with his rifle in hand, the butt poised to strike again.

Vega nodded toward the driver. "Tie him to the chair."

The driver picked up the rope and looked at me. "The easy way? Or the hard way?" His bass voice sounded like a bear's.

Wincing as I tried not to groan, I climbed to my feet and sat in the chair. A knot on the back of my head throbbed as if ready to burst.

The driver tied my wrist to a chair arm. His strong hands drew the loop tight and strangled my circulation. Beer-soaked breath washed over my face as he spoke again. "If you know what's good for you, you'll keep your mouth shut."

When he finished, my hands and feet tingled. My limbs wouldn't budge. The situation was growing worse every second.

Vega stood directly in front of me. "I referred to my proposition as an offer, but your aborted attack changed that. Consider this a hostile takeover." He tossed the key ring to the driver. "Bring a girl here. The sassy one will be perfect. The one you call Puddin.'"

The driver caught the keys and walked down the hall toward the girls' rooms.

"You see," Vega continued, "Topper kept me up to date. I know of your attempted rescue of two of the girls here. It is fitting that they be punished for agreeing to go—" Something chimed. Vega withdrew a phone from his jacket pocket and looked at the screen, scrolling with his thumb as he read. "Well, that's interesting. Very interesting. This will require some thought, but I can still continue with a demonstration of my resolve."

I concealed a tight swallow. I had to put a stop to this. "Look. Why don't you just tell me what you want? A demonstration isn't going to change anything."

"So you think." Vega slid his phone back to its place. "You rescue sweet innocents who have loving parents desperately begging for their return, parents who are willing to pay." He crouched close and looked me in the eye. "But what about the other girls? Many have no parents who care where they are or what they do, certainly no one who would cough up cash for your services. These girls are unloved. If they never come home, no tears would be shed."

I shot a fiery glare at him. "What's your point?"

"I want to see what value you place on this second class of girls." He straightened. "The knowledge I gain will help me construct my takeover."

I squinted at him. This lunatic "businessman" was making no sense at all.

The driver reappeared in the hallway, pushing Jessica. Propelled by a final push, she stumbled into the lobby and fell to her hands and knees in front of my chair. When she looked up, she glared at me. A raging fire crackled in her eyes.

Vega nodded at the driver. "Do it."

The driver shed his topcoat, revealing a three-inch-wide strap attached to his belt. "With pleasure."

CHAPTER TWELVE

DEBORAH SAT IN an aisle seat again, her laptop perched on the tray table as she stared at the email screen. Earlier, she had written to Maria as much history as possible, including Tommy's accidental revealing of the family's secret and her phone-role-playing of a sex-trafficking madam. Maria answered once in a while with a quick "OK" message. Since she was driving, she couldn't type much.

And now it had been at least half an hour since Maria's most recent update, a note saying that Emma had stowed away and that they were closing in on where Mike was supposed to be. They would probably arrive in a few minutes, depending on the snow.

Deborah glanced at the clock on the screen. That was forty-five minutes ago. And every minute ticked by in slow motion.

Soon, the computer chimed. She clicked on the new-message icon and read. *With Emma. Parked out of sight near address. Motel. Lots happening. Just wait.*

Deborah leaned back in her seat. That wasn't an update. That was a cruel teaser. Sure, Maria was trying to type on a phone screen and was probably nervous, but that didn't help the worried wife sitting six miles high in the air, helpless to do anything.

She drummed her fingers on an armrest. Five minutes passed. Ten minutes. Fifteen. Would this torture never end?

Finally, the chime returned. Deborah sat up and read the note. *An FBI agent came. He was helping Mike but had to run. He has a plan.*

Deborah whispered, "That's it? He has a plan?"

After a moment or two, another message came in. *This is Special Agent Reese Spencer. Your husband is in great danger. I fear he could be killed at any moment. I have a plan to rescue him, but I need your help.*

Deborah typed, *Of course. Anything.* and sent the message.

Through the next few minutes, Deborah drummed her fingers again and shifted in her seat multiple times. The delays were maddening.

Another message chimed. *Heard from Maria about your Paulette deception. Let's use it. I will send a photo to you. You send it on to Sugar Daddy. I will give you email address and tell you what to say. Be ready to be Paulette when you get here.*

Deborah stared at the screen. What? Become Paulette? How would Paulette have acquired Sugar Daddy's email address? The same way she got his phone number?

After another minute, a new message arrived. *Send clothing size info to Maria. She will pick up something for you.*

Thirty seconds later yet another email popped up. *Info coming in five minutes. Be ready to act fast. We have to time this perfectly.*

Deborah leaned back again. After all the anxiety that mounted while waiting helplessly for news, now she had been pulled into the thick of the action. If she made the slightest mistake or delayed too much, it could mean death for Mike.

She leaned close to the computer, set her fingers on the keys, and whispered, "Come on, Special Agent Reese Spencer. Let me have it. I'm ready."

.   .   .   .   .   .

The driver walked to Jessica's side, towering over her as she braced herself on her hands and knees. As he lifted the strap, she looked up at him with pleading eyes and whimpered, "Papa … please … no."

"It's your own fault, bitch." He grabbed the hem of her T-shirt and slid it up to her neck, exposing her back.

I jerked at my bonds. They didn't give an inch. So this beast was Papa, an enormous animal ready to ravage a little girl. This torture was exactly what she feared, exactly what I promised to protect her from. But I was powerless to stop it.

Flexing his muscles, Papa swung the strap down with a heavy lunge. The thick material slapped her back.

"Argh." Jessica bit her lip and turned her glare on me. Pure hatred shot out and stabbed my heart.

I spotted the knife, still on the floor but out of reach of my immobilized hands. I could try to tip over and grab it, but the two gunmen would end that plan in a hurry.

When Papa raised the strap, it left a red welt that bled along one edge.

Jessica heaved shallow breaths. "Papa, I'm … I'm sorry. I promise. I promise I won't do it again."

"Too late for begging." Papa whipped the strap down with all his might. The smack echoed in the lobby. Blood droplets flew and spattered across Jessica's back.

She locked her hate-filled stare on me again. Lifting a hand, she extended her middle finger and thrust it at me. It jabbed like a serpent's fang. Her venom burned.

I rocked the chair from side to side, but the ropes held fast. "Wait. Let me take her place. I told her to come with me."

Vega raised a hand, prompting Papa to stop. "Did you force her?"

"I …" I looked at Jessica's eyes. For a moment, the fierce hatred eased, as if her anger waited for my response.

I took in a deep breath and nodded. "I forced her. She threatened to squeal to Mama. I made her go with us."

Vega folded his hands at his back and strolled toward me. "Why didn't you say that earlier?"

"Because …" I tried to think of a plausible lie, but only stupid ideas came to mind.

"Because you're lying." Vega took the strap from Papa. "So you want to take her place, do you?"

I nodded vigorously. "If you want to beat up on some-one, then do it to me."

Vega ran a finger along the strap's edge. "But watching her causes you far more pain."

"I can't see why—"

Vega whipped the strap down on Jessica's bare skin. A loud smack pierced the air.

Jessica screamed. Her mouth locked wide open as she gasped for breath.

I strained against the bonds—jerking, thrashing. The rope cut into my wrists and drew blood. My voice rasped as I spat out, "Leave … her … alone."

Vega gave me a solemn look. "Leave her alone? Is the demonstration making a difference after all?" He slapped the strap down once more.

Jessica wailed.

"I think it's quite effective." He ripped the strap across her back once more.

New blood splashed. Her arms and legs gave way, and she collapsed to the floor. As blood oozed from the raw welts, she writhed, clawing at the carpet. "Please … please … no more."

Gasping with her, I echoed her cry. "No more. Please. Just tell me what you want. Leave her alone."

Vega rolled up the strap and handed it to Papa. "Take her to her room."

The huge man slid one arm under Jessica's stomach, lifted her, and hauled her away like a sack of dirt. As he walked down the hall, her arms and legs dangled. Blood dripped to the carpet, marking the trail.

Vega spoke with a casual tone. "Now you see what I mean by a hostile takeover. I will not hesitate to repeat my demonstration if you fail to cooperate."

"What do you want from me?" A tremor erupted. I swallowed to quell it. "Maybe we can work something out."

"We will definitely work something out, but first I need to ponder a new development." He turned toward Goose. "Escort him to her room. Lock him inside with a first-aid kit until I'm ready for him."

I fumed. These animals needed to die. I could take one of them out, but what good would that do? I would probably die in the process. I had to help these girls, especially Jessica. But would she let me?

Goose picked up the knife. When he cut the ropes, I stood and rubbed my wrists. The circulation slowly returned with a painful tingle.

He set the knife's point at the back of my neck. "Move."

As I walked down the hall, I stared at the red trail. The drops were like acid that burned in my gut. The image of that strap splitting Jessica's bare skin assaulted my mind again and again. With each repetition, I winced as if the beating were still happening before my eyes. The vision was clear. Too clear. Maddeningly clear.

A new migraine stabbed through my skull. The headaches always debilitated me, though they also enhanced my scent-tracking gift. But I wasn't tracking anyone, and the throbbing torture was sure to make it harder to maintain my sanity.

When we arrived at the door, Goose opened it. "Get in there. I'll be back with the first-aid kit in a minute."

I stepped into the dim room. Jessica lay prostrate on her mattress, her shirt pulled up near her shoulders, exposing her back down to her shorts. Tiana's bed was empty. Neither coat lay in sight.

When Goose closed the door, the shaft of light from the hallway vanished. Complete darkness prevailed. I stood motionless and inhaled slowly. Although the odor of cigarettes and cheap perfume infused the air, the scent of Jessica's soul had no trouble filtering into my senses with its varied flavors. Anger. Hurt. Despair. ... Betrayal.

"Who's there?" she mumbled. "I hear someone."

Following a mental path to her bed, I stepped close. "Jessica. It's Mike."

"Go away." Her tone sounded more despondent than angry.

I knelt and felt with my fingers until they touched the edge of the mattress. "I can't go away. They're forcing me to stay with you."

"The strap wasn't enough punishment?"

I almost said that the beating was really designed to punish me, but that would have been stupid. "I hope I'm not punishment."

The door opened a crack, providing a splinter of light. Still on her stomach, Jessica now faced me, her eyes narrowed against the light.

"Here you go." Goose set a foot-long white box on the floor and gave it a push with his shoe. The box slid halfway across the room and stopped. The door closed, and a padlock snapped shut.

In darkness again, I crawled to the box and brought it back, my head pounding with every move. "I have a first-aid kit. Do you mind if I take care of your wounds?"

Silence burned in the air. After a moment or two, she sighed. "Why not? You're the reason I got them."

I let the barb pass without retort. It was well deserved. "I'll have to turn the light on."

"Go ahead." Her voice was now muffled.

I rose and walked toward the light switch near the door. With each throb of the migraine, darkness pulsed ahead, ready to swallow me as I advanced.

When I reached the wall, I felt around until my hand ran across the switch. I flipped it up. The bulb flashed on, filling the room with harsh yellow light.

As I walked closer to Jessica, my eyes slowly adjusted. She had buried her face in the pillow. The raw, bloody welts on her back blared like a siren.

I knelt again, opened the kit, and found a can of benzocaine. "Jessica, I'm going to spray your back with an anesthetic. I doubt it will take away all the pain, but it might blunt it a bit."

"Go for it." The pillow still muffled her voice.

I sprayed the rawest looking spot at the center of her lower back and spread outward in a circle until wetness covered every welt. During the process, she flinched now and then, but when I finished, she settled and let out another sigh.

"Is that better?"

"A little." She turned her head and faced me, her expression suspicious. "Why are you helping me? Feeling guilty?"

"Definitely. Very guilty." I put the can away and picked up a roll of gauze. "But that's not the only reason." I reeled out a few inches of gauze and cut the strip with a pair of tiny scissors.

Jessica shifted to get a better view. "What's the other reason?"

"Well ..." I found a small bottle of hydrogen peroxide and soaked the gauze. "Because I care about you."

She let out a huff. "Give me a break. Nobody cares about me. Not you. Not Chock. Not my parents. Nobody."

"Believe what you want." When I touched the wet gauze to the worst of the oozing welts, she winced tightly. I pulled away. "I guess it stings pretty bad."

"Like hell." She nodded. "Don't stop. I can take it."

I patted the gauze on each open wound until the material became too bloody to use. As I cut a new strip, I studied her expression. She seemed subdued, surrendered. "You don't look like you're ready to kill me anymore."

She fingered the edge of her pillow. "Yeah. Well, trust me. If I could've, I would've."

"And now?" As I added peroxide to the new gauze, she let my question hang in the air. I patted more wounded areas, but these weren't as deep. She no longer winced at the touch.

Finally, she gave a little shrug. "I guess I decided to let you off the hook. You were clueless about what goes on here, so you didn't know that these guys always find you. You can't get away for very long."

"Then why did you decide to come with me? Because I mentioned a raid?"

"That was part of it. And what you texted to your dearest one. I figured she must trust you, so maybe you were worth trusting. I was wrong, but ..." She shrugged again. "I learned my lesson."

"That you can't trust anyone?"

"Pretty much."

"I can't blame you for that." Once I had cleaned the area, I rummaged through the kit and found a tube of Polysporin. "I'm going to dab the open wounds with an antibiotic ointment. The pressure might make it sting again."

"It's all right. That stuff you sprayed is helping."

The process raised reminders of Emma as she nursed my shoulder at the other motel. I had forgotten about the stab wound. The pounding headache masked all other pain.

I squeezed out a dollop of ointment, dabbed an oozing welt on her lower back, and lightly rubbed it in. "It'll probably be best to leave the wounds open to air. Just don't lie on your back."

She laughed under her breath. "Get real. You know what I do here."

Warmth spread to my ears. "Right. I'd better bandage it. I think I have enough gauze to do a wrap."

"A wrap?"

"Yes. You'll have to sit up."

Grimacing, she rose to a sitting position.

I picked up a full roll of gauze. "Lift your arms a bit."

She complied, again wincing with the effort.

"I'll try to hurry." I wrapped the gauze around her torso. As I repeated the process, her body tensed. At one point, my hand touched bare skin. She sucked in a quick breath and closed her eyes tightly, as if anticipating pain. Or maybe something else?

I whispered, "Don't worry. You're safe with me." When I finished, I grasped her wrist and set her hand over the bandage's endpoint at her stomach. "Hold it right there."

Again, she complied. I cut strips of white tape from a spool and applied them to the gauze to secure it. When I attached the last strip, I pressed it down. "There. That should hold, at least for a while."

"Yeah." She ran a finger along the tape. "I think so."

I slid back on my knees and made eye contact. "I'm sorry, Jessica."

She blinked. "For what?"

"For failing you. I made promises I couldn't keep. I said I'd get you out of here. I said you wouldn't get the strap." I heaved a deep sigh. "I failed."

"Yeah. You did. But ..." She gave me a sincere nod. "Thanks for trying."

"So you don't hate me anymore?"

She narrowed her eyes. "Is that what you want from me? Just no hate?"

"What do you think I want?"

After staring at me for a few seconds, she averted her eyes. "Never mind. It was stupid."

The redness in her cheeks gave away her thoughts. "No, Jessica, it's not stupid. But I'm not like the other men in your life. I really am here to help you. Nothing else."

She nodded but stayed quiet, her gaze still to the side, maybe not yet convinced.

"Jessica, no decent man would ever …" I bit my lip. She didn't need a sermon. She just needed to get out of this perverted pit and learn about better men. "Besides all that, I'm married to a wonderful woman, and I could never betray her. She's my dearest one, like you saw in my text."

She regained eye contact. Her lips parted, then closed again. Slowly, ever so slowly, wetness filled her eyes. Finally, a single tear dripped to her cheek, and she whispered, "Okay. I get that."

"This is what I want from you." I offered her my hand.

She looked at it. "A handshake?"

I nodded. "Just a sign that you don't hate me anymore."

After studying my face for another long moment, she slid her hand into mine. "All right, then."

As we shook hands, we exchanged no words. Her expression—skeptical, yet inquisitive—said it all. She no longer hated me, but she wasn't quite ready to trust me, this strange guy who didn't want to use her for pleasure.

I pulled my hand away. The migraine eased, and my muscles relaxed. "Well, it looks like we're going to be together for a while longer." I rose, pulled the two chairs closer, sat in one, and gestured toward the other. "You said I'm a talker. Let's talk."

She eyed the empty chair. "About what?"

"About you."

"About me? Why?"

"Because I want to know more about you. Tell me what you want to do when we get out of here. What are your hopes? Your dreams?"

She smiled. "You really are a piece of work, aren't you?"

"Yeah, maybe. But humor me. Dream with me." I extended a hand. "Need a lift?"

She stared at my gesture, skepticism thick in the air. Finally, she grabbed my hand, rose with my pull, and sat in the chair, again wincing.

"Does it hurt too much?"

"I'm okay." She looked upward for a moment, as if in thought. When she regained eye contact, she leaned forward a bit, her arms braced on her legs. "So you want to know my hopes and dreams."

"Very much so."

"Okay. You asked for it." She took in a deep breath. "When I was like seven, I wanted to be a nurse, but my parents said I daydreamed too much to make it. Well, I did daydream a lot, so maybe they were right. Anyway, Scott was one of the older boys at school. I guess he was maybe thirteen. He got a horse, so I started going to the library and reading about how to take care of horses. I thought maybe I could help him and make a friend. I mean, why would he turn me down, right? So I learned how to ride, but that wasn't easy. I fell off and bruised my butt a few times, but Scott kept telling me, 'Get back on the horse, dammit.' And that was a big lesson for me. It's how I survive. Like when Papa found me at the shelter and whipped me. When I fall, I always get back on the damn horse. I can't think about the stupid things I did before."

Jessica chatted on and on, and I listened intently, asking questions and laughing at her surprisingly sharp wit. Joy sparkled in her eyes. How long had it been since someone really paid attention to her? Had anyone truly probed her mind, her heart, or listened to her voice, how her words rolled off her tongue, how her thoughts altered her expression, how her story transformed her mood?

She laughed. She pondered. She mourned. Most of all, she poured out the longings of her soul.

And I drank in every drop. This girl, this young woman, was a priceless gem. I didn't know how many hours I would be spending with her, but I was determined to savor every moment.

CHAPTER THIRTEEN

A FTER TALKING almost nonstop for nearly an hour, Jessica's shoulders sagged. "I think I'm getting sick." She got up and laid a hand on her stomach.

I rose from my chair. "Do you need a bucket?"

"Just bed." As she hobbled to her mattress, I noted her bent-over form. The anesthetic had probably worn off.

She lowered herself to the mattress and lay on her side. With every movement, she winced, but when she settled, her face calmed.

"Lights off?" I asked.

"Sure. Just leave the bathroom light on so we can see."

I turned on that light, then strode to the door and turned off the ceiling bulb. As I walked back to my chair, Jessica nestled into her pillow. "Are you tired?"

"Exhausted." I sat heavily in the chair.

"You can rest in Tiana's bed." Her tone seemed hospitable, perhaps apologetic. "The sheets are pretty fresh for a change."

"Thanks. I think I will." I shuffled to the mattress and laid my aching body down. Although my migraine had eased, my shoulder resumed its painful throb. The bandage

Emma applied shifted a bit and pulled against the dried blood, but I was too tired to try to fix it.

I closed my eyes and took in the room's aromas. The antibiotic ointment mixed with perfumed tobacco to create an odd blend. As before, Jessica's scent hovered and now Tiana's.

"Mike?" Jessica said with a soft voice.

I kept my eyes closed. "Yes?"

"When you told Tiana and me your story, you mentioned your missing daughter. What's her name?"

"I didn't say her name?"

"Nope."

My throat narrowed. I could barely speak the word. "Emily."

Jessica echoed in a whisper. "Emily." After a moment of silence, she added, "What does she look like?"

"After three years, I can't be sure. I don't know if I would even recognize her. But she had dark hair and brown eyes. Narrow face and frame. Some Latina features."

"I get the picture. I'll bet she's really pretty."

"She is." I opened my eyes and looked at Jessica. "And she loves pretty things, especially anything purple. So I'm always on the lookout for a girl who wears purple."

Jessica propped herself on an elbow. "Since you found other girls, why couldn't you find Emily? The smell thing, I mean."

"Long story, but I didn't learn about my gift until a while after she was kidnapped. Then it was too late."

After a pause, Jessica whispered, "What does a soul smell like?"

"Well, it depends on the person. Emily's soul is ... fruity, I guess. I noticed it while packing away some old clothes she outgrew, about the same time I discovered my gift. Anyway, no one else smelled quite like her until I started tracking Emma, the most recent girl I rescued."

Jessica smiled. "Her name's Emily. Likes purple. Soul smells fruity. Got it."

I laughed softly. "Yes, you do."

When I closed my eyes again, a new silence descended. Except for the hum of a heater somewhere, all was quiet. The warmth was comforting. From what I had read in the article Mahoney sent, some stables had far worse conditions than this one. At least the girls here had heat and decent bedding. Of course, royal finery couldn't make up for the abuse they endured. These slavers were just protecting their income generators. Nothing more.

As I waited for sleep to arrive, I tried to imagine what Emily might look like today. In my dreams, she was always the eleven-year-old girl who smiled and played with puppets and dollhouses, but by now she might have suffered the ravages of sexual abuse, drug addiction, and beatings. Perhaps she had become hardened and emotionally callous. Maybe I wouldn't recognize her at all.

I slept. For how long, I had no clue. Tortured dreams skewed time. The strap fell on Jessica again and again, and her thrusting finger knifed at my face with every blow. Then, the dreamscape shifted to her room. As I wrapped the bandage around her body, she transformed into Emily.

When I taped the bandage in place, she gave me a forlorn stare and whispered, "Don't you love me, Daddy?"

I tilted my head. "Of course I love you, sweetheart."

"Then why wouldn't you carry me?" She held Rupert the parrot, his body in one hand and his head in the other. "Fix him."

I took the decapitated parrot and tried to push the two parts together, but they wouldn't stay in place. "I'll need some glue. I don't have any right now."

Her lips moved again, but Deborah's voice emanated. "Glue won't fix what you've broken, Mike."

Then Emily's image burst into a million pieces. I tried to catch the multicolored fragments, but they slipped through my fingers and dissolved on the floor in puffs of smoke.

I covered my face with my hands and wept. I had lost her once again, and it was my fault. All my fault.

The smoke drifted to my nose. I inhaled. Emily's scent permeated the room—so strong, so real.

An odd scratching noise pierced the dream. I opened my eyes. The sound continued. I scrambled to my feet and faced the door.

Jessica rose and joined me. "Just survive, Mike. That's what I always say to myself. I just gotta survive."

"Thanks, Jessica."

The door opened. The hallway light framed Papa. His huge form filled the doorway as he twirled a ring of keys on his finger. "We have a surprise for you."

Emily's scent stayed constant. It wasn't a dream. "Just tell me what it is. I hate drama."

"Can't. Vega's orders. He wants to see your expression when he springs the surprise."

Emily's face blazed across my mind. Had Vega brought her to this place?

Goose stepped into view, an assault rifle in hand. "They're here."

"Good. You can take him." Papa eyed Jessica. "I got something to do."

Goose gestured with his head. "Let's go."

As I walked, Jessica followed. When we reached the door, she looked at Papa. "Is it all right if I go with him? He's about to collapse."

Papa shook his head. "You got more coming to you for what happened to Mama. She's still out cold. If she doesn't wake up soon, I gotta take her to the hospital. That costs big bucks."

"But I didn't hit her."

"Maybe not, but you're gonna pay for it." Papa grabbed her arm, forced her into the room, and thrust her toward the rear corner. She stumbled and fell to her back on the mattress. As she cried out in pain, Papa stepped into the room and began loosening his pants. He looked back at Goose and me. "Go on. This ain't no peep show."

When Goose reached for the doorknob, I blocked his hand. "Wait. I want Puddin to come with me."

Goose wrinkled his brow. "Why?"

"Because if she doesn't, I'm telling Vega that you ruined any chance of me cooperating." I lowered my voice to a whisper. "Show Papa who's boss."

"Well it ain't you." Goose looked into the room. "I'm taking the girl."

Papa glared at him. "What if I don't let you? You gonna shoot me?"

Goose rolled his eyes. "C'mon, man. You can do her later. Let's get this thing done."

Papa zipped up his pants and stormed out, bumping Goose with a shoulder as he passed through the doorway.

Jessica struggled to her feet and joined us, her face solemn as we walked abreast along the hallway.

When we reached the lobby, I scanned the area for Vega. No one was in sight.

From the glass doors, sunlight poured in, enhanced by a blanket of snow piled up at the edge of the parking lot. What time was it? The angle of the sun indicated at least noon or maybe early afternoon. Had I slept that long?

The Carver chair stood in the middle of the room, severed ropes scattered at the legs. I inhaled. Emily was close. The scent of her vibrant soul infused every particle of air.

Goose motioned toward the chair. "Sit. If you don't want to get tied up again, just do what you're told."

With Jessica still at my side, I lowered myself to the chair. When I settled, she whispered, "Thank you. Papa's always really rough on me."

"You're welcome." I took her hand. "Stay close."

"Okay." She looked at our clasped hands, her whisper lower than ever. "But do we have to hold hands?"

"Uh … no." Heat radiated to my cheeks as I released her. "Sorry."

She backed away a step. "I'll stay here as long as they let me."

Goose stood five paces in front of me, shifting from foot to foot as his eyes darted.

"Nervous?" I asked.

He averted his eyes. "If you knew Vega like I do, you would be."

Less than a minute later, Vega appeared down the hallway, striding quickly as he looked at his phone and tapped the screen with both thumbs. Still wearing a full suit, he looked like an urban businessman hurrying to a meeting. Evans followed, armed with a rifle.

When they arrived, Evans joined Goose, and the two stood like sentries. Vega slid his phone into an inner jacket pocket and smiled at me. "I see you and the young lady became friendly. You must have really put on the charm." He squinted at Jessica, his focus on the bandage around her waist, exposed by her bare-midriff T-shirt. "You patched her up nicely. A gentle touch is often an effective aphrodisiac, even for a whore."

Although an urge to stab him with insults raged within, I spoke with a calm voice. "Jessica and I came to an understanding."

"Fair enough. I see no need to probe further, though I find your attachment to her intriguing." He withdrew a folded sheet of paper from the same inner pocket. "I hope you and I can also come to an understanding."

With Emily nearby, I mentally begged for him to cut the drama and get to the point, but again I kept my cool.

Vega opened the paper and turned the printed side my way. "This is a purchase order for twenty girls for a convention in Dallas. They want young girls, under eighteen. If I could send them, I would be paid handsomely, but you have pinched my supply line."

I gave him a skeptical stare. "I killed a few kidnappers. I'm sure you have a bigger network than that."

"Oh, I do, but your efforts don't end there. Your exploits have emboldened others to oppose my business dealings. Citizen action has spiked as has compassion for the girls. The police are raiding more places like this one, and they're taking the girls to charity shelters instead of to jail. We can't get them out and put them back to work as easily as before." He tucked the note into his pocket. "By yourself you're a minor annoyance, but the people you inspire are the real supply-line pinchers. They multiply what you do a thousand-fold."

"So if you kill me, the influence will fade."

"Not at all. You would become a martyr, which would instead enhance your influence. I have grander plans." He inhaled dramatically through his nose. "It is said that you can sniff out troubled girls. Track their scents for miles and miles."

"What about it?"

"I can use that talent." He wrinkled his nose as if smelling a foul odor. "At one time, I did the catching myself. Dressed as a clown, I sought girls who were easy targets, baiting them with drug-spiked candy—a tedious job. Fortunately I have others to do that now, but the craft of ensnaring is still too slow for my liking."

Jessica whispered, "This guy is a freaking lunatic."

"I know. Shhh."

Vega continued without a hitch. "Girls from broken homes are usually deeply troubled and needy. They're safer for us to procure and keep. No one answers their calls. Often no one even cares. This is why I tested your compassion for this type of girl, to see if you would be likely to resist my new business plan for you."

I tensed. His twisted logic was becoming clear.

He folded his hands at his back. "Your compassion, even in spite of her wrath, was extraordinary, which told me that your resistance would be high. That's why I moved to preempt your objections by having your daughter brought here." He nodded at Goose. "Bring them in."

Goose opened the motel's entry doors and walked out.

I swallowed hard. Even though Vega planned to use Emily as coercion, and it would be best for her to stay far, far away, I longed to see her again.

While we waited, Evans walked to my chair and set the barrel of his rifle behind my ear. "Just remember I'm close by." As he stepped back a few paces, Jessica, still standing within my reach, let out a wordless growl.

Soon, Goose returned and held one of the doors. A black woman with platinum-blonde hair strutted in. Wearing a long, fur-trimmed coat and tight leather pants, she stopped, disgust obvious in her overly painted expression as she looked around. "What a dump."

Vega leaned close to me and muttered, "Her name is Miss Paulette. Uppity bitch has no clue that she's out of her league."

Miss Paulette looked outside through the open door and waved a hand. "Well, if you're so cold, get in here."

A girl walked in, hugging herself and shivering. Goose bumps covered her bare legs and arms. Wearing pink short shorts, a tight black T-shirt, and dark purple lipstick and eye shadow, she looked like a youthful hooker. Only her ragged sneakers and white socks spoiled the image. She squinted at me as if confused.

My entire body trembled. I tried to look past the mask of makeup. Yes, she did look like Emily. I inhaled and took in her scent, that long-lost scent that I had sought for so many months. It was true. It had to be true.

I whispered, "Emily?"

"Daddy?" She took a step toward me, but Miss Paulette grabbed her arm and pulled her back.

"No, honey. Not yet. He has to earn you. Nothing's free in this business."

I shot to my feet, but someone grabbed my shoulder and shoved me back to the chair.

The rifle barrel appeared inches in front of my eyes. "Stay put," Evans said.

I clutched the chair's armrests. My facial muscles twitched as I tried to talk without squeaking. "Emily, are you all right?"

Again hugging herself, she stared at the floor, biting her lip.

Vega walked to her and lifted her chin with a finger. "Don't you want to look at your father? Don't you have anything to say to him? He's been searching for you for three years."

When he drew back, Emily focused on me. Her lips tightened, and a hand waved though she kept it tucked under her arm. "Hi, Daddy."

I could barely form words. "Hello, sweet daughter."

"Well …" Emily watched her shoe as she slid it along the carpet. "I'm not so sweet anymore."

"What makes you say that?"

"Because of what I do." She kept her eyes averted. "I'm a whore."

Bile erupted into my mouth. I nearly choked but managed to swallow it. "Emily …" My voice rasped. I cleared my throat and forced the words out slowly. "Emily. All of that is in the past. We'll get a fresh start. We'll get out of here and—"

"Wait." Vega held up a hand. "How do you propose to work that miracle? Emily belongs to Miss Paulette."

I growled, "Spill the plan. How do I get her back?"

He sported a triumphant smile. "I will give you more details later, but the bottom line is simple. Use your gift to locate troubled girls. Procure them and bring them to me. This will fill my immediate need, and the icing on the cake is that we will announce that the Guardian Angel has switched sides. The instant firestorm will destroy your heroic image as well as the spirit of those you have inspired."

I shook my head. "You're out of your mind. I would never help you kidnap and enslave girls."

"Out of my mind?" Vega laughed. "Actually, you are out of your league."

I clenched my teeth. "I suppose you're going to tell me you'll kill her if I don't join you."

"Oh, no. Of course not. If Emily dies, my leverage is gone. You would no longer have a reason to acquiesce. I plan to coerce you in another way." Vega unbuttoned his suit jacket and unclipped a strap from his belt. "Shall we see if Emily's bare skin is as tender as Puddin's?"

CHAPTER FOURTEEN

JESSICA WHISPERED, "Oh, my God." My heart thumped wildly. I could barely breathe.

Emily shuddered while Miss Paulette held her wrist firmly. "Don't you dare whip her," Miss Paulette said. "She's mine until I see some cash."

"Very well." As Vega reclipped the strap to his belt, he smiled. "I just wanted our friend to understand the consequences if he should resist my demands."

Swallowing again to cool my burning throat, I focused on Vega. "Listen." A tremor throttled my voice, but I couldn't help it. "Suppose I agree. Who will have Emily? You or Miss Paulette?"

"For now, Miss Paulette." Vega buttoned his suit jacket, concealing the strap. "She and I are negotiating with regard to a number of girls she has for sale, and I am acting as her broker. Until the deals are completed, Miss Paulette is incentivized to hold Emily, so they will remain in this area until you finish your task."

"You mean, collecting girls."

"Twenty, to be exact. I don't care if they're fresh or already hustling on the street, but they have to be under eighteen." He withdrew the purchase order from his pocket and slapped it against his palm. "That will be enough to fill this request and to forever damage your reputation along with your inspirational influence."

"You're a madman!" My shout escaped unbidden. I opened my hands to strangle Vega, but when I caught a glimpse of Evans stepping closer, I inhaled deeply and relaxed my muscles. "Okay. Okay. Listen. Once I help you get twenty girls, what's to stop you from demanding twenty more? Then fifty more? You'll never let me quit."

"That dilemma has already been resolved." Vega gestured toward Miss Paulette. "This savvy businesswoman knows that she can get more than market value for Emily from you, so when you get the twenty girls, she sells Emily to you, and I have no more leverage."

"But Emily's also worth more than market value to you, so you might buy her to keep me hunting for girls."

Miss Paulette wagged a finger at me. "Listen, Mister Mike. I'm a woman of my word. When I make a deal, I keep it. I wouldn't sell Emily to him for all the tea in China. So when you get the girls for him, it's over. Then you and I can negotiate a price."

I gazed into her eyes. Her voice, even the words she used, sounded so familiar.

"Exactly." Vega stalked toward me. "But until that time, if you show any hesitance to cooperate, I will send word to have Emily gang raped and whipped on camera, and we'll post the video on the Internet for all of my associates to see." He crouched and touched my knee in a condescending manner. "Whom will you allow to suffer? Twenty strangers, or your own daughter? I await your decision."

I tightened my jaw, calling on every ounce of strength to keep from spitting in his face. His sick drama was infuriating. But I had to give him an answer. Obviously I couldn't let Emily get raped or beaten, but I couldn't help him kidnap twenty girls either. I had to feign cooperation until I could find other options. "Okay." I exhaled heavily. "I'll get the girls. Anything for Emily."

Vega's smile grew nauseatingly smug. "As expected. A father's protective instincts for his own daughter surpasses all else. He is willing to allow twenty other girls to suffer in her place."

I glared at him. "Don't rub it in."

"As you wish. I see no need to further salt your wounds." Vega rose and backed away toward Miss Paulette. While they conversed, Jessica stooped at my side and whispered, "I can't let this happen. It's not fair to make you choose like this."

"If you have another option, let's hear it."

"I do. Get ready."

"Ready for what?"

"To fight with me." She lunged at Evans and clawed at his eyes.

I leaped after her and jerked his rifle away, but something slammed into my head. I dropped the rifle, toppled over, and landed on my side. Horrific pain ripped across my skull from ear to ear. I writhed. Bells rang. Dark spots flooded my vision.

In the midst of the spots, Goose stood close with his rifle aimed at me. Evans, his face bleeding, picked up his rifle and set the barrel against Jessica's head as she sat crying nearby.

Vega strolled toward me in a nonchalant manner. "Have you already violated our agreement? How do you expect me to trust you while you're collecting my girls?" He kicked me in the stomach.

The impact punched the air out of my lungs. I curled into a tight ball and gasped for breath. The blow cleared some of the spots away, though new pain sent hot peals through my eye sockets. Near the motel entry doors, Miss Paulette called out, "I saw the whole thing. That girl attacked your man. Mister Mike was trying to make sure your man didn't shoot anyone. He was probably worried about his daughter getting shot."

Vega's gaze shifted from her to Jessica to me. "A fair assumption, though that doesn't explain Puddin's attack."

"She's in love with him," Goose said. "It happens. Even to whores."

"Understood." Vega nodded toward the door. "Escort our guests outside. I'll take care of things here."

Goose guided Emily and Miss Paulette out. The moment the motel doors closed, Vega turned to Evans. "Take Puddin to her room and kill her. Do whatever you want to her first. Just keep it all quiet."

"Gladly." Evans grabbed a fistful of Jessica's hair and jerked her to her feet. As he began leading her away, she cried bitterly.

The sight sent a new shockwave through my body. Air shot into my lungs, and the last spots in my vision cleared. "Wait." I sat up and pointed at Jessica. "I want Puddin to come with me."

Vega raised a hand. "Evans. Hold a moment."

Several paces down the hall, Evans huffed but released Jessica's hair.

Vega refocused on me. "Why do you want her?"

"Let me get up." I struggled to my feet, shuffled to the chair, and sat down heavily, my stare now locked on his. "She can be useful to me. Why lose an asset?"

He smiled and wagged a finger. "I like how you appeal to my profit motivation. Very well played."

"So you'll let her come?"

"Perhaps." He began walking around me in a slow orbit. "The biggest potential flaw in my plan is the freedom I must allow if you are to apply your talent. If I give this whore to you, I double the risk that you will cross me."

"But you'll also double my speed. I can find the girls, but she'll be the one who'll convince them to come with me."

Vega stopped, an eyebrow lifting. "I see your point. And another angle just occurred to me. The two of you together will create a juicy bit of gossip. The Guardian Angel has a slutty mistress helping him track down wayward girls. He's getting some action on the side."

I let the comments roll off my back. I had to get Jessica out of this place. I couldn't let her down again. "Call it whatever you want. I need her help."

"Very well. It is so ordered." He nodded at Evans. "Get her things and bring them here."

Evans shoved Jessica toward me. She staggered for a moment before regaining her balance. Tears streaming, she hurried to my side, knelt, and grasped my hand as she wept. "I'm sorry ... I ... I had to do something. I just—"

"Shhh. It's all right. No harm done."

Vega stood at my opposite side and laid a hand on my wounded shoulder. "Harm will come if you fail to do as you're told. Do not call anyone, text anyone, or try to contact anyone but me, and then only if you have a girl for me to take off your hands. For that purpose, I will supply you with a mobile phone. I will also give you that van outside, which has been repaired, but be aware that it has a GPS tracker that we will monitor. We will also have someone tailing you. If you stay at a motel, we will check phone records and any security cameras to see if you tried to access on-site computers."

"That really narrows my research abilities. I usually rely on Mahoney for that."

"I will make sure you have plenty of incentive to sniff out the feral kittens without your Mr. Mahoney." He compressed my shoulder, but the new pain seemed minimal compared to the pounding throbs in my head. "I will arrange for Miss Paulette to send daily video updates to the phone so you will see that Emily is alive and well. That should keep you on task."

My headache grew worse and worse. My brain felt like it was ready to explode. "I'll stay on task."

Vega extended a hand. "May I help you up?"

"I can manage." Bracing my hands on the armrests, I pushed myself to my feet. As usual, the migraine enhanced my senses. Jessica's scent poured forth with pungent agony, and Emily's scent still hung in the air, thinly distributed but easily detectable. Hers seemed worried. And no wonder. Who could tell what the future held for her now?

Trying to settle my dizzied vision, I helped Jessica rise. Her arms tucked against her chest, she stood close, as stiff as a statue. I slid an arm around her, careful to avoid her wounds. She flinched but stayed put.

Vega pushed some items into my free hand. "The keys to the van, your new phone, and a credit card for expenses. I will be monitoring your purchases. I expect to see gas, lodging, and food. Nothing else. And one room. Not two. I'm not paying extra just because you want to bring your whore along."

I slid the items into my pants pocket. "Clothing. I need warm clothes for Jessica. She has nothing decent to wear."

"Evans will be back soon with her possessions, but I will make an allowance for anything she's missing. Nothing but the basics."

I nodded. I didn't want to say another word to this monster. I ached to get out of his sight, plan how to escape his sticky web, and rescue Emily.

When Evans returned with Jessica's coat and a plastic trash bag, she put on the coat. I took the bag, guided her to the door, and walked outside to the van.

The following minutes flew by in a fog. I must have started the van and somehow navigated through town without cognizant thought, because the next lucid moment, I found myself driving into a mall parking lot with Jessica in the front passenger's seat. Snow had been plowed into high drifts, reducing the number of available parking spaces. I crept slowly past tightly packed cars in search of an opening.

Maybe I had suffered a concussion and lost short-term memory. The last clear memory was of Vega giving me the keys, the phone, and the credit card. The phone sat on the console between Jessica and me. The credit card was probably still in my pocket.

"Um ... what were we talking about?" I asked.

Jessica looked at me, her hands tucked inside her coat. "Nothing. You haven't said a word other than asking a guy how to get to the mall."

"Yeah. Sorry about being quiet. My head really took a hard blow."

"No problem. I like it quiet." She inhaled through her nose. "I smell French fries. I haven't had any in a long time."

"Then we'll find the fries." I found a parking space pretty far from the mall entrance and looked at Jessica's bare feet and shorts. The sight brought back another memory—Evans giving us the coat and bag. "Couldn't find anything to wear in the bag?"

"My skirt and top. And my underwear. The skirt's kind of short, so I thought I'd wait. You said we'd get clothes."

"Right. I'll go first and get you some socks and shoes. Then we'll go together and shop for something warmer."

"Great. Size seven. Cheap gym shoes will be fine. Vega said just the basics."

"Good shoes *are* basic." I got out and jogged toward the mall. Still without a coat, I shivered, but it couldn't be helped. At least I wasn't barefoot.

Inside, I found a department store. After buying a pair of thick socks and top-of-the-line Nike shoes, I returned to the van and waited while Jessica put them on. Then we hustled through the biting air back to the mall.

At the same store, she chose a pair of jeans and a long-sleeved top. I picked up a coat and underwear, though Vega hadn't approved purchasing what I needed. When Jessica emerged from the dressing room wearing her new clothes, I inserted the card in the reader and signed the screen with an indecipherable scribble. After that, we stopped at a drug store and bought some toiletries for each of us and a bottle of Excedrin for me.

As we passed the food court on the way out, Jessica gave me a coy smile. "I found the fries."

"Sure." I dug in my pocket and pulled out a twenty. "I don't know when we'll have time to eat again, so go ahead and get an extra large."

"And a diet Coke." She snatched the bill. "How about you?"

"Fries and a Coke would be great. Just no diet stuff."

She lifted her brow. "And smokes?"

"If you have to." Just as she turned, I touched her shoulder. "Wait. Aren't you too young to buy cigarettes?"

"No worries." She grinned. "I can hustle a guy to buy them for me."

"Well … like I said. If you have to." I looked at the exit. "I'm going to the van to see what I can detect. I'll meet you there."

"You got it." She walked toward one of the restaurant counters.

I hurried to the van, got into the driver's seat, and lowered the window. As a fresh, cold breeze blew in, I inhaled. Although I always needed a starting scent to follow a particular trail, it seemed reasonable that I should be able to track down a dense population of troubled souls. Once there, I could find a motel close by.

Dozens of aromas entered, a curious mixture of emotions. Sadness flowed like a slowly creeping mist. Anxiety blended in. Then anger pierced the air. Not a storming fury that stings like a hornet. It smelled like an embarrassed anger. Shame. Self-loathing. Bitterness that bites itself and leaves an acidic taste that slowly burns—mental mutilation that might lead to suicide.

A moment later, like a trembling child, the scent of a worried woman sneaked in. The aroma seemed compressed, as if huddled in a corner. The scent was familiar.

Could it belong to Deb? I had forgotten all about her. Had she arrived in Spokane? If so, where was she now?

I shook my head. The concussive blows had addled my brain. Insanity was creeping in. Here I was driving around town with an underage sex worker, buying her nice things, planning to go to a motel with her, and I hadn't given a single thought toward my wife.

The scent of shame returned. But this time it was my own.

When Jessica arrived, she climbed into her seat, handed me a box of fries, and set a soft drink in one of the cup holders between us. She set her own drink next to mine and began munching a French fry.

I searched around her. "Where are your smokes?"

"You said if I have to." She pulled another fry from her bag and smiled. "I decided I don't have to."

I smiled in return. Her joy was contagious. She looked like a bird set free from a cage.

I started the engine. While she brushed her hair, looking at herself in the rearview mirror, I scanned the inside of the van for sound-detection devices but found nothing. No surprise. If Vega had planted a microphone, he probably wouldn't have added so many other precautions. We could probably talk without worry that anyone was listening in.

Soon, Jessica had brushed her hair into silky tresses that draped her shoulders. I shifted the mirror back to its place. "Next on the agenda. You can probably pick up a local transit bus here. I know a wonderful family who'll help you get wherever you want to go. Maybe then you can catch a bus back to Oakland—"

"Oakland?" She pointed the brush at me. "You said you needed my help."

"Do you really want to help me kidnap girls and hand them over to that monster?"

"You won't do that. You have a plan." Her eyes narrowed. "Don't you?"

"Not yet." As the pounding threatened to crack my skull, I massaged a temple. "I just need to think. They have GPS monitoring. Someone tailing me. No phone calls. If I try to sneak out from under Vega's thumb, he'll hurt Emily. You can't make contacts for me, because whoever's tailing us will see you leave."

"Don't worry about that." She wagged her brush at me. "I've been ducking cops since I was eleven."

"But they'd notice you're gone." I raised a finger. "Unless we can find a girl who looks like you."

"You mean to sit in my seat?"

"Right. But we'd have to wait until dark to be sure it'll work."

"That's cool, 'cause you need to take those pills for your headache and catch a nap. Most of the girls won't come out until later anyway."

A black sedan with tinted windows appeared behind us, seemingly searching for a parking spot. That could be the car Vega assigned to tail us. I would have to be watchful for it or any suspicious vehicle from now on.

After taking a couple of Excedrin, I drove out of the parking lot, followed my nose into Spokane's downtown area, and, tracking a growing scent, turned eastbound onto Sprague Avenue.

"Look." Jessica pointed out her window. "A bus pulled in over there. I'll bet it's a station. A perfect place to start."

"All right. We'll look for a motel close by, get some rest, and come back later."

After driving around a bit, I chose a Comfort Inn about a mile from the station. Earlier, we passed the Davenport where Spencer had said he was staying. The motel raised questions that my concussion had hidden away. Where was Spencer now? Since I killed a man to save his life, maybe he would eventually help me out behind the scenes. In any case, I couldn't trust him. Since he played trafficking games while girls were being raped, he had to be dirty.

When I parked in the Comfort Inn's lot, the same black sedan I had seen at the mall drove slowly past on the access road.

I gestured with my head. "Check out the black car. We were followed."

Jessica turned. Her eyes moved with the vehicle's progress. "I'll be watching for it."

Carrying our new purchases and Vega's phone, we checked into a room with two double beds. When we walked in and I turned on the bedside lamp, Jessica stopped just inside the door. She stiffened and pulled in her bottom lip.

I set my purchases and the phone on the bed farther from the door. "Something wrong?"

She stared at the closer bed. "Um ... Do you mind switching?"

"No problem." I transferred my things. "What's the matter?"

"Well ..." She walked past the first bed, sat on the second, and folded her hands in her lap, her eyes scanning the room. "I've never been in a motel room without getting raped."

I sat across from her. The tragedy of her words burned a hole in my heart. "You want me between you and the door."

Her eyes sparkling with tears, she nodded. "I know it's stupid, but—"

"It's not stupid. I'll do whatever it takes to help you feel safe."

She brushed a tear from her cheek. "Thank you."

After shedding our coats and using the bathroom, we again sat on the beds and faced each other over the gap between them.

"Okay. Here's the deal." As I gestured with my hands, Jessica stared at me as if ready to memorize every word. "No one's home at my apartment, and my wife's supposedly on her way to Spokane. She might already be here. Her mobile phone was stolen, so we can't call that. She has a replacement, but I didn't memorize the number ." I pulled the phone book from a drawer and searched without success for Fred Horowitz. If only I had thought to keep the business card they had put in their purple bag. "Fred and Maria Horowitz have her number. I rescued their daughter, Amy."

I wrote their names on the motel's notepad. "I don't remember their street, but I do remember seeing a place called Manito Park real close by." I wrote the park's name as well. "That's something to go on."

Jessica tore off the page and pushed it into her jeans pocket. "I can find Internet somewhere, maybe go to a different motel and use their computer. I'll find Amy's family somehow."

"I don't doubt that." I reclined and laid my head on the pillow, not bothering to pull back the covers. "What time do you think we should go to the station?"

"Maybe five or so. Like I told you, I left my parents when I got home from school. That happens a lot. Kids come home to all kinds of crap and just can't take it anymore. So they try to get out of town."

"Around five sounds like a plan." I glanced at the room's clock—2:30 p.m. "We have two hours to rest. That should help."

Jessica set the clock's alarm, got under her bed's covers, and turned to her side, facing me.

I noted her position. Lying on her back probably hurt. "Do you want me to check your wounds?"

"I looked at the bandage while I was in the bathroom. Blood's not leaking through. It's probably fine."

"Good. Let's get some sleep." I turned off the lamp and closed my eyes. As I tried to drift off, Jessica's scent wafted my way. Earlier she emanated determination, resolve. Now the flavor was different, a trembling wariness. But she would be all right. I was there to protect her.

Just as sleep began to hold sway, a voice broke the silence.

"Mike?"

I opened my eyes to darkness. "Yes?"

Her voice quavered. "Talk to me."

"Uh … all right." I imagined her staring at the same darkness. She was scared. She needed comfort. "Do you like poems?"

"I guess so. I haven't heard any in a while."

"I have one memorized. When Emily and I cuddled on stormy nights, she liked hearing it."

"Because she was scared?"

"Sort of. I think she just wanted company."

"That's really sweet."

"So do you want to hear it?" Silence ensued. Only Jessica's breaths and my thrumming heart broke the stillness as the quiet moment ticked by. The sound of rustling covers followed. My mattress sank a bit, and her voice drew close. "I need some company."

"Sure." I sat up, propped the pillows behind me, and leaned back against the headboard. My eyes now adjusting, I could see Jessica as she scooted close.

She laid her head on my shoulder. "I'm ready."

Although her body trembled, her warmth felt good. "It's a nonsense poem called Jabberwocky." I took a breath before starting. "'Twas brillig, and the slithy toves did gyre and gimble in the wabe: All mimsy were the borogoves, and the mome raths outgrabe."

Every time I inhaled to continue, her scent drifted in. Her tremors, both body and soul, eased into peaceful contentment. It seemed that she had finally decided to trust me.

With each line, I slipped closer and closer to sleep. Whether I reached the part where the boy killed the monster, I don't know.

A dream took over—Jessica on hands and knees bracing herself as the strap slashed her bare flesh, then her terrified expression as the strap lifted to make ready for another strike. All the while, I sat watching as the failed rescuer who betrayed her.

The sight enraged me, sickened me. And, for some reason, it puzzled me. The beating, of course, was a device to torture me as well, and a way to expose my empathies.

Vega's words returned to mind. *I want to see what value you place on this second class of girls.* At that moment, I had no clue what he was talking about, but his insane demonstration soon explained his methods.

Yet, he miscalculated. No amount of force could make me do his bidding. I didn't simply have empathy for Jessica.

I loved her. She was no second-class girl. She was a human being—a smart, courageous, sacrificial, loving human being. She just wanted to be loved in return.

And Vega's demonstration and the follow-up first-aid treatment taught me that lesson. Love begets love. Real love looks beyond the ravages that cruelty inflicts. It sees through masks no matter how scarred they are on the surface.

Jessica was scarred. So was I. We both needed love to remove our masks.

The dream drifted away. I opened my eyes. I lay on my back with my shoes off, still on top of the spread, though half of it covered me, folded over from the side. Jessica was now in her own bed snuggled under the blanket, her respirations deep and even.

Dim light from the window illuminated her face—serene, angelic. Her fear of rape had flown away, and she had found peace.

Closing my eyes again, I searched for sleep. Although the headache had eased, dreams would come, most likely the Halloween kidnapping again. That would be more than enough to upset my rest.

Yet, if I could dwell on Jessica's newfound trust, maybe it would be different this time. Maybe everything was different now. A healing miracle had taken place—the result of forgiveness freely poured out from one injured heart to another. Love had torn away my mask. The scent of my own soul was likely sweet indeed.

CHAPTER FIFTEEN

DEBORAH DRIED HER face with the motel room's hand towel. The last of the dark-skin makeup was gone. Looking at the bathroom mirror, she straightened her black jacket's sleeves as well as the sleeves of the white shirt underneath. Now wearing loose black slacks instead of those ridiculous skin-tight leather pants, she finally felt normal.

From the counter she grabbed a shopping bag filled with the pants and blonde wig and walked into the main room where Fred, Maria, Emma, and Special Agent Spencer sat in a circle of furniture—a sofa, a loveseat, and an armchair—pulled together from the walls of the suite with a square table at the center.

Deborah sat in the loveseat next to Emma, who had also broken free from her makeup mask. Wearing her jeans and a shirt Mike had bought for her, she snuggled close and locked elbows with Deborah.

Sitting in the single chair, Agent Spencer leaned forward. "Now that Mike is safe from immediate harm, we have a chance to breathe and make sure we're all up to speed. The next step is to get word to him that the girl he thought was Emily is in no danger. He can stand down from Vega's plan. We're assuming Vega took Mike's phone. Deborah, what do you think he would do in this situation?"

"He'll be trying to contact me somehow." She nodded toward Fred and Maria. "Or one of them."

Agent Spencer shook his head. "Let's assume that Mike thinks the slightest deviation from the plan will jeopardize Emily. We have to go to him. Find him somehow before he starts kidnapping girls."

"But he won't do that," Deborah said. "I know he won't. He'll figure out a way to turn the tables."

Agent Spencer gave her a condescending smile. "We'll just have to make sure he doesn't have to, won't we?"

Deborah tried to ignore the patronizng snub, but this agent's manner seemed too phony to overlook. Yet, what could she do but play along and learn everything possible? So far nothing else had worked, not even when she risked exposure to speak directly to Mike with one of her common phrases. *I'm a woman of my word* seemed to register in his eyes, but only for a fleeting moment. "Can you find out where Mike is?"

"I wish. Even though I've been pretending to work with Vega for a while, he doesn't trust me. I barely convinced him to go along with this plan. He knew I had been searching for Emily, but it still took some doing to convince him that I found her. The photo was the clincher. But now Vega's shut me out."

"Why were you at the stable motel this morning?" Fred asked.

"To take Vega down. My goal was to lure him to the stable so I could place him at the location and get some video evidence of his connection to the prostitution ring. But that didn't work out. My associate betrayed me. If not for Mike, I'd be dead. Fortunately, Vega decided to give me this second chance to help him."

"Agent Spencer …" Deborah's hands quaked as violently as her voice, but she had to go on. "During your search, did you find any sign of the real Emily?"

He shook his head. "All I know is that Vega sold her in the Fort Lauderdale area soon after he kidnapped her. When Vega learned about Mike's identity a short time ago, he sent an operative looking for her, but when I presented Emma as Emily, he might have canceled the search. I'm not sure."

"So when we get Mike back," Deborah said, "will you start a new search for Emily?"

"Definitely." Agent Spencer blew out a sigh. "Okay. Are there any more questions?"

Deborah lifted a hand. "Do you think Mike trusts you?"

Agent Spencer shook his head. "He thinks I'm the lowest form of life. That's the risk I take being a double agent of sorts."

"So you can't be the one to track him down and tell him it's safe to stop looking for girls."

"Not me personally, but local police are on the lookout, and we're monitoring security cameras all over town. We know Mike's driving the motel's van, so maybe someone will spot it." Agent Spencer withdrew a phone from his pocket. After tapping the screen a few times, he turned it where everyone could see a photo of a navy blue cargo van. "This is it."

While Fred and Maria studied the van, Deborah pictured Mike driving it around the city, his expression worried. "Where are the best places to look for him?"

"Places runaways might go. Shelters. Churches. Soup kitchens. Parks. Abandoned buildings. Anywhere they can sleep. Some kids try to leave town, so I've got a man at the bus station on Sprague just down the road. Mike might also go to prostitute hangouts. Pick up street girls who are already sex workers. There's a likely spot several blocks away. Doing that is risky, though. Their pimps might give him trouble."

"You mean risky for the pimps." Deborah exhaled loudly. "Okay. I'll walk to the bus station and check it out, then I'll go to the prostitution area."

"Not alone," Fred said. "I'll come with you."

Maria picked up a purse at her side. "I'll go home, and Amy and I will start calling churches, shelters, and soup kitchens."

Agent Spencer rose from his seat and focused on his phone's screen. "And I'll monitor any leads the police get."

Deborah looked at Maria. "Will you take Emma?"

"No." Emma tightened her grip on Deborah's hand. "I'm coming with you."

"It's too—" Deborah caught herself. She almost said *too dangerous*, but after what Emma did at the motel, walking public streets was nothing. Besides, knowing her, she would find a way to follow. "All right. You can come."

"Okay," Agent Spencer said, still looking at his phone. "I got something. The van was spotted on a security camera at the bus station. It was heading east on Sprague, so we were on the right track."

"Let's go." Deborah rose from the sofa and grabbed hers and Emma's coats. "I programmed your number into my phone. I'll contact you if we find anything. And you do the same. Keep me up to date."

"I will." Agent Spencer tapped in a number and paced as he waited for an answer.

Fred, Maria, and Emma joined Deborah and put on their coats. The foursome took an elevator to the lobby, a quiet ride save for the humming of the lift mechanism.

When the doors opened and they began walking toward the hotel's main entrance, Fred spoke up. "Deb, what do you think of Spencer?"

"Think of him?" She stopped near the center of the cavernous lobby. "Are you asking if I trust him?"

"Well, he's working with the man who stole your daughter. He set up a roadblock to catch Mike. His officers kept me at the station way longer than necessary, at least until the snow was too deep and I couldn't go looking for Mike. Not exactly a great résumé."

"Yeah. His story stinks."

"What I want to know," Maria said, "is if Vega really believes our Emily is the real one. I mean, maybe we're the ones being gamed. I'm not sure Vega would let Emma go if he really thought she was Emily."

Fred nodded. "Good point. Vega needed to convince Mike, not us. As long as Mike's on board, Vega gets what he wants."

"But where does that put Agent Spencer?" Deborah asked. "Is he for us or against us?"

"I say he's against us. Maybe he's getting a cut of the action. If Mike collects girls, Spencer collects money. So Spencer wants Mike out on the street finding girls. Vega and Spencer don't care if Emily is real as long as Mike thinks so and brings in the catches."

Deborah shook her head. "Then they don't know Mike. He's simply not going to grab girls and throw them to the wolves." She hammered each word home. "It. Won't. Happen."

"But would Mike sacrifice Emily to keep from carrying out Vega's plan?"

"No, but he'll sacrifice himself. If he can't figure out another way, he'll mount a one-man stampede to kill Vega or die trying."

"After talking to Mike, I believe it." Fred raised a finger. "But here's the bottom line for us. If we find Mike and tell him what's going on, Vega's scheme is sunk, so if Spencer is on Vega's side, he'll want to make sure we fail. We have to watch our backs."

"Then this search might be a lot more dangerous than I thought. Maybe Emma had better go with Maria and—"

"No." Emma buttoned her coat. "It's only more dangerous if Agent Spencer is on Vega's side. You don't know that. He could've stopped us way before now. Maybe killed us all up in his room."

"Kind of morbid, but true." Deborah ran a hand across Emma's hair. "I guess we can't be running from shadows."

"Then I'll leave Emma with you." Maria pointed toward a side exit. "I'm parked out there. I'll see you later."

Fred kissed her tenderly. "See you in a little while."

When she left, Fred walked toward the front door. "I'll go first. Check for possible trouble."

As Deborah followed with Emma alongside, she scanned the lobby—an exquisite chamber with high ceilings, gorgeous furniture, a grand piano, and tapestry-like engravings on the ceiling. Why would a federal agent stay in such a pricey place? Maybe he really was getting a cut of Vega's action.

When they reached the door, Fred waved to them from the outside. Deborah led Emma to the sidewalk and joined him. Cold wind funneled down the street from the west and beat against their coats, forcing them to duck low and face eastward.

"The wind's pushing us the right way." Fred pointed. "About five blocks to the bus station."

Deborah and Emma walked abreast, while Fred stayed behind. Deborah glanced at him. Hunched over with his hands in his coat pockets, he looked all around, watchful for an ambush. Every minute or so, he gave an update about how far they had to go.

Soon, they turned right onto Bernard Street and arrived at a red brick building on the left—the Spokane Intermodal Center—which housed bus and train depots. A gust of wind swept them into a trot and ushered them through the main entrance.

Inside, people walked this way and that along a tiled floor. A few stood in line at a train ticket window. One man leaned against a wall reading a schedule pamphlet, sweat-shirt hood up and head down.

Deborah studied every face. Mike was nowhere in sight.

Fred walked toward a set of restrooms. "I'll check the men's room."

"Maybe I'd better go," Emma said. "We might not have another chance for a while."

"Good idea." The pair hurried to the ladies' room, relieved themselves, and washed up. When they walked out, Deborah searched for Fred, but he wasn't in sight. "Do you see him?"

Emma glanced around. "Maybe he saw someone who looks like Mike and followed him outside."

"Worth a shot." They walked briskly to the exit and into the cold, blustery wind, but there was no sign of Fred anywhere.

When they reentered the depot, Deborah marched straight toward the men's room. "Emma," she called. "Stay close."

Emma hurried to her side.

Deborah stopped at the door and knocked. When no one responded, she pulled the door open and called, "Fred? Are you in there?" Again, no one answered.

She stepped in and gestured for Emma to follow. Once inside, Deborah called again. "Fred?" Her voice echoed in the tile-and-porcelain room. She pushed open each stall door. Inside the last one, Fred sat on the toilet, fully clothed and leaning back against the wall, a bullet hole in his forehead and blood spattered on the wall behind him. His eyes open and vacant, he stared straight ahead.

Deborah gasped. Emma screamed. Deborah grabbed her wrist and bolted for the door. They dashed into the depot. Deborah shouted, "Police? Security? Anyone?"

While everyone stopped and stared, a uniformed officer, lean and lanky, jogged toward them. "What's the trouble?"

Deborah gestured toward the men's room with a trembling arm. "My friend. In there. He's been shot. I think he's dead."

The officer barked into a shoulder-mounted radio. As the world began spinning, his words seemed garbled. Deborah pinched herself. She had to stay in control.

The officer drew his gun. "So you were in there, ma'am?"

"Yes, yes. He didn't come out, so we went in to check on him."

"And was anyone else in there?"

Deborah shook her head. "No one."

"Stay right here. Backup's on the way." Leading with his gun, the officer pulled the restroom door open and walked inside. Some of the gawking crowd dispersed and went about their business, while a few milled around.

Emma pulled Deborah's sleeve. "We'd better go. We'll be the next targets."

Deborah looked for the hooded man she had seen earlier. He was gone. She whispered, "You might be right. When the police show up, we won't be able to go anywhere."

She jogged with Emma to the exit. Once outside, they walked at a brisk pace, heading eastward again as the wind pushed them along. Deborah pulled Emma's hood up, then her own. "Keep your head low."

Sirens wailed, drawing closer. Deborah and Emma marched on, their faces as hidden as possible, but it would be easy for the police to locate two females of their description. They would have to find a place to hide.

As Deborah walked, grief swelled to the surface. It seemed that her phone burned in her pocket. Maria needed to know about her husband, but calling would slow their pace. Besides, the police would find Fred's phone and call the most frequently used numbers, unless, of course, the murderer took it from him. And then who would tell Maria she was now a widow? How would Amy learn that she had lost her father?

"We have to stop." Deborah halted and pulled out her phone. "I need to call Maria."

"Okay." Emma looked westward, blinking at the cold wind. "I'll keep watch."

Deborah brought up her contacts and found Maria's number. Just as she raised a finger to call, her phone rang. She juggled it before grabbing it again.

She looked at the caller ID. "It's Fred's number." She tapped the answer icon and raised the phone to her ear. "Hello?"

"Deborah. This is Special Agent Spencer. What in the world is going on?"

"Going on?" She swallowed. It was time to get aggressive and reach deep for a strong voice. "I found Fred's body in the bus station men's room. Why do you have his phone? Did you have him killed?"

"Don't be ridiculous. I'm at the station investigating his murder. I recovered this phone from his body. Your number was on his recently called list, so I checked it out. Since you took off, it makes you look suspicious."

"Would you have stuck around to see what was going to happen next? We have bulls-eye targets painted on our backs."

"Just tell me where you are, and I'll send someone for you. We'll put you in protective custody."

"Protective custody? Who will protect us from you?" She tapped the End key. It was a good thing she had disabled the GPS locator earlier.

Two seconds later, her phone rang again. This time it showed Agent Spencer as the caller.

Deborah slid the phone into a coat pocket and took Emma's hand. "Let's go."

They jogged ahead. After nearly a minute, they came upon a beauty shop on the left. Deborah pulled Emma inside, and they sat on padded wooden chairs in the waiting area.

As they tried to catch their breath, the proprietor, a thirty-something woman with long brown tresses and perfectly made-up face walked from a room that held four vacant barber-style chairs. "May I help you?"

Deborah tried to settle her heart. The reality of seeing a murdered friend and then running from police and Agent Spencer was crashing down like an avalanche. She spoke with labored breaths. "May we … please … just sit here … for a little while?"

The woman looked through the window. "Someone chasing you, honey?"

"You could say that."

"Trust me. I understand." She closed a set of blinds, pulled up a chair, and sat. Her expression exuded sympathy. "Boyfriend? Husband? Ex-husband?"

"I'm not sure you'd believe me if I told you."

"Trust me, sweetie, in this part of town, you see it all."

Deborah looked her straight in the eye. "Sex traffickers. This girl was just rescued, but they're after us. We need to get away."

"Traffickers?" Her brow bent double. "Well, you've come to the right place. I've got wigs and makeup. When you leave here, your own mama won't recognize you."

"Thank you. But we both had disguises once before. They'll probably be watching for that. It's hard to disguise that we're a woman and a teen girl traveling together."

The woman pinched her chin. "Maybe not as hard as you think."

"What do you mean?"

"All I need is a wig, scissors, and skin glue. Just sit right there. I'll be back in a minute." She hustled toward the rear of the vacant shop, her voice fading. "I'm Julie, by the way."

When she disappeared in a back room, Deborah took Emma's hand. It was cold and trembling, and her own trembling hand could do nothing to restore calm. "It's pretty obvious now," Deborah said softly. "Agent Spencer is on Vega's side. He has no intention of finding that van. He wants Mike to kidnap girls and bring them to Vega. That means we're on our own. We're the only ones who'll tell Mike what's going on."

"But we don't have any way to tell him." Emma picked up a business card from a table next to her chair. "Maybe write your number on a card and give it to Julie. If she hears something, she can call you."

"That's a long shot, but it won't hurt." Deborah got up and found a pen at the service counter. She sat down again and, her hand shaking, wrote her number on the back of the card. Her unsteady grip made the pen slide and smear the ink. She lifted the card to the light and frowned. "That's not very readable."

Emma took the card and looked at it. "Nope, but I'll keep it in case we need to call Julie." She put it in her coat pocket and picked up another one from the table. "Try again. Just be calm."

Tightening her fingers, Deborah wrote the number legibly this time. "That should do it."

Deborah got up again, set the pen on the counter, and returned to her seat. Emma stared at her lap. Although her lips moved, no sound came out.

Leaning toward Emma, Deborah whispered, "Are you praying?"

She nodded. "For Amy and her mom."

As Deborah imagined a grieving mother and daughter dressed in black, both touching a closed coffin, tears welled.

A family had been fractured, and now the survivors needed to leave home to stay away from a stalking FBI agent.

After whispering a prayer of her own for Mike, Deborah withdrew her phone and brought up Maria's number. "Pray for me, too, Emma. I have to call Maria and tell her she's a widow."

CHAPTER SIXTEEN

WHILE I SLEPT, the usual dream arrived, Emily's kidnapping. Deb, Tommy, Emily, and I walked on a sunny, paved path through the park. Yet, something was different this time. We weren't holding hands.

Still, we wore our pirate costumes with the accessories—eye patches and foam swords. Rupert the parrot teetered on my shoulder, making Emily's pins dig into my skin. The pain seemed much worse, like hornets stinging, but I could ignore it, at least for a while.

Right on time, clouds blanketed the sky, and thunder announced the expected storm. As always, Tommy shuddered and slid an arm around Deb's, though this time he sucked the thumb on his free hand, another odd alteration to the dream.

When it came time to run, Emily reached up and said, "Carry me, Daddy."

I waved her away. "We'll be faster if I don't."

She pouted, but when I began a slow jog, the others ran alongside.

My mind cried out, "You fool. Carry her. Tell her you'll keep her safe from the wolves."

Yet, my dream persona ignored the warning.

Soon, Rupert toppled off my shoulder. I stopped and turned. When Rupert hit the pavement, his head broke off and lay apart from his body.

"He's broken." Emily collected the two pieces and held them up to me. "Fix him."

I took them and fitted them together, but they fell apart again. "I'll need some glue. I don't have any right now."

Deborah whispered from behind me. "Glue won't fix what you've broken, Mike. You should've carried her like she asked."

I ignored the barb. "It's too late now. Let's just get going." We jogged on, Emily still carrying Rupert's head and body, one part in each hand.

With the pavilion in sight, rain fell in chilling torrents. Thunder crashed nearby. Tommy pulled his thumb from his mouth and reached for my hand, but the sight of the slobbery digit made me jerk away. "Man up," I said. "You can handle this."

Tommy recoiled and began crying. Deborah glared at me but stayed quiet.

We ran under the shelter and huddled near the center, finally safe from the storm. The clown showed up as before, Sugar Daddy sticks in hand as he called out his hideous name. My mind anticipated the lightning strike that would drive the clown away, but it didn't come. Instead, he joined us under the pavilion. My dream persona greeted him with a handshake.

My mind whispered, "No. Don't welcome him. He'll take Emily." But the Mike under the pavilion paid no attention.

The clown said that the party venue had changed due to rain, and he had come to show everyone where to go. While

Deb and Tommy stayed to give other arrivals a heads up, Emily and I followed the clown, Emily still trying to piece Rupert together.

The clown took a path that led us into a secluded section of the park. Along the way, he picked up a metal rod that looked like a fallen fence post, saying it didn't belong there. He would throw it away.

As rain fell harder, warnings blared in my mind. The path was getting darker. Thunder rumbled. Yet, the clown seemed to be in no hurry. Not only that, walking in a storm while carrying a metal rod didn't make sense.

I called a halt. When he turned and faced me, I said, "This path just leads deeper into the woods."

"We're fine." He pointed down the path. "If you walk that way a few more yards, you'll see a clearing."

That did it. This clown was bogus. We weren't going another step. I whispered to Emily, "Let's run" and grabbed her hand.

My fingers knocked Rupert's body from her grasp. She pulled away and reached for it. I lunged to stop her, but the clown's metal rod swung toward me. I tried to duck, but it crashed down on my head.

Darkness flooded my mind. Within the inky soup, a man's silhouette scooped a screaming girl into his arms and carried her away.

I tried to shout, but no sound emerged. Why had the dream taken such a horrific turn? In this version it was all my fault. If I had carried Emily, Rupert wouldn't have fallen. We would have gotten away. She would still be in my arms, and this three-year nightmare would never have begun.

Finally, my voice returned in a wail. "Emily, come back. I'm so sorry." I curled into a fetal position and wept. "I'll carry you, Emily. I'll carry you all you want. Just come back to me."

"Mike?"

The call came from above as if spoken from the storm.

"Mike, wake up."

Something shook my body. I opened my eyes. A wall lamp illuminated a female, vague and blurry, standing at my bedside.

She whispered, "You were having a nightmare."

I sat up and blinked. Her face finally came into focus. "Jessica?"

"Yeah, it's me." She rubbed my arm. "Everything's fine. You're all right."

I shook my head to scatter the cobwebs. "That dream. It was different."

"Different?" Jessica sat on the bed with me. "Different from what?"

"Whenever I get a migraine ..." My throat felt like it was full of sand. "I need some water."

"I'll get it." She hopped up and walked to the bathroom. "You were shouting for Emily. Something about carrying her." She returned with a plastic cup of water and handed it to me as she sat on the bed across from me. "It was pretty intense."

After drinking the water, I nodded. "Whenever I get a migraine, I dream about Emily's kidnapping. It's always the same, except this time it wasn't. I always carry Emily when she asks me to, but tonight I wouldn't. So the parrot fell and broke, and that led to the clown having a chance to ..."

I let my words die and looked at Jessica. Her head tilted as if she were trying to interpret my insane ramblings. "Sorry," I whispered. "It's just a dream. Thanks for waking me up."

She took the empty cup. "Want more?"

"No. I'm fine. Thanks."

"Do you think the dream means something?"

"Maybe." I slid out of bed and stood. My legs shook a bit, but they quickly settled. "I wouldn't carry Emily. I wouldn't hold Tommy's hand. I acted like a total jerk." I pointed at myself. "I was the reason Emily got kidnapped. It was my fault. If I had been a halfway decent father, she'd be safe."

Jessica set the cup on the bedside table. "But it was just a dream, right? That's not the way it really happened."

I bit my lip hard. As the dream replayed in my mind, the previous dream ran alongside it. The lightning strike, the tree falling on the pavilion, the collapse over our heads now looked like an absurd parody.

Then Deb's words echoed. *Glue won't fix what you've broken, Mike.*

The pain in her voice stabbed my soul. Her disappointment in me as a father ... as a man ... twisted the blade.

I sat on my bed again. Tears streamed. A spasm erupted. I buried my face in my hands and sobbed. "Deb, I'm so sorry. I'm so, so sorry. No wonder you don't want me to come home."

Jessica sat next to me and massaged my back. Her strong fingers pushed deeply into my trembling muscles. "It's all right, Mike. Just go ahead and cry."

"It's all true." I lowered my hands and looked at her, my vision blurred by tears. "The new dream is the true one.

It's my fault I lost Emily. It's my fault she's with that Miss Paulette woman, threatened with rape and whippings."

Jessica bent her brow. "Then get back on the horse, dammit."

I blinked at her. "What?"

"Get back on the damn horse." She slid off the bed and grasped my wrists. "You gotta forget the stupid things you did before. It's the only way to survive."

"But it's worse than falling off a horse. I hurt someone else. Not myself."

"All the more reason." She pulled me to my feet and looked up at me, her eyes aflame. "You gotta get on that horse and go after that bastard and kill him."

Her confident voice washed over me—a contagion that spread heat from fingers to toes. Every muscle flexed. The headache eased. My mind cleared. Yes, the dream was real. Yes, it was my fault. But now it was time to right my wrongs and stop whitewashing them with fake memories.

As I curled a hand into a fist, I growled. "Vega's game is over. It's my turn to dictate the moves."

She punched my arm. "That's what I'm talking about."

"Thanks for the boost." I gave her a firm nod. "You're amazing. Did you know that?"

She smiled. "Keep saying it, and I might believe you."

"Well, it's true. You are amazing."

"I'm not Emily, but ..." She slid her hand into mine. "You can hold my hand. You can even carry me if you'd like. If it'll make you feel better."

I pulled her into my arms and held her close. "I feel better already."

Letting out a long sigh, she laid her head against my chest. She whispered, "I wish I had a father like you."

Tears crept to my eyes again. I could barely control my voice. "I would be proud to have you as a daughter."

She drew back. "Okay then." As she brushed away tears of her own, her voice perked up. "So we'll do what we planned. We find a girl who's willing to go with us, and you call Vega pretending you're going to deliver her. I'll sneak out to try to contact Amy's parents."

"That sounds good."

"Yeah, but what then?"

"I don't know. I'll figure it out on the way." I glanced at the clock—4:23. I grabbed my coat from the bed and Vega's phone from the night table. "Let's go."

After throwing our coats on, we hurried to the van, made our way to Sprague Avenue, and headed west toward the bus station. As we approached, flashing police lights appeared ahead.

"Not a good idea." I made a U-turn at the next intersection and drove eastward. Soon, we passed a mission shelter on the right and a seedy motel on the left. With darkness falling, this might be the perfect place to look around. "I sure could use Mahoney now."

"I heard Vega mention him," Jessica said. "Who is he?"

"My research guru. I don't know if Spokane has a well-known track. Keep your eyes open for a porn shop or a strip joint. Something like that."

"A strip joint might be a good place to start. We could talk to the girls there."

I shook my head. "They're usually older than what Vega's looking for. Besides, they're not the kind of girls I focus on."

"What do you mean?"

"Strippers, independent escorts, agency girls, any girl who isn't trapped. Some *want* to be doing what they're doing. They make decent money, and they get to keep it. Some even enjoy it. They prefer to be called sex workers, entertainment professionals, or whatever label makes them sound respectable."

"Yeah. I've met a couple of them. They were pretty nice to me."

"I suppose they're nice." I tightened my grip on the steering wheel. "Well, they can do what they want. It's not my mission to stop them. Unless they're underage. That's where I draw the line. There's no such thing as an underage prostitute. They're all coerced, even if they've convinced themselves otherwise."

"I know what you mean. I tried to convince myself it was cool. When I first started on the streets, I pretended I was a big shot, strutting my pathetic skinny stuff in short shorts and a push-up bra with nothing to push up. But that didn't last long."

"What changed your attitude?"

Jessica gave me a skeptical look. "You sure you wanna know?"

"Trust me. I've heard it all."

"Okay." She took in a deep breath. "The first oral I did on a guy. It was in his pickup truck. He smelled like a pig. Made me want to puke. When I finished, he called me a skinny little bitch and threw a crumpled dollar bill at me. He said that's all I was worth. Then he pushed me out and drove away."

Anger simmered, but I kept a straight face. "Did you tell your pimp?"

"I had to. First, he slapped me and said I'd get lots more practice. Then he took off to find the guy. I never heard what happened after that."

"So you get just a dollar and you get slapped for it. I guess that knocked you down a peg."

"It did." She looked out the windshield, her countenance gloomy. "But you know, I don't think it was the dollar so much as what he called me. A skinny little bitch. Ever since that day I've hated the word bitch. Nothing makes me madder."

"And you were eleven." I shook my head. "I can't imagine what you went through."

We drove on in silence. I glanced at her from time to time, but she kept her gaze forward. Maybe she was embarrassed about what she said, wondering what I thought of her. The images she painted of herself were far from pretty.

I reached for her hand and whispered, "Jessica, like I told you before, I think you're amazing. You're a courageous young woman, and I'm proud to be with you."

She looked at me with piercing eyes as if searching my soul. Finally, she said, "Thank you," grasped my hand, and held it as we drove on.

A couple of blocks later, I spotted a black girl leaning against a brick building. She wore tight jeans and a shirt that revealed a substantial waist, not fat, but certainly heftier than Jessica and Tiana. She had to be cold, but to her, the skin advertisement was probably more important than comfort.

"A candidate?" I asked.

Jessica shook her head. "She doesn't look like me at all."

I touched Vega's phone, now on the console between us. "At this point, we just need a girl so we can contact

Vega and tell him we have one. If we can't sneak you out, then so be it."

"If you say so." Jessica lowered her window. "Let me handle it."

As I pulled over to the roadside, she leaned her head out. "Hey, girl. You getting any action here?"

The girl pushed away from the wall. "Who wants to know?"

"Just someone who's been where you are. I was walking the streets when I was—"

"Don't preach to me, girl. I can get that at the mission."

"I'm not preaching. Just trying to help. We can get you off the streets. You can get cleaned up. Find a job that's—"

"I got a job."

"So you think standing out like that in the freezing cold waiting for some John to buy your goods is a job?"

She shrugged. "It's money. A girl's gotta live."

"Then your man just takes it all. What does that leave you?"

She wagged her head in a cocky manner. "I ain't got no man. I keep every dime." She waved us on. "Just move along. You stopped at the wrong corner."

"A renegade," Jessica muttered. "We might as well go."

I pressed the pedal and eased away. "That's a hooker without a pimp, right?"

"Yeah. Most of them don't last long, though."

"Did you ever try to go it alone?"

She shook her head. "One girl I knew tried. A pimp beat her to a pulp. That kept me in line."

I drew a mental picture of a pimp throwing the black girl up against her leaning wall and approaching her with a clenched fist. "I guess pain is an effective deterrent."

"Yeah. I'm not a fan of pain. That's why I hate the strap."

I winced. Her words scalded like a hot iron. She probably didn't mean for them to hurt, but they did. Her whipping would probably haunt my nightmares for years to come.

I swept the thoughts to the side. Concentrate on Emily and protect Jessica at the same time. I could do this. "I guess I'll just follow my nose for a while."

With Jessica's window down, the air in the van freshened with new odors. A number of scents entered, perhaps both girls and boys. Without a source to go by, the aromas in a breeze were often hard to separate.

Soon, the scent of a troubled soul drifted in—pungent, urgent. "I got something. Smells like trouble."

I turned left at the next intersection. The aroma grew stronger. It seemed to call from somewhere to the right, but no road led that way. I drove into an abandoned car lot and parked. As I unbuckled my seatbelt, I turned to Jessica. "This could be dangerous."

"Yeah, but you might need me to talk to her."

"True." I scolded myself again for putting her in danger, but rationalization took control once more. She wanted to come. "Stay close, but be ready to run."

"Don't worry. Like I said, I don't like pain."

When we got out, I walked toward a narrow alley that divided two single-story buildings, my hands in my coat pockets. Jessica kept pace at my side. Dusk had arrived, but streetlamps here and there provided enough light to dispel the approaching darkness.

As we neared the alley opening, the sound of flesh striking flesh reached my ears, then a stifled cry.

I whispered, "Come on."

We jogged together to the alley. About fifty feet in, a man stood over a woman as she cowered against a wall. He slapped her face and barked, "If you ever hold out on me again, I'll kill you."

"Wait here." I ran and tackled him to the pavement. As I rolled past, I used my momentum to leap to my feet. With both hands, I grabbed his arm, jerked him up, and forced him to the wall, pinning his back against the bricks. "You're no man," I growled, my face an inch from his. "A real man never hits a woman. Never."

His terrified eyes darted around. "She … she owed me money. I was just collecting—"

"Shut up." My spittle sprayed his face. "You make me sick. Your money comes from forcing girls to swim in sewage, and if you don't get enough, you beat them up. You must really think you're tough, slapping around little girls like that." I backed away a step and began shedding my coat. "Come on. Show me how tough you are. I want to see it for myself."

He took off in a wild sprint to the opposite end of the alley and disappeared around a corner.

Jessica ran to the woman and crouched next to her. "Are you all right?"

She nodded. "I'm okay."

I refastened my coat and joined them. The girl appeared to be in her late teens or early twenties, dressed for the cold weather in multiple layers and gloves.

"What happened?" Jessica asked.

The girl looked up at me. "Are you a cop?"

I shook my head. "Just a guy who heard the noise and decided to help."

"Thanks." She lowered her gaze. "But I'm used to it. He said he'd kill me, but he won't."

"Was that your man?" Jessica asked as she helped the girl rise. "Or just a runner?"

"A runner. He—" She cocked her head. "You a working girl?"

"Used to be." Jessica gestured toward me. "Until this guy helped me. We can help you, too, if you want. Get you out of the life, I mean."

She touched a darkening bruise on her cheek. "How old are you?"

Jessica set a hand on her hip. "Sixteen. Why?"

The girl looked at me with scorn. "You think you found a hero." She patted Jessica on the cheek. "He'll let you down. Men always do." She pushed past us, bundled her coat close, and walked toward the alley opening where we had come in.

Her words reverberated in my mind. *He'll let you down.* Each echo brought a twinge of pain. How many girls had I let down? Emily. Deb. Jessica. And so many still in chains.

Jessica crossed her arms. "No loss. She's too old for Vega."

"True. Wish we could help her, though."

We walked to the van in silence and reboarded. When I started the engine and turned on the heater, I leaned back and looked at Jessica. She stared straight ahead with a blank expression. "Something wrong?" I asked.

"Not really. Just thinking."

"About what?"

"Just what she said." She took in a deep breath and exhaled. "You know. The thing about men."

"I heard. It kind of opened a wound."

"Yeah. I figured it might."

I hoped for a reassuring follow-up, like, "Don't let it bother you." But it didn't come.

I drove out of the lot and back to the street.

"What now?" Jessica asked. "Try the bus station again?"

"Sure. We'll see if the police are still around." I returned to Sprague Avenue and headed west. We drove past other girls who might be prostitutes, but they all appeared to be older than eighteen. Of course, I couldn't be certain. Underage girls often tried to look older, and for some, "the life" drew age lines of its own.

Now well into evening, I scanned the road ahead. In the growing darkness, any strobe lights would have been visible by now. The police were probably gone.

We parked in a public lot and walked to the depot, a combination bus and train station. Once inside, we searched for a likely candidate. I immediately detected a strong scent—a devastated soul—crushed, lost, and lonely.

I reached for Jessica's hand. "I think I got something. Let's play father and daughter. It might work better than the former-prostitute angle."

As I followed the scent, we hurried hand in hand toward a ticket counter for the train station. Near the end of the line, a white girl wearing jeans and a black hoodie was talking to a dark-skinned man, perhaps Middle Eastern. Dressed in garb similar to the girl's, he had one hand on her shoulder and the other in a sweatshirt pocket. No older than thirteen, the girl wiped a tear as he spoke, her eyes fixed on his tender gaze.

"He's got the hooks in," Jessica said. "Got a plan?"

"I'll draw the guy away. You see what's up with the girl."

"Got it. She's perfect. Even looks like me."

From the ticket counter, I grabbed a schedule pamphlet, walked straight to the man, and faked a confused expression. "Excuse me, sir. Could you explain the schedule to me?" I grasped his arm and opened the pamphlet. He was my height and build. I could probably take him on if it came to a fight. "I'm trying to get to Seattle, but I don't see where to find the right train."

I sneaked a look. Jessica was talking to the girl and guiding her slowly away. So far so good.

The man shook my hand loose. "I don't work here. Go to the ticket window if you got a question."

"But before I can buy a ticket, I need to know—"

"Buzz off." The man strode past me toward Jessica. "Hey, where you taking my girl?"

I pushed between them and faced the man. "Your girl? You've got to be fifteen years older than she is. She can't be your girl."

"That's none of your business." He grabbed my arm, but I jerked away, locked his thumb with mine and pushed his hand toward his body, making him twist until we were side by side, my arm braced under his.

As I added a dose of painful torque, I spoke calmly. "Listen, you can walk away, or you can fight, but if you fight, I'm going to break some of your bones. Your choice."

He grunted, "Okay. Okay. I'll walk. Just be cool."

I let go and pushed him away. He sauntered toward the exit, though he kept glancing back. If he decided to return with some friends, I'd be in trouble. I had to hurry.

I turned to Jessica. "What's up?"

She set a hand on the girl's shoulder. "Dad, this is Kaitlyn. She's thirteen. She got thrown out of her house by her mother. Kaitlyn was hoping to go to Las Vegas where her aunt lives, but she doesn't have the money to get there. That guy you chased off promised her enough cash. All she had to do was come to his car and help him flag someone down to jumpstart it."

I nodded. "Nice pitch. Probably something like, 'Hey, a pretty girl like you can flag someone better than I can.' Right?"

Kaitlyn lowered her head. "Yeah. Something like that."

I whispered to Jessica. "Did you ask about coming with us? That guy had daggers in his eyes. He might be back with reinforcements."

"I started asking." Jessica ran a hand up and down Kaitlyn's arm in a soothing way. "Listen, there's a reason my father knew what was going on. He's heard every trick in the book to get girls like you. Get into your pants, I mean."

She cocked her head. "Into my pants?"

"Yep. If you'd've gone with him, within an hour you'd be at a rape party, and you wouldn't be the one celebrating. A bunch of guys would bang you until you couldn't stand up."

Kaitlyn's eyes narrowed. "How do you know?"

"Like I said …" Jessica gestured toward me. "He knows. He's the Guardian Angel."

Kaitlyn took a step back, gasping with a hand over her mouth. "Really?"

I squelched a protest. At this point my identity didn't matter. I kept scanning the area, searching for any possible trouble.

"Yes. Really." Jessica grasped Kaitlyn's elbow. "So what we were wondering is if you would come with us to help us rescue some other girls. They're locked up in a motel nearby."

"Me? How could I help?"

Kaitlyn's "boyfriend" walked back into the depot, accompanied by two other men of similar build and ethnicity.

I broke in. "Kaitlyn, I need you as a decoy so I can save the girls." I looked straight at her and gestured with my eyes toward the men. "I can explain later. Decide now. In ten seconds we won't have a chance."

She glanced at the men, then nodded. "I'll go."

We quick marched three abreast around a bank of stairs, leading the men away from the exit, then completed the circle and headed for the door. Just as we neared it, a man in a suit walked in—Agent Spencer. He stopped and drew his head back. "Mike. I'm glad I found you. Listen, I have news about—"

"Save it." I turned and nodded toward the approaching men. "They're ready to skin my hide."

"I'll scare them off." Spencer opened his suit jacket, exposing a holstered gun. "Wait for me at the door. I have a lot to tell you." He reached for his gun as he walked toward the men.

I whispered, "Let's go" to the girls and guided them toward the door.

Just before we reached it, a bearded man walked in along with a boy. The man wore a ski mask with the face portion folded up at his forehead, while the boy had his ski mask pulled down over his face.

Spencer called, "Mike, wait."

I tried to dodge the two, but the boy stepped in front of me. We collided, and he stumbled back, though he managed to stay on his feet. "Excuse me," I said to him. "I'm sorry." I grabbed a hand of each girl, and we ran outside.

When we arrived at the cargo van, I opened the side door for Jessica and Kaitlyn. While they climbed in, I dashed to the driver's seat and started the engine. The moment they seated themselves on the floor in the back, I took off.

Jessica whispered something to Kaitlyn, but the sound of the rattling motor drowned her out. Then Kaitlyn, wearing Jessica's coat, made her way to the front and sat in the passenger's seat.

With the new "Jessica" visible to anyone who might peek in, I drove from the parking lot, now in search of a motel to get Internet access. I looked at the rearview mirror. A dark car closed in. When it passed under a streetlamp, its size and shape became clear—Vega's spy car. Since one headlight was burned out, it would be easy to spot.

Ahead, a traffic light turned red. I slammed down the accelerator and turned left just as a delivery truck approached from the right. Our tires screeching, I careened in front of it. Its horn blared, but we avoided colliding.

I looked back. Vega's car stopped at the light and eased forward, trying to wedge itself into the flow as more horns honked.

Soon, a Holiday Inn Express motel loomed ahead on the left. I pointed. "See that, Jessica?"

"Yep." She crouched in the back, her hand on the side door's handle. "Ready."

"I'll give you half an hour." I turned left at the next intersection, putting the motel on the right. As we neared the entry drive, I slowed. "Here we go."

When I stopped. Jessica threw the door open, jumped out, and closed it again, then bolted into the darkness.

I pressed the gas pedal and accelerated at a normal rate. At this point, there was no use trying to evade the tailing car. With the van's GPS enabled, they would eventually track me down. I would just have to elude them again when it came time to retrieve Jessica.

I turned left once more to begin a route that would eventually take me full circle back to the Holiday Inn. In the dim light of streetlamps, Kaitlyn seemed pale as she stared straight ahead.

"You all right?" I asked.

She nodded. "I think so."

"Scared?"

"Sort of." She turned toward me and pushed a dark lock from her eyes. "This is, like, real, right? I mean, it's not a trick you're playing on me."

"It's real. The guy who's tailing us is a sex trafficker who's keeping an eye on me. It's a long story, but we needed you to impersonate Jessica while she's getting information."

"She told me that part."

"There's a lot more." I gave her a brief description of the stable and my hope to take her there as an excuse to show up and kill the sex-trade mastermind.

When I finished, I took in a deep breath. "It's dangerous, so if you're not up to it, I'll take you to a shelter or back to the bus station after I pick up Jessica. I'll figure out another way to do what I have to do."

She focused straight ahead again. "I'll think about it."

For the next few minutes, I slowed our pace to give Jessica the allotted time. I made sure every traffic light caught us, and while crossing bridges, we crawled along as if ogling views of the city.

After about fifteen minutes, I stopped at a light and idled in the right lane of two south-bound lanes. The tailing car approached, its dark headlight giving it away. When it caught up, it stopped to my left. Goose sat alone inside. He looked at me, then leaned forward as if to get a view of my passenger. Without changing his expression, he looked forward again.

When the light changed, I accelerated, while the tailing car lagged behind and merged into my lane.

Kaitlyn, her body stiff, wrung her hands in her lap.

I needed to get her to relax, make conversation. "Do you mind telling me more about yourself? Maybe why your mother threw you out?"

"I don't mind." She crossed her arms over her stomach and aimed her stare out the side window. "She found a joint in my room. I didn't remember leaving it there. I guess I was high and dropped it by accident."

"She kicked you out because of one joint?"

"That's just what started the fight. She accused me of messing with her boyfriend. That he paid me with pot. Which wasn't true." Kaitlyn shook her head. "She went crazy. Slapping me. Throwing stuff. I finally ran outside, and she said don't come back and slammed the door."

"So then you went to the bus station."

Kaitlyn nodded. "I was sick of fighting. I have an aunt in Las Vegas. My mom's sister. I already called her, and she said I could come. She's always been nice to me, so I thought I'd try to hang out with her a while. Maybe get a job there and pay rent."

"You're thirteen. The job market is pretty narrow for girls your age. You might not like the openings you'd find."

"I know what you're gettin' at." Kaitlyn sighed. "It was a dumb dream, I guess. I was thinking it would be easy money. No sense giving it away."

"Like to your mom's boyfriend?"

She stayed quiet, her eyes low.

I let the silence rule for a moment before continuing. "So the part that wasn't true was him paying you with pot. You *were* messing with him."

"More like he was messing with me." She shrugged. "But I let him, so I guess I couldn't call the police."

"You could have called. It's statutory rape. In the eyes of the law, you're too young to give consent. He coerced you."

"Yeah. In a way." She lowered her head. "But I don't want to talk about it."

"Sure. No problem." The poor girl was so naïve, so misinformed. She seemed to think she could walk the Las Vegas strip and collect cash for her body. At least she knew better now. Jessica's wake-up call about a rape party probably shook her up.

I drove in silence back toward the depot and turned left on First Avenue to continue the square. "Kaitlyn, the station's coming up. What do you say? Come with me, go to a shelter, or catch a bus?"

She stared at the station lights as they drew closer. "I'll stay with you."

I smiled and gave her a nod of thanks. When we passed the station, I glanced at the people milling about. No sign of Spencer. He said he had a lot to tell me. Since he kept a finger on Vega's pulse as well as the police department's, the information might come in handy, but I couldn't risk checking it out.

I made my way back to Division Street and headed north toward the Holiday Inn Express. The tailing car followed. Soon I would have to come up with another way to shake him.

After making the final left turn, I closed in on the motel's entry drive. No one stood anywhere nearby. It had been only twenty-eight minutes.

Hoping Goose wouldn't follow, I turned into the parking lot and drove toward the lobby entrance. Maybe he would think I was tracking a girl's scent. It was worth a try.

I glanced at the rearview mirror. Goose's car eased into the lot but lagged well behind. I might be able to pull up to the door and collect Jessica without her being noticed, but only if she happened to be waiting close by.

"Kaitlyn, watch for Jessica. When you see her, let her in quietly. I'll try to distract the guy who's tailing us."

Kaitlyn grasped the door handle. "Got it."

I drove under the portico, parked, and stepped out to the pavement. When the tailing car drove within sight, I turned my nose up and sniffed the air several times, then shook my head.

Goose's car stopped about ten paces back. I pushed my hands into my coat pockets and walked toward his window. My fingers touched a card of some kind, maybe a business card. I couldn't remember picking one up, but since I was half-comatose for a while, it was hard to be sure.

When I arrived, Goose lowered the glass. "Got something to say?"

I pointed at the front of his car. "Just that your left headlight's burned out. You wouldn't want to get pulled over."

His forehead wrinkled. "Uh … thanks."

"Don't mention it." I drew close and set both hands on the window frame, hoping he would lock his attention on me. "Look. I know you're following me, and you know I know. So let's stop playing games and talk straight up."

"Stop playing games? You're the one who's driving like a wild man."

"Can you blame me? When I find a girl, just one car's enough to scare her away. Two cars looks like an invasion."

"I ain't gonna stop following you, if that's what you're hoping, but I'll hang back if I see you with a girl."

"That'll help." I kept my stare on him. "You know how many girls I have, right?"

He nodded. "Two. Puddin and one you picked up at the bus station. She's sitting in the back."

"And you know why I came here, right?"

"I saw you sniffing. Figured you tracked a girl."

"Yeah, I thought I had another lead, but it dried up."

"I guessed that, too."

"It's been a rough day. I might have to take this girl to the stable and try again tomorrow. I figure with a fresh start I can get five or six girls in a day." I leaned even closer and shifted to a furtive tone. "Since we're being straight up, can I ask one question?"

"You can ask. No guarantees."

I lowered my voice to a whisper. "You know who Agent Reese Spencer is, right?"

"Maybe. What about him?"

"I saw him at the bus station. He said he had news for me, but I didn't have time to talk to him. Any idea what the news was?"

He narrowed his eyes. "How the hell would I know that?"

"I got the impression Spencer and Vega might have some kind of business relationship, so maybe you overheard something."

"Get lost. I'm not telling you anything."

"Okay. Okay." I pushed back from the car and strolled toward the van, my hands in my pockets. Again I fingered the card. I withdrew it and tried to read the stylish print on the front, but the dimness wouldn't allow my eyes to focus on it.

When I re-entered the van and closed the door, Jessica sat in the front passenger seat, and Kaitlyn again sat on the floor in the back. I laid the card on the dashboard, shifted into gear, and drove away slowly.

I looked at Jessica. "What did you find out?"

Her brow knitted deeply. "That girl you rescued? Amy? Her father's dead."

My throat caught. "Dead? What? How?"

"Murdered in the bus station restroom. Amy and her mom are okay."

"And Emma?"

She shook her head. "I didn't read anything about Emma, but take a look at this." She withdrew a folded sheet of paper from her back pocket. "Someone at the station took a video with a phone camera. I printed out this still-shot. The police are trying to find these two." She unfolded the page and showed it to me.

I stopped at the end of the motel driveway and looked at the photo. A woman and a girl stood with a security officer, both with alarmed expressions. Although the printout was a bit grainy, their identities were clear enough.

I whispered, "Deb and Emma."

"Deb's your wife?"

I nodded. Barely able to move my lips, I said, "What … what time was this taken?"

"Around three-thirty, I think."

"So my wife was there with Emma. Fred was murdered. They were probably all three together. And now they can't find Deb or Emma. That means they're in big trouble." My heart pounded, but I ignored it as I continued thinking out loud. "Obviously Spencer knows about Fred, and the police would've picked up Fred's phone. It has Deb's number in it, so Spencer might've tried to call her. It's much more likely that Spencer would've tried whatever number Fred most often called."

Jessica folded her printed page. "His wife, maybe?"

"Right. That's Maria. So Maria knows about Fred by now, and Maria has Deb's number, so she would've tried to call Deb. But if Maria reached Deb, would she tell Spencer about it?"

"Maybe," Jessica said. "Spencer seems like a smooth operator. She might trust him."

"And Spencer said he had a lot to tell me. Maybe news about Deb and Emma."

Jessica touched Vega's phone where it lay on the console. "Do you think Spencer has this number? He could just call you if it was important."

"Maybe. I got the impression from Goose that he knows Spencer. If so, Spencer might be more in cahoots with Vega than I realized, but he still might not call this phone even if he knows the number. The line's not secure. Maybe he was going to tell me something he doesn't want Vega to know. Like Deb and Emma being in town."

She nodded. "Right. Didn't think of that."

I lifted my brow. "Did you pick up any body language from Spencer, any non-verbal cues? Good news? Bad news?"

"Bad news, I think. But maybe he was going to tell you about Amy's father, not Deb or Emma."

"Could be." I replayed the quick meeting in my mind. "Spencer's expression did seem morose. So did his voice when he called out to me. That's when I ran into that boy and nearly knocked him—"

"Boy?" Jessica drew her head back. "You mean, that girl."

I blinked at her. "Girl? Are you sure?"

"Pretty sure, but with that mask on, I couldn't see her hair. The weirdest part is she looked like she got in your way on purpose. But we were in a hurry, so I didn't mention it."

"Why would she do that?"

Kaitlyn spoke up from the back. "I thought she might be a pickpocket. She stuck her hand in your coat pocket, but she didn't pull anything out. I figured, no harm, no foul, so I kept my mouth shut."

"My coat pocket?" I pushed a hand into each pocket. Where did I put that card? Right. The dashboard. I plucked the card and squinted at the text. "Blush Beauty Bar?"

"Does it have a phone number?" Jessica asked.

"I think so. I can't make it out."

"Let me look." She took the card, then transferred it to her other hand and pressed her thumb and index finger together. "It's sticky. Is something sticky in your pocket?"

"Not that I noticed. The coat's brand new."

Jessica turned the card over. "Wait a minute. There's a number on the back. Someone smeared the ink." She drew it close to her eyes and read the numerals out loud.

"Maybe that girl was being kidnapped by the bearded man." I ran a hand through my hair. It seemed that my thoughts were flying everywhere. Words kept spilling out. "Did he try to disguise her as a boy, and she gave me that card as a cry for help? Did I miss a chance to save her? That poor girl might be—"

"Mike." Jessica grasped my wrist. "Chill. Not every girl is being kidnapped. We'll just call the number and check it out."

Heat filtered into my cheeks. My own trauma drama had erupted. Another sign of insanity. "You're right. Sorry." I touched Vega's phone. "But we can't call. Vega tracks this one."

"Then Kaitlyn and I'll switch again. I'll get out and borrow a phone from someone."

"Too risky. Mr. Genius behind us will be watching closer now. I think I raised his suspicions."

"Wait a minute," Kaitlyn said from the back. "You need a phone?"

I turned toward her. "Yeah."

She withdrew a phone from her sweatshirt pocket. "You can use mine."

CHAPTER SEVENTEEN

I SLAPPED THE STEERING wheel. "I can't believe I didn't ask if you had one."

"I told you I called my aunt," Kaitlyn said. "I figured you knew."

"But needing a phone is the whole reason Jessica sneaked into that motel. To get some news and try to make some contacts."

"I saw you had one, so …" She shrugged. "I just now figured out it's bugged."

I blew out a sigh. "I should've told you. My fault."

"Water under the bridge," Jessica said. "Let's use it."

Still parked in the motel driveway, I glanced at the rear-view mirror. The one-eyed car had stopped directly behind us. "If our buddy back there sees me using a phone, he'll think he should be able to monitor it."

Kaitlyn set her phone on the floor. "Just use the speaker. He won't see a thing."

"I'll call out the number," Jessica said as she looked at the back of the card.

Kaitlyn tapped the speaker icon. "Let's have it."

While Jessica read the number, Kaitlyn punched it in. The phone on the other end trilled once ... twice ... three times.

"Hello?"

The woman's voice was beautifully familiar. I could barely squeeze out her name. "Deb?"

"Mike?"

My voice broke through the pinch. "Yes, Deb, it's Mike. I found your number on—"

"Wait. Listen. In case we get disconnected. That girl you saw at the motel with Miss Paulette. She wasn't Emily. She was Emma in disguise. Miss Paulette was me in disguise. Emma's with me, and we're both safe. We did it to save your life. Vega would have killed you if you refused to cooperate with him, and we knew you would have refused unless you were sure Emily was in danger."

Jessica gasped. "Oh, my God."

Deb's words tumbled in my mind like scattered puzzle pieces. "Then ..." I licked my lips. "Then do you know where Emily is?"

"She's still missing, Mike."

Tears crept to my eyes. "Then ... then we'll start searching again. I ... I can try to find Emily's scent ..." My throat tightened. As tears spilled, my voice squeaked out a whispered, "Dear God, help me."

Jessica snapped up the phone, hunched low in her seat, and turned off the speaker. "Deb, this is Jessica, the one they called Puddin'. What should we do now?" She looked at me as she listened. "Uh-huh. ... Uh-huh. ... Yeah, we heard about him. It's terrible. ... Right. ... We don't trust Spencer either. He's a snake ... Well, we have a girl, so we have a reason to go. ... Good. We'll need that. ... Yeah. I think so.

Her name's Kaitlyn. ... Yeah, Mike's all right. Just needs to recover from the shock. He's taken a few hard knocks on the head. ... Emma put it in his pocket? Smart girl. ... Oh, your beard looked real. Mike thought you were a man kidnapping a kid. ... Yeah, same here." Jessica smiled. "I'll let you tell him that." She pressed the speaker button and aimed the phone my way, the view from the rear window blocked by her seat. "You're on."

I spoke toward the phone, my throat looser now. "Hi, Deb. Sorry about that."

"I understand. We were worried that might happen once you found out."

"Yeah, it's another kick in the head. That's for sure."

"Mike ..." A tremor invaded her voice.

I swallowed. "Yes?"

"I love you, Mike. I love you with all my heart."

I brushed a new tear away. "I love you, too, Deb." I smiled, but my quivering lips could barely hold the smile in place. "I guess we have a new master of disguises in our family, don't we?"

"Not really. It scared me to death, but it was kind of fun at the same time."

"I guess Jessica will tell me what you talked about."

"Yes, but call me if you have any questions."

"I will. Bye, sweetheart."

"Bye."

Jessica pressed the End button and stealthily handed the phone back to Kaitlyn.

I nodded at Kaitlyn. "Thank you."

"No problem." She slid the phone back to her pocket.

"Here's the deal ..." Jessica gestured with her hands. "Spencer worked with Deb to set up the Emily bluff, but

Deb's not sure if Vega knows about it or not. Maybe he knows and he's just playing along. Even though Spencer helped, she thinks he's a crook, but she's got no proof.

"Anyway, Deb met a beauty shop chick who gave her and Emma their disguises, and she also came up with a safe place for Deb to meet up with Amy and her mom and her grandma, so Deb and Emma took a bus to get there. That's when we saw them at the station. When met up, Amy's mom gave Deb the minivan you rented and a gun, so Deb's mobile and armed now. The gun is a semi-automatic something. I don't remember. But it'll hold a lot of bullets. She said to meet her at the airport. That should be a safe place to get back together."

I checked the side mirror. The car still sat behind us, patiently idling. "If we can shake Vega's man."

Vega's phone rang. I glanced at Jessica, then picked it up. "Hello."

"Mike, it's Spencer."

I repeated his name for Jessica's sake. "Agent Reese Spencer. Since you're calling me on Vega's phone, you must be in on this girl-collecting scheme, even after I killed a man to save your life."

"Listen, it's not what you think. I'm pretending to be on Vega's side. All I do is warn him if any raids are planned for his stable, and being close to him gives me access to information I can't get otherwise. And I'm the one tracking this phone, so we can talk."

"Give me one good reason I should believe you."

"Easy. I'm blowing up Vega's scheme right now. The girl you saw at the motel. She isn't Emily. She's Emma, the girl you saved in Seattle. And Miss Paulette is your wife.

They were both disguised. That's what I wanted to tell you at the bus station."

I faked a surprised tone. "What? Then where's Emily?"

"Still missing. It's a shocker, I know. But we cooked up the plan to save your life. It was the only way Vega would let you leave."

I winked at Jessica and put on a trembling voice. "If … if you're pretending to work for him, then why did you bolt at the motel?"

"I was there to arrest him until Topper blew up the sting. After I made a run for it, I convinced Vega that Topper thought I had double-crossed him because it looked like I was helping you, so I had to run for my life. When I told him that I found Emily, I got back in his good graces, and I'll stay there as long as it looks like I'm cooperating."

"So … so what's the next part of your plan?"

"Now's our chance to take Vega down for good. He knows you picked up a girl. He wants you to bring her immediately to prove you're doing what he demanded. I'm already at the motel. I'll meet you there, and we'll figure out how to take him down."

"Should I really bring the girls?"

"Definitely. They'll help with the deception in case anyone sees you before I get to you."

"I'll be there in about thirty minutes, depending on traffic."

"That should work. But I need to warn you about something that's going on. I'm sending a video to your phone to explain. I'll see you soon."

The call terminated.

I handed the phone to Jessica. "He's sending a video. Find it and play it for me." I shifted to drive and pulled out of the motel entryway. Goose followed.

"I don't get to use one of these very often." She tapped on the screen. "Wait. Here it is." She set the screen where I could see it and twisted her body so she could look on.

Two news anchors sat at a TV studio desk, a man and a woman. "We have breaking news," the man said. "Authorities have named the so-called Guardian Angel a suspect in multiple murders in Spokane, and they are asking for help in locating him. We have exclusive videos of the man believed to be the suspect, mobile phone recordings sent to us by citizens."

The display switched to a view of the bus station's interior as the female anchor spoke. "This shocking video shows the Guardian Angel leaving the Spokane bus station with two teen girls."

In the recording, I collided with the "boy." As I watched Emma putting the card in my pocket, I couldn't resist a smile. Her quick thinking saved the day.

"One of the girls," the reporter continued as the video showed us leaving the station, "is believed to be under fourteen years of age. An eyewitness says that he tried to save her, but the Guardian Angel nearly broke the witness's arm in order to escape."

An image of the thug who tried to kidnap Kaitlyn appeared. "Yeah, he put me in a kung-fu hold, or something like that. When he let go, I ran out and came back with a couple of my friends, but he took off. I feel sorry for that girl, but I did the best I could. I talked to an FBI agent who was there and told him everything. I hope they find her."

The screen switched to the two reporters as the man continued. "Police believe the other girl is the Guardian Angel's accomplice. She is a known prostitute, but since she is a minor, police are not divulging her name." The video switched to a view of the Comfort Inn where we stayed. Fast-changing snapshots showed Jessica and me checking in at the front desk and walking to the elevator. "In this surveillance footage, the Guardian Angel and the under-age prostitute can be seen at a Spokane Comfort Inn. Police raided their room, but they were no longer there."

The female reporter appeared again. "Police are asking citizens to report any sightings of either of these suspected child snatchers, but do not try to confront them. The Guardian Angel is a suspect in the killing of two local men as well as four others in the Seattle area. He is considered armed and dangerous."

The camera panned out to show both reporters. The man shook his head sadly. "And we all thought he was a hero. Maybe we should start calling him the Fallen Angel."

The video ended. Jessica stared at me, her mouth hanging open. "The whole world thinks we kidnapped Kaitlyn."

I pointed at myself. "And that I'm hooking up with an underage prostitute."

"The Guardian Angel's reputation is shot to hell. Literally."

I gritted my teeth. "Vega's dream came true."

Kaitlyn pulled out her phone. "I'm going to make a video right now and post it."

"Not a good idea. Vega's people might see it. I want him to think we're still cooperating."

"Mike," Jessica said, "if people see you in action, it'll turn their heads. They'll stop believing the bullshit they're hearing on TV. It might be your only chance."

I felt like a politician sniffing for a photo-op. "Go ahead, but don't let our shadow back there see what you're doing. And set it to private. I'll let you know when to make it public."

"No problem." Kaitlyn tapped on her phone's screen. "Starting in a second. I'm not going to show myself, though. I don't want a bull's-eye on my butt."

I turned west out of the motel's driveway, then south on a road that would take us to the Interstate. "I'm supposed to bring you and Jessica with me to make Vega think I'm doing the job, but you don't have to come. No one will question your courage."

Kaitlyn pointed at Jessica. "If she's staying, I'm staying."

"Then find a place to hang on. I'm going to try to lose this guy again."

Kaitlyn grabbed a strap on the side panel. "Ready."

I studied the road ahead. The Interstate was coming up, but there was no access ramp. I drove under the overpass and turned left on Fourth Avenue eastbound, the Interstate to our left, running parallel and elevated on a bridge well above. Now I just needed to find a ramp to get up there.

Kaitlyn pointed her camera toward Jessica and me. "I'm the girl the police think the Guardian Angel kidnapped. It's not true. He saved me from a pervert who wanted to rape me. The girl he's traveling with *is* a prostitute, like they say, but … well, she *was* a prostitute, but she and the Guardian Angel are not hooking up. She's there on the right."

Jessica waved at the camera. "She's telling the truth. He hasn't laid a hand on me. We're working together to rescue girls, not kidnap them. Don't listen to the media crap. The Guardian Angel's a hero."

"That's him on the left," Kaitlyn continued. "He's trying to get away from people who want to catch me and make me a sex slave." She turned the camera toward the back of the van. "You can see that we're in the van they mentioned on TV, so what I'm saying is true. Like the other girl said, don't believe those reports you're hearing. Think of all the girls he's rescued. Like Amy here in Spokane and lots of others." She shouted, "He's a hero, dammit!"

She turned off the camera and smiled. "When I make it public, I'll tag the TV station."

"Thanks." I stopped for a traffic light at Division Street. At this point, Vega's man might have thought I wasn't familiar with the city, that I was searching for an Interstate access. A ramp lay immediately to my left, but it was the off ramp from the eastbound lanes. I needed to go westbound, and no on ramps heading in that direction lay in sight. The off ramp would have to do.

I tightened my grip on the steering wheel and glanced at the girls. "Jessica, check your seatbelt. Kaitlyn, hang on."

Kaitlyn again grabbed the side-panel strap, this time with both hands.

Jessica checked her seatbelt. "Are you thinking about—"

"Yep." I ran the light, spun a U-turn, and headed up the ramp. Honking my horn, I forced the van to hug a barrier on the right. The side panel scraped the barrier, making a loud squeal. An oncoming car blared its horn and dodged to our left.

I glanced back. Vega's man had turned up the ramp as well, but now he was trying to reverse course.

After avoiding several more honking cars, I reached the main highway, turned into the flow, and merged with the eastbound traffic.

I exhaled. "We lost him."

Kaitlyn released the strap. "That was a wicked ride."

"Whew." Jessica slumped in her seat. "You sure know how to show a girl a good time."

"I can't outrun the satellite, but maybe we can get to the airport before any of Vega's men catch up with us."

I took the next exit ramp, a lengthy stretch that carried us well north before I could get off and turn around. When I finally returned to the Interstate in the westbound direction, we hit some heavy traffic and had to settle for about thirty miles per hour.

"Jessica, can you call Deb and tell her we're running late? I'm guessing we'll be there in twenty minutes. Ask her to meet us as close as possible to the Interstate on the airport access road."

"I'll text her," Kaitlyn said. "I'm watching the upload. It's almost done."

"Fine, but if she doesn't reply, give her a call."

"Sure." Kaitlyn tapped on her screen for several seconds. "All right. Text sent. And ... video's still uploading. It's pretty slow."

As I drove, passing as many cars as I could without attracting too much attention, I imagined people watching Kaitlyn's video. Would they believe her? Some might say that I manipulated her into thinking she was safe, that I was still a fallen angel. Most people believed whatever they wanted to believe, especially dirt. Even eyewitness testimony didn't matter.

After I drove a couple of miles in silence, Kaitlyn piped up. "Your wife answered the text. Well, Emma did. They're five minutes from the airport. They'll look for a place to meet."

"Okay. So far, so good."

Jessica looked out the back window. "I don't see any cars with a missing headlight."

"Keep watching. They'll find us eventually."

After another minute, Vega's phone rang. I picked it up. "Is that you, Spencer?"

"Yeah. Vega's tracking the GPS. He's furious. Where are you going?"

"To the motel. I got turned around. The streets are confusing, but I'm back on track now."

"Confusing?" he shouted. "You drove the wrong way on an exit ramp."

"I know. Scared us half to death. But we made it."

"Do you really want me to tell Vega that lame story? If you keep pulling stunts like that, he'll threaten to whip one of these girls again."

I growled into the phone. "Just tell him I got sick of seeing his dog-faced stooge in my rearview mirror. I'll be there soon."

"I'm not telling him that. I'll think of a better excuse."

"You do that."

Spencer's tone softened. "I'm told you're on I-ninety heading west. Do you need directions?"

"I remember how to get there from the airport, so I'll take that exit. It shouldn't be too far out of the way."

"Just hurry. To make this sting work, we can't have police showing up. I told them you were heading eastbound.

They think you're skipping town for Idaho. The state patrol is setting up a roadblock at the border."

"Perfect. Thanks." I tapped the End key and set the phone down.

Jessica picked it up and looked at the screen. "So what's the plan?"

"When we meet up with my wife, I'll get the gun from her and drive alone. You two will stay with her. I don't want either of you anywhere near the motel."

"But if you're alone, they'll know something's up. And I don't trust Spencer. He'll screw you over."

"Don't worry about me. Since they don't really have Emily, I have a lot more options."

I drove on. Kaitlyn stared at her phone screen while Jessica shifted nervously in her seat. The situation felt surreal. In a few minutes, I would see my wife after many weeks away from home. On the phone, her words of love sounded heavenly, so different from the cold good-bye she murmured when I last saw her. Something had changed. What? I had no clue. But I didn't care. A warm reunion was coming, and I could hardly wait.

And what then? I would pass two troubled girls into Deb's protection and leave her behind … maybe forever. Although Emily was no longer in danger from that devil clown, I had to kill him so no other Emilys would get dragged down his road to hell.

When we drew near to the airport exit sign, Vega's phone rang again. I picked it up. "What now, Spencer?"

"Mike … I can't believe it." His voice rattled. "Vega. He found her."

"What are you talking about?"

"Emily. Vega found Emily. I mean, one of his men found her in SeaTac and brought her here. To the motel. She's with me now."

My hands shook. Fire burned in my ears. I glanced at Jessica. She stared at me and mouthed, "What?"

I ignored her and growled into the phone. "Prove it's Emily. Let me talk to her."

Jessica covered her mouth. "Oh. My. God."

"I can't," Spencer said. "She's sedated. When she saw Vega, she lost it. Went into hysterics."

I shouted, "Why should I believe you? Maybe you're really working for Vega after all."

"Because …" Even over the phone Spencer's loud swallow came through. "Because I have proof. When the sedative calmed her down, I told her I needed evidence that she was the real Emily so you would come and rescue her. She showed me something she said you'd understand. It looks like a parrot's head. She was getting really groggy, but it sounded like she called it Robert, and she said something about him falling off your shoulder, that she saved it all this time to remember her family. Then she fell asleep."

My heart thumped in my throat. If Spencer somehow learned the parrot's name without having Emily there, he would have said it correctly. The name spoken by a groggy Emily could easily have sounded like Robert. The mistake proved his story. Even if not, how could I risk believing otherwise?

"Mike, I'll do everything I can to keep her safe. I'm sure you think I'm a two-timing rat, but I'm trying to save everyone. You don't know what's going on behind the scenes."

"Listen closely." I tried to keep my voice from shaking, but it didn't work. "You can make excuses all you want, but if Emily gets a single bruise, just one scratch—"

"Threats aren't going to help, Mike. But don't worry. No one's going to hurt her. Just get here with those two girls, and come straight to the lobby. We'll work it out. I don't know how yet. I'll think of something."

"Can you get Goose off my tail?"

"No worries. He hit some bad traffic and won't catch up to you anytime soon."

"Good. I'll see you in a few minutes." I terminated the call and set the phone down. A new headache pounded against my skull.

I whispered, "They have Emily. For real this time."

"So now what?" Jessica asked. "Your plan's in the toilet. You need two girls to go with you."

"I can't ask you to go. You'd be risking—"

"Asking?" She laughed under her breath. "I was already planning to stow away. I'm coming."

The off ramp lay straight ahead. As I slowed, I adjusted the rearview mirror until Kaitlyn appeared. "You can go with my wife. You'll be safe. Since this van has no side windows, Vega won't notice you're missing, at least for a while. I can handle it."

"Thanks." Kaitlyn looked at me in the mirror, teary-eyed. "I hope you get her back. Your daughter, I mean."

"I appreciate it. You've been great." We reached the end of the exit ramp and merged onto route two. At the first exit—the access highway to the airport—my rented mini-van sat on the ramp's right-hand shoulder, its emergency lights flashing.

When I pulled the van onto the shoulder behind the rental, my headlights illuminated two figures standing at the rear of the car. Both wore ski masks.

My heart raced. The taller one was Deb. The shorter, Emma. My arms ached to hold them both.

The moment I stopped and shifted to Park, I called, "Okay. Let's go. No need to run, but we can't dawdle."

Kaitlyn opened the side door and jumped out, while Jessica stayed put in her seat. I opened my door and strode toward Deb and Emma. Deb's ski mask raised reminders of the "momma-bear" fan girl who took Amy. This masked woman in front of me was the only fan girl I ever wanted.

My arms spread unbidden. Deb pulled her mask off, revealing her beautiful smiling face, though a few fake whiskers clung to her cheeks and chin.

I took her into my embrace and held her close. She felt so good. So warm. So strong. Then she kissed me. Her lips, soft and supple, caressed mine with sweet-smelling balm, sliding sensually as she hummed. Her pleasure motor. I hadn't heard that lovely purr in years.

When we separated, I smiled at Emma. She removed her mask, letting her dark locks fall to her shoulders. Her pretty brown eyes and bright smile sent another wave of warmth straight to my soul.

I extended a hand. She joined our huddle, an arm around each of us as she leaned her head against me. Kaitlyn stood nearby, patiently waiting as she hugged herself and blew streams of vapor. Jessica emerged from the van and walked slowly toward us.

My head pounded once again. Urgency called. I had to get going. "Sorry," I said as I drew back, "but we have to move fast. I was planning on sending both girls with you while I took the gun and went to the motel on my own, but now ..." Deb stared at me with trusting eyes. How could I break this to her? "Sugar Daddy has Emily there. No faking this time. Spencer said she has Rupert's head."

Deb raised a gloved hand to her mouth and bit it. She threw herself back into my embrace and held me close. "Mike, I can't stand this. When is it all going to end?"

I grasped her arms, pushed her back, and looked into her watery eyes. "It ends when I kill that demon and rescue Emily. But I have to get going. They're monitoring the van. They think I'm bringing two girls, so Jessica's going with me." I gestured toward her. "She'll be sitting in the front, and they won't be able to see that no one's in the back. Maybe it'll work."

Deb's voice spiked. "Maybe? Maybe? Mike this is your life. This is Emily's life. And Jessica's. We can't afford maybe."

"We don't have a choice. I'm not putting Kaitlyn in any more danger. Jessica volunteered, and I couldn't keep her away even if I wanted to."

"I'm going, too." Emma marched over to Jessica and hooked arms with her. "You can't keep me away, either. I'd be dead without you, Mike. You need two girls. I'm going."

Deb bit her lip hard, tortured fear in her eyes. Finally, she pushed me toward the cargo van. "Okay. Go. Hurry." She waved at Kaitlyn. "Get in my van, sweetheart. I'll be right there."

While Kaitlyn walked that way, I extended a hand to Deb. "The gun?"

"Here it comes." She embraced and kissed me again as she shifted the gun from her coat pocket to mine. When she pulled back, tears glistened on her cheeks in twin streams. "I believe in you, Mike. Bring Emily home."

"I will. I promise." I pivoted and jogged toward the cargo van. "Let's go, girls."

We hustled to the van and climbed in, Jessica in front, Emma in back. When we set out, I followed the route I had taken before. Jessica and Emma stayed quiet, apparently sensing the danger. In just a few minutes, people would die. I had to make sure these two girls stayed out of the body count.

Jessica's scent, determined yet worried, blended with Emma's, which still mimicked Emily's. It was no wonder she fooled me when she disguised herself. If the challenge ever came to tell their scents apart, could I do it? It seemed unlikely.

I withdrew the gun. Driving with my knees, I looked it over—a Glock 9mm. I popped out the magazine. Seventeen cartridges loaded and ready. Regardless of my earlier queasiness about killing people, this gun would soon pound the death drum for every scumbag at the stable.

I pushed the gun back to my pocket and gripped the wheel again. As I imagined escape scenarios, every option included me driving away, but if I had to wield the gun to cover Emily, these two girls, and any others who escaped, an alternate driver could make all the difference.

"Jessica, do you know how to drive?"

She shook her head. "Never had a chance."

"I can," Emma said. "When Mom wasn't home, my dad sometimes made me drive to the corner store to buy stuff for him when he was too drunk to get out of bed."

"No problem reaching the pedals? Seeing over the wheel?"

She crossed her arms. "I'm not that short."

"Okay, okay." I smiled in spite of the tension. "I'll keep that option in mind."

I looked at the rearview mirror. Headlights appeared, maybe a half mile back. Was Deb following? I didn't warn her not to. "Jessica, we forgot to take Kaitlyn's phone with us, didn't we?"

Jessica offered an apologetic grimace. "Yeah. Sorry."

"No worries. We all forgot." I glanced between the two girls. They were so smart, so courageous. And their fidgeting proved that they were also nervous. Maybe it would be best to brainstorm an escape plan and get them emotionally prepared.

"Okay. First things, first. We have to find Emily. Vega has to show her to us. I can probably bait him into that with an appeal to his ego. He'll check me for a gun, so I'll need one of you to carry it."

"Let me," Emma said. "If I play a scared little girl, they won't think I have a gun. And they saw me with all that makeup on, so I don't think they'll recognize me."

Jessica touched her chest. "They know me, but that's a good thing. I can say I'm taking Emma to a room for lockup. Probably only Papa will go with us, so when we go into a room, we can take him out."

"You mean shoot him?"

Jessica's eyes turned fiery. "I won't even blink."

"I believe you."

"Then we'll see if any of the other girls want to leave."

"Okay …" I stretched out the word as I inhaled deeply. "That could work, but try to muffle the shot with a pillow."

"Yeah. Good point." Jessica reached over and laid a hand on my arm. "How're you going to defend yourself without the gun?"

"Not sure yet." I touched the key ring in the ignition. "Emma should carry the van key. If you can get out, run for it. Don't wait for me."

"No." Jessica shook her head hard. "I'm not leaving without you."

"You have to. You two leaving in the van might be just the distraction I need." I looked at the mirror again. The headlights stayed the same distance behind. "I'm pretty sure Deb's following. She'll probably hide her vehicle close by. Emily and I will have a ride."

Emma blew out a long breath. "This is going to be rough."

"No doubt. Vega's unpredictable. We'll have to think fast. Don't be afraid to change the plan if you have to." As I imagined these two precious girls driving away in a hail of gunfire, my throat narrowed, making it hard to talk. "Listen. You two are really amazing. I trust you both. With my life. With Emily's life. I know you can do this."

"Thanks, Mike." Jessica's eyes misted. "I trust you, too."

"Same here." Emma extended a hand, her expression determined. "Now show us how to use that gun."

CHAPTER EIGHTEEN

Deborah drove the minivan slowly along the narrow road, following Mike's cargo van. When she visited this place earlier posing as Miss Paulette, Agent Spencer was driving, and she forgot to memorize the turns. She had to stay close enough to keep Mike's taillights in view and far enough back to avoid detection from anyone at the stable. If she could park within walking distance of the motel while staying out of sight, that would be perfect.

Kaitlyn sat in the front passenger's seat, staring at her phone.

"Something interesting?" Deborah asked.

"A big upload. It's almost finished." She looked at Deborah. "I took a video of your husband and Jessica. I want to show the world that he's not a murderer."

"Or a whoremonger. I saw some of that nonsense. The media spews whatever appeals to sewage drinkers."

"He told me not to post it publicly yet, because Vega might see it."

"What would be wrong with that?"

Kaitlyn shrugged. "I'm not sure. It's hard keeping up with everything. But it was before he found out that Vega has the real Emily."

"Then his reason is probably out the window." Deborah nodded. "Do it. We need public opinion on our side."

"You got it." Kaitlyn looked at her phone's screen again. "Upload's done. I'll post a link on the TV station's Facebook page and tag a couple of their reporters. I'll also link it on Reddit and Twitter with a Guardian Angel hash tag. That should get things going."

"Good. At least we're doing something." Deborah sighed. "I feel so useless. My husband's walking into hell with two young girls, and I'll just be sitting out in the cold waiting for him. He'll either save all the girls or die trying. For him, there won't be a third option."

"Yeah. I guessed that. He's really intense. In a good way, though."

"I know exactly what you mean."

"Hey, look." Kaitlyn pointed at her phone. "The video's already getting views. The reporter reposted it with a comment that they're going to put it on TV right now. A special bulletin."

Deborah leaned to try to see the screen. "Are there any comments? What are people saying?"

"Um ..." Kaitlyn tapped the screen a few times. "A flame war started. Some say he's a hero, and some say the video's fake. They're calling each other names."

Deborah shook her head. "Comment sections are the toilet of the Internet. Just let me know if you see anything important."

"You got it."

Deborah focused on the road again. A sense of helplessness flooded in once more. Sure, she just authorized an attempt to boost Mike's reputation, but that mattered nothing compared to the battle about to take place. If only she could come up with a way to lend a more tangible hand.

"They played the video on TV," Kaitlyn said. "The comments are going wild. It's about three-to-one saying the video's fake."

"Idiots," Deborah huffed. "If you got his face on the video, how could it be fake?"

"I know. Right?"

"Exactly." Deborah followed the van over a bridge that crossed a river. Now in a more open area, the surrounding buildings and trees were easier to see. Snow blanketed everything, covering roofs and weighing down evergreen boughs, making them sag.

Driving onward, she imagined one of the laden trees giving way to its burden. With so much snow, it was a wonder that power outages hadn't been a problem.

She whispered, "Power outages."

"What?" Kaitlyn looked up. "Were you talking to me?"

"No. Just thinking." Deborah gestured toward Kaitlyn's phone. "Can you live stream?"

"Probably. I never tried it."

"Maybe mine can." Deborah pulled her phone from her pocket. "My regular phone was stolen. I'll see if this one can do it."

"So you're a geek?"

"Proudly." With one hand on the wheel, Deborah set the phone on the center console. "I have to drive. Can you download a streaming app for me? Search for Ustream. I have a channel there."

"Sure." Kaitlyn grabbed the phone. "I know what you're thinking. I'll post a link to your channel on the TV station site and tag the reporter again."

"Great." About a half mile ahead, Mike slowed the van and turned into a parking lot. This show's curtain was about to rise, for better or for worse. "We're almost there. I need to find a place to hide the van."

"Got the streaming app. It's ready to go." Kaitlyn looked at Deborah. "What's your Ustream channel?"

"Deborah's Computer Shop."

"You really *are* a geek. You got your own shop." After a few taps on the screen, she aimed the phone's camera toward the driver's side. "The link's posted, and you're live."

"Perfect." Deborah looked at the lens. "This is Deborah Pritchard. The Guardian Angel, Mike Pritchard, is my husband. He's getting ready to risk his life to rescue girls, including our long-lost daughter, from a sex-slave stable in Spokane, Washington. I'm driving a getaway car to help the girls escape. If you have any doubt about the truth of my statement, Google my name and my computer shop in Fort Lauderdale. My photo is there. You can also look up the story about our daughter, Emily Pritchard, who was kidnapped three years ago."

Kaitlyn used her free hand to manipulate her own phone on her lap. "Forty viewers already, including the reporter. I recognize her screen name."

Deborah furrowed her brow as she continued. "We're about to pass the stable in a few seconds. Local residents might recognize the place, but I urge you to stay away. Knowing my husband, this place will explode with gunfire at any moment. Let the police handle it."

"More than a hundred viewers. How many can your channel handle?"

"It should be unlimited." Deborah nodded toward Kaitlyn's window. "Get a shot of the stable. We'll pass it in a second."

Kaitlyn turned the camera. A streetlamp illuminated the parking lot and Mike's van but not the motel's façade.

"Not a great view," Deborah said. "I'll get a better one in a minute."

Kaitlyn turned the phone back toward her. "Do you know the address?"

"Only that we're somewhere between the airport and downtown." Deborah found a clear place at the shoulder and pulled over. The snow-laden boughs of a tree provided cover, and the van would be out of the motel's view. It looked like the perfect spot.

"I'm going to get closer." She killed the engine and handed Kaitlyn the key. "Start it only if you're freezing." She retrieved her phone and pointed the camera lens at herself. "Try to stay out of sight."

"Will do." Kaitlyn slid low in her seat. "But I feel like a scaredy-cat sitting here while everyone else risks their lives."

"You're not a scaredy-cat." Deborah set a hand on Kaitlyn's shoulder. "You're amazingly brave just to be here. And besides, I need you to monitor Internet activity."

"All right." Kaitlyn looked at her phone screen. "Almost a thousand viewers now. The comment window's going nuts. Most people still think Mike's a dirt bag, but at least they're all saying the live stream's real."

"Too real." Deborah opened her door, stepped out, and shut it quietly. As a cold breeze buffeted her cheeks, she aimed the camera ahead and walked toward the motel's entry drive. "This stable used to be a motel," she whispered directly into the phone, "but there's no sign in front. My guess is that if the police are watching, they've already figured out where it is, but FBI Agent Reese Spencer is probably directing law-enforcement away from us. We think he's part of the sex-trafficking gang. I hope the Spokane city police aren't in his pocket."

When Deborah arrived at the lot entrance, she stopped and let out a long breath. The van had parked near the front door, and Mike was just stepping down on the driver's side. As she edged closer, she spoke again to the phone. "Okay, all you viewers out there. Hang on. The real show's about to start."

. . . .

After parking in a space near the motel's front entry, I leaned close to Jessica and Emma and gave them a super-quick lesson on how to use the gun. Once they both seemed comfortable with it, I handed it to Emma and turned off the engine. When the noise silenced, I nodded firmly. "Let's do this."

They stared at me with grim expressions. "We're ready," Jessica said. "I hope."

I got out and walked calmly around the rear of the van to the right side. I opened the sliding door and helped Emma down to the pavement. Her head low and her hands deep in her coat pockets, she sucked in quick breaths as if stifling sobs. The little actress even had me convinced.

Jessica hopped down to the pavement on her own, her eyes sharp and steely. Choosing to go without the coat I had bought her, she defied the cold with shoulders back and head erect. Although lean from head to toe, she looked as strong as a tiger.

I led them to the entry, opened one of the first set of doors, and waited for them to go in. Beyond the second set, Vega sat at the center of the lobby in the Carver chair. A floor lamp stood at his side, shining its light on him. It seemed that no one else was in the room. If Spencer had a plan, he wasn't showing his hand yet.

"Here we go." I opened the next door and ushered the girls inside. Emma wept. Jessica glared at Vega with an expression that could slay a dragon.

I marched toward him, gesturing for the girls to follow as I urged myself on. The walk felt like balancing on a thread. But I could do this. For Emily. For Emma, Jessica, and the other stable girls. I had to do it.

Emily's scent entered my nostrils, though maybe it was Emma's. They were so much alike. Or were they?

My mantra came to mind. *Every girl is unique. Every girl is loved. Every girl needs a hero.* But now *I* needed a hero, and the two girls behind me might be the heroes I was hoping for.

Vega crossed his legs and propped his chin with a hand. His blank expression gave away no emotion, no hint of what he planned to do, though he ran a finger along the whipping strap, rolled up and attached to his belt.

When I drew within a couple of paces, I halted. The girls stopped a step or two behind me. Emma's weeping grew louder. When Jessica whispered shushes, she calmed down somewhat.

I gave Vega a genial nod. "I'm here. I brought Puddin back and a new girl."

Vega stayed nearly motionless. Only his lips moved. "Just so you know, a hidden gun is aimed at your head."

"Understood."

"Take off your coat."

I shed it and laid it to the side. Spreading my arms and rotating slowly, I made sure he could see my empty holster and waistband. "It would be stupid to come here armed."

"Indeed it would." Vega uncrossed his legs. "Agent Spencer told me that he informed you of my recent acquisition."

"He did."

Vega leaned forward. His pudgy face looked almost friendly. "Are you convinced? After Miss Paulette's version of Emily, I would be doubtful were I in your position."

I studied his eyes. Like Deborah guessed, he knew from the start that her version of Emily was fake. He went along with the ploy just to gain leverage. "I'm not one hundred percent convinced. Spencer hasn't exactly been reliable."

"Maybe to you, but his loyalty to me has been unblemished, though he might have told you things that made you wonder where his alliances lie. Topper was foolish to doubt him, and that cost him his life."

I brushed off the story. With lies abounding, it seemed impossible to know what to believe. "Loyal or not, I want to see Emily. You have to prove that she's here."

"She's asleep, and I fear that you seeing her might provoke an irrational response on your part." He inhaled through his nose. "Perhaps you can detect her scent. She's close by."

"The scents from these two girls have been pretty overwhelming, but I'll give it a try." I walked a few steps away from the girls and began sniffing the air. Several scents entered. The strongest were Jessica's and Emma's as well as one from a female who seemed angry, ready to lash out. Might Mama be in the vicinity?

I inhaled again. No change. If Emily was really close by, I couldn't distinguish her scent from Emma's, as I had feared. Yet, Emily likely was here. Otherwise, Vega wouldn't have suggested that I try to detect her.

I walked back to him. "I believe she's here."

"Very well." He leaned back in the chair. "Special Agent Spencer and the man who tailed you have reported your, shall we say, erratic behavior, but also that you have not deviated from our agreement." He gestured toward Emma. "You brought me a girl. An excellent specimen. Young and pretty. She will do fine."

Wishing I could kick him in the face, I stared at him. I had to keep playing the game. "Okay. What's next?"

"Just a question to satisfy my curiosity. How did the fake Emily convince you? With all that makeup I wouldn't have been able to tell her apart from a young showgirl, but I don't have your nose."

"I got conked on the head a few times. I was under a lot of pressure. And it's been three years." I shrugged. "I thought I detected her, but I was wrong. Wishful thinking, I suppose."

"Yet you're sure now."

"I didn't say I was sure. Just that I believe she's here. I detected a familiar scent, but, like I said, it's been three years. It's a reasonable conclusion, especially since Spencer told me something Emily said that was pretty convincing."

"Oh, yes. The parrot's head. What an odd keepsake." Vega rose to his feet. "You owe me nineteen more girls. But now I will keep Emily, and I will allow her to talk to you on a daily basis so you will know she is safe." He extended his hand. "Are we agreed?"

I kept my arm pinned at my side. "I understand."

"I see." He lowered his hand. "I should know better than to expect a gesture of cooperation."

Jessica piped up with a scornful tone. "If it's all the same to you, can I go to my room? I'm sick of being next to this so-called Guardian Angel. He's screwed me over twice now."

"Of course." Vega turned toward the hall. "Papa, come here and take these two to a room."

Papa appeared from a shadowed area in the corridor and walked toward us, sliding a handgun behind his waistband. "Let's go."

Emma's sobs erupted afresh. Jessica hugged her and looked at Papa. "Can we be roommates? She's really upset."

"I can arrange that after I initiate her." Papa gestured with his head toward the hall. "Move it."

"Get some video," Vega said. "It'll be good for the income stream."

As they walked away, Jessica and Emma arm-in-arm, hot blood surged through every part of my body. He planned to rape Emma. She and Jessica would have to be ready to take him down as soon as possible. But Papa was so big and powerful. Even with a gun, their chances of success were low. If Spencer didn't show up to help in less than a minute, I would have to make a run for it and save them.

Vega faced me. "We're still not alone. Mama has recovered, and she is watching with a scope-mounted rifle. Don't be fool enough to try anything rash."

My heart thumped. I glanced around, but Mama was nowhere in sight. "You have Emily. That's all the leverage you need."

He extended an arm toward the exit door. "Be on your way, then. Since you have nineteen to go, you had better—"

"Vega." Spencer walked into the lobby from the hall, a computer tablet in his hands. "I need to show you something."

Vega's eyes lit up. "You're supposed to be with Emily."

"Don't worry about that. She's not going any—"

"I told you not to let her out of your sight."

I sneaked a look into the hall. The first door on the left stood ajar, a light on inside. Emily had to be in there. If

I were to run to stop Papa, she would be vulnerable no matter whose side Spencer was really on.

"I know," Spencer said as he showed the tablet to Vega, "but you need to see this."

Vega squinted at the screen. "What am I looking at?"

"Someone's streaming live from here. Says she's Mike's wife. It looks like she might be inside the building now. Maybe she came through the back door."

I raised my brow. Deb? Was she really here? Or was Spencer setting up a diversion, some way to free me up to rescue Emily? But did he know about the danger the other girls were in? I couldn't save all of them without help.

Vega's cheeks blazed cherry red. "Where are Goose and Evans?"

"On their way. Maybe ten minutes."

Vega hissed through clenched teeth. "Find that bitch and kill her."

"I'm on it."

When Spencer turned, Vega grabbed his arm. "Wait. I need to show our Guardian Angel what happens when someone double crosses me. Bring Emily here. I don't care how groggy she is."

"Will do." Spencer hustled to the hallway and disappeared inside the room with the open door.

My time was up. I had to make a move. I took a stealthy step toward the hall. Emily first, then the other girls, then Deb, if she really was out there.

"Don't get any ideas." Vega turned toward the lobby desk. "Mama, show yourself."

She rose from behind the desk, the rifle aimed straight at me. Wearing a bandage around her head, she didn't say a word, but her hate-filled expression said plenty.

I froze. All I needed was a distraction. Anything. Then I could run for it.

Spencer returned in a rush, one hand holding the tablet and the other clutching a girl's elbow. He stopped with her between me and the hall entry, just five steps away.

I stared at the girl. Her eyes appeared dazed as she wobbled in place. Although she wore a short skirt and a tight halter, and although she had aged more than three years, there was no doubt. After hundreds of nightmares, Emily stood almost within reach.

"Daddy?" Emily blinked drowsily. "Is that you?"

I swallowed hard. "Yes. Yes, it's me."

I took a step toward her, but Vega blocked me with an arm. "No, you don't. Sit in the chair."

New heat rushed to my face. "Just let me hug her. Touch her."

Emily staggered toward me, but Spencer grabbed her wrist and jerked her back. "You have to stay with me."

Tears streamed from Emily's eyes. Her face, worn and weary, twisted as she wept and reached out with a trembling arm. "Daddy, please take me home."

"I will." My heart raced wildly. What about Jessica? Emma? Deb? "I will. Just stay calm." My head pounded, the worst migraine in history. I couldn't lose control of my senses. Not now.

Vega grabbed the chair's arm and lifted two legs from the floor. "This is too light, and my rope is shredded." He dropped the chair. "Spencer, find something that'll hold him and handcuff him to it."

After setting the computer tablet on the reception desk, Spencer unclipped the set of handcuffs from his belt and fastened a cuff around my left wrist. A gun in his shoulder holster was visible and within reach.

I couldn't wait another second. I lunged for the gun. Just as my fingers touched it, he twisted away. He whipped the gun out and slammed the butt against my skull. I crumpled to my knees. Pain throbbed from ear to ear, and darkness flooded my vision.

He jerked me to my feet and into a headlock with the gun barrel pressed against my cheek. "Cool it," he hissed into my ear. "I'm not going to hurt your wife. Just play along or Mama'll shoot you. I can't control her."

I swallowed past the pressure on my throat and whispered, "But Emma is about to get raped by Papa."

"I can't stop that either." Spencer pulled me to the entry door and slapped the other cuff around the handle. Now several steps from Vega and Emily, Spencer stood between me and them and closed the cuff, making the ratchets click. He slipped something cool and metallic into my free hand. "Do what you can. I'll provide the distraction."

As he walked back to the desk, I stealthily opened my hand. In the midst of pulsing dark spots, a small silver key lay in my palm. I quickly enclosed it and spied the keyhole in the cuff.

Spencer picked up the tablet. "I'll track her down." With his stare on the screen, he walked out, turned toward the motel's rear exit, and faded into the darkness.

Vega pushed Emily to the floor and straddled her.

"What're you going to do?" Mama asked.

"Show the Guardian Angel that I mean business." Vega unhooked the rolled-up strap from his belt. "Mama, watch him. If he manages to break free, kill him."

CHAPTER NINETEEN

MAMA AIMED THE rifle at me. "You best stay calm. He's not gonna kill her."

"I'll kill *him*." I grabbed the cuff and pulled. The links jerked tight. As I struggled, I shielded the cuffs with my body, slid the key in, and turned it. The cuff clicked open, still hidden from Mama's view. I was free. But when would the distraction come?

Vega held the strap and let it roll out to its full length. On the floor, Emily lay on her back, sobbing, her hands over her eyes. Drugs and terror had sent her into panic mode. She was shutting down. Giving up.

I couldn't wait for Spencer. I shook the cuff loose and ducked. Mama fired. The bullet whizzed by my ear and smacked into the door's glass, shattering it.

The lobby lights flicked off. Darkness veiled everything. I threw myself out of the line of fire. More shots popped. The gun's flashes gave away Mama's position. I sprinted across the lobby and dove over the desk. The momentum sent me bulldozing into her. She slammed into a wall. Her body crumpled under my weight.

"Emily," I called as I pried the rifle from Mama's hands. "Crawl away from him and stay quiet."

Pain throttling my shoulder and chin, I listened. Neither Vega nor Emily made a sound. Her scent proved that she was still close, but was she safe? As I felt my way around the desk, I called out, "Turn the lights back on. I have control now."

The lights flashed to life. With the rifle ready at my hip, I scanned the lobby. Emily sat with her back to the reception desk, her knees pulled up to her chest, shivering as she stared at me with terrified eyes. Vega was gone.

I set the rifle down, dropped to my knees in front of Emily, and gathered her into my arms. I wept as I ran my hand across her back. She was here. She was really here. "Emily, are you all right?"

"Daddy …" She sobbed against my chest. "Daddy, tell me this isn't a dream. Tell me right now."

"It's not a dream. This is all real."

"Are you going to take me home?"

"Soon, sweetheart. Very soon." I couldn't bear to tell her that it wasn't over yet. With Vega and Spencer missing, and with Goose and Evans on their way, the worst was likely yet to come. Not only that, Papa must have heard the gunshots. He might charge in at any moment. It seemed strange that he hadn't come already.

I picked up the rifle, helped Emily to her feet, and held her hand. "Come with me. I have to save another girl—"

"Mike?" Deb appeared from the rear exit hallway. "Are you all right?"

"I'm fine." I gestured with my head toward Emily, a quiver in my voice. "So is our daughter."

Deb's mouth dropped open. She wrapped Emily in her arms and swayed with her chest to chest. "Oh, dear God. Thank you. Thank you. Thank you."

"Listen. We'll trade stories later. Right now I have to—"

A shot rang out down the hall, then another, then a third.

"Stay close." I jogged into the hallway. At the far end, Jessica and Emma burst from a room. They ran toward us, their faces etched with fear.

Papa staggered out with the Glock in his grip. Blood covered his shirt. When he raised the gun, I waved an arm and shouted, "Everyone drop!"

Deb and all three girls dove to the floor. Papa fired. A bullet ripped into my thigh. My leg gave way. I toppled forward and landed on my stomach between Jessica and Emma.

Papa stomped toward us. Now in sniper position, I peered through the scope and set the crosshairs on his chest. In the tiny view, he looked like a charging rhino—wounded and crazed.

I squeezed the trigger. With a crack, the bullet zipped out and thumped into his chest. He stumbled back and stared at his bleeding torso as if confused. I fired again. The second bullet sent him reeling backwards until he fell with a skidding thud. After writhing for a brief moment, he lay still.

I exhaled. "Finally."

Deb climbed to her feet and helped the three girls rise. "Mike, you're bleeding."

"I think he just grazed me." I rolled to my back and extended a hand. "Vega and his men might show up at any second."

All four joined in hauling me up. While Deb braced me, I looked the two girls over. A bloody gash marred Emma's arm, and a deep scratch striped Jessica's face. "Did Papa give you those wounds?"

"No." Jessica grimaced as she shifted her weight, apparently bruised somewhere. "Madison scratched us. Papa brought her to make a video, but she went freaking nuts when I shot Papa. I'll tell you about it later."

"Where's Madison?" Deb asked.

Emma pointed down the hall. "In the room. Crying. She's a basket case."

"She might be trouble," Jessica said as she marched toward the room. "I'm going to lock her in."

Emma followed. "I'll do it while you tell the other girls what's going on." Along the way, Jessica picked up the Glock from the floor.

Deb set a hand on my back. "We need to get you to a hospital."

"I'm not leaving until the girls are safely out of here."

"What about a first-aid kit? Don't you usually travel with one?"

I nodded. "In the minivan."

"I'll ask Kaitlyn to find it. I parked by the road out of sight." Deb withdrew a phone from her pocket and tapped out a message. "Maybe I can go and get it."

"Not by yourself. Too dangerous. Vega's lurking."

"So's Agent Spencer. He helped me find the power box, but when I turned the lights back on, he was gone."

"*You* controlled the lights?"

She nodded. "And I live streamed everything. I'm hoping that will draw the police here."

"Good job." I looked at my reddened wrist where the cuff had been. "I guess Spencer was on our side after all."

"Don't bet on it. He has Fred's murder to answer for. I still don't trust him."

"You won't get any answers soon. He's probably long gone by now." I leaned against the wall. Emily leaned with me, still groggy. Blood trickled down my leg. Not a gush. I could manage, though the pain was crippling. Still, Deb was right. First-aid would help. Jessica and Emma needed some patching up, too. "They have a kit around here somewhere. When Jessica gets back, I'll ask her to check the room where I last saw it."

Deb tapped on her phone. "Kaitlyn found your kit. She says a few commenters on the feed recognize this place. But no way to know if anyone's coming. Not a word about the police."

"Spencer misdirected them. It might take a while for them to get here." I looked down the hall. Jessica and Emma had padlocked the far door and entered another room. Gathering the other girls could take a while, and Kaitlyn was vulnerable out there by herself. "We have to make a move."

I pushed away from the wall and limped toward the lobby, the rifle aimed forward. "Stay close. I'm getting you two out of here. Jessica and Emma have a gun. They should be safe until I get back."

Just as I reached the end of the hall and entered the lobby, Goose and Evans burst in and aimed their rifles at me. They both fired. I lunged back into the hall and collided with Deb and Emily, knocking myself and them flat. Bullets zinged over us and ripped into the wall.

Deb gasped. Emily cried out. I rolled off them and shot a barrage in return. A bullet clipped Goose's arm. His rifle went flying. Evans dropped to his belly and kept shooting. More bullets zipped past, nearly hitting Deb and Emily.

I lunged to my feet and ran stiff-legged toward the reception desk. A hail of bullets in my wake, I dove behind the desk and fell on top of Mama's body. No breaths emanated from her. She was dead.

Several bangs followed. Holes riddled the back wall above desk level. Then all fell silent. After crawling off Mama's corpse, I peeked around the side of the desk. Goose sat against the far wall holding his wounded arm in his lap. Evans, rifle in hand, belly crawled across the carpet toward the door. Being exposed, he was vulnerable. He knew he had to escape.

But I couldn't let him. Looking through the scope, I set the crosshairs on Evans and let the barrel drift with his progress. I fired three shots. Each bullet slammed into his side. He fell limp and moved no more.

My thigh throbbing, I climbed to my feet and hobbled toward Goose, the rifle trained on him. "If you want to live, you'll stay put."

He closed his eyes and nodded.

I waved toward the hall. "Deb. Bring Emily. Let's go."

They rose and shakily walked into the lobby, Deb propping Emily from the side.

Jessica and Emma hurried in as well. Jessica, the butt of the Glock barely visible behind her waistband, seemed ready to break into tears. "Tiana's the only one who's coming. She'll be out in a minute."

I compressed her shoulder. "Then we'll wait for her. We'll all leave together."

Emma handed me the cargo van's key ring. "The others are scared. They heard the gunshots."

"They won't come," Jessica said. "No use waiting for them."

I slid the key ring into my pocket. "Okay. As soon as Tiana—"

"Mike, put the gun down, or this girl is dead."

I swiveled toward the voice. Vega walked through the front doorway holding a handgun to Kaitlyn's head. As she clutched the first-aid kit in both arms, tears seeped from her tightly clenched eyes. She swallowed back sobs and whispered, "Please ... please."

"It appears she was on an errand of mercy." Vega took the kit from her and tossed it to the floor. "I assume you will show her the same kindness by dropping your gun."

I glanced at the other girls and Deb. Terror blazed on their faces. If I disarmed, they would all be at risk. My only hope was to pretend to go along and look for an opening.

"Take it easy, Vega." I laid the rifle on the floor. "What do you want?"

"A vehicle out of here. I'll let her go once I'm safely down the road."

Jessica walked forward. "Take me instead."

"Jessica," I hissed, reaching for her arm. "No."

She pulled away and stepped within Vega's reach. "I'm a more valuable hostage."

Vega squinted at her. "How so?"

"Because ..." She licked her lips. "Because Mike loves me. He and I are ... well ... more than friends."

"You're such a bad liar, but ..." He grabbed Jessica's arm, twisted her around, and transferred the gun to her head. "I do think he's attached to you." He shoved Kaitlyn toward us with his foot. Deb caught her and held her close.

Jessica blinked rapidly. Her body shook. As she focused on me, she whispered, "I love you, Mike."

"How sweet." Vega extended a hand. "Now the keys to the van."

When I fished the ring from my pocket and laid it on his palm, his smug expression returned. "Like I said before, you're out of your league."

As Vega edged backwards with the gun barrel pressed against Jessica's head, she kept her chin firm and stared straight at me. I had to do something, and I had to do it now. But what?

Headlights flashed outside. Car engines roared, then silenced.

"Goose," Vega called. "It's the cops. Get your rifle and cover me. This bitch is our ticket out of here."

Jessica screamed, "I'm not a bitch!" She jerked away from Vega's grasp. He fired. Jessica staggered into my arms, groaning. As warm liquid soaked my shirt, I braced her to keep her from falling.

Vega stepped closer and set his gun at the back of her head. "It's just a shoulder wound. Give her to me. Now."

"All right. All right. Just cool it." I drew an arm back and slid the Glock from Jessica's waistband, then pushed her to the side and shot Vega in the chest. Once. Twice. Three times.

His eyes flared. His gun dropped to the floor. Blood soaked his shirt. After teetering for a second, he fell to his back and looked up. His lips moved, but no sound came out.

I straddled him and tried to imitate his voice. "It seems that you're out of your league." I fired once more, this time at his forehead. Blood splashed around the entry point. He closed his eyes and stopped breathing.

I spun toward Deb and Jessica. They now sat on the floor, Deb with a hand compressing Jessica's shoulder. "The bullet passed right through a fleshy part," Deb said. "The bleeding's not too bad."

Kaitlyn knelt and fished a gauze pad from the first-aid kit she had brought. "Yeah. We can take care of her. If I can stop shaking."

I blew out a relieved sigh. "Perfect."

Two huge men carrying double-barreled shotguns burst in. Wearing jeans and flannel jackets, they looked like a blue-collar rescue squad. One of them eyed me from under the brim of his John Deere baseball cap. "Are you the Guardian Angel?"

I nodded. "Thanks for showing up. You scared the trafficker into making a mistake."

The men lowered their guns. The first man pinched the bill of his cap. "Glad to be of service."

An officer entered. The insignia on his uniform spelled out Spokane City Police—Alan Petrie, the officer I met at the bridge. "Sorry it took so long. We were called on a wild goose chase. More are on the way."

Although the pain in my thigh returned with a vengeance, I forced a smile. "Thanks, Alan."

"Trust me. It's my pleasure." He nudged Vega with a shoe. "Looks like you took care of business."

"One survivor named Goose leaning against the wall. Two corpses in the lobby, Vega and Evans, and you'll find another body down the hall, a pimp they call Papa." I gestured toward the reception desk. "And a dead woman's back there."

"I'm sure you have quite a story to tell, but …" His face reddened as he shifted nervously. "I'm going to radio that I have you under arrest. That'll keep the state off your back. I'll have to take you in for questioning eventually."

I nodded. "Understood."

Emma dragged the chair closer. "Mike. You look kind of shaky. Sit."

"Gladly." I lowered myself to the seat. "Thanks."

While Alan and the two shotgun-wielding rescuers hauled Goose outside, Deb helped Jessica rise. "Are you sure you're okay?" Deb asked.

"Yeah. Fine. I'll be right back." Jessica walked into the hallway, a slight limp in her gait, and disappeared from sight.

Deb shot me a worried glance. "Should I follow?"

I shook my head. "She's strong. She'll be all right."

Deb gathered Emily, Emma, and Kaitlyn close to my chair. A girl walked into the lobby from the hallway, her lovely eyes brilliant against her dark skin.

I whispered, "Tiana."

Still wearing Jessica's jeans, sweater, and shoes, she carried a plastic bag of belongings and wore a heartbroken expression. "No one else would come."

"I heard. I'm not sure what we can do about it."

Soon, Jessica returned with a cup of water and picked up Kaitlyn's first-aid kit. After giving me the cup, she knelt next to the chair, flipped open the box, and plucked out a pair of scissors. "I'll be your nurse today. The touching might get kind of personal, but it's only fair, right?"

"Right." Smiling, I winked at Deb. "I'll explain later."

"No need." After returning the smile and wink, Deb looked at her phone. "I'm calling a shelter. No one can stay here."

Jessica cut my pant leg off several inches above the knee, exposing a bleeding flesh wound on my inner thigh. While she cleaned and bandaged it, she rattled off her story about her encounter with Papa. When the lights went out, she grabbed the gun from Emma. Then the moment the lights came on, she shot Papa in the shoulder. That dazed him for a while, but Madison came at her and Emma like a lioness with claws extended. When they fought Madison off, Jessica made ready to shoot Papa again. He charged at her, so she shot repeatedly, though she wasn't sure how many times she hit him.

As she continued, I tried to listen, but her words swirled, whether because of my exhaustion or the loss of blood, I couldn't tell. I drank the water, but it didn't help much.

After a final wrap, she taped the bandage in place. "Now be careful."

I gave her the biggest smile the pain would allow. "I will."

Soon after Alan and the two rescuers carried the corpses outside, a van from the shelter pulled into the parking lot. Two counselors, middle-aged women who revealed that they were once prostitutes, carried warm clothes and blankets into the motel and distributed them.

The women convinced Kaitlyn and the stable girls to come to the shelter, though Tiana considered that to be a short-term option. She hoped to go home to her brother but agreed she needed some time to recover.

When the girls began boarding the van, one of the counselors—Peggy, a graying, heavyset woman with kind eyes—stood by my chair and explained to Deb and me that rescued girls were often severely traumatized. They could take weeks, months, or even years to recover from the torture and regain a semblance of normalcy. Many ended up returning to "the life" simply because it was all they knew.

"What about Emily?" I asked. "You had a chance to talk to her. How's her emotional stability?"

Peggy looked toward Emily as she stood at the motel entrance, watching the girls who had lined up at the van. "She's a bit withdrawn, but there's a lot of life in her. And she has parents who love her. That's an advantage a lot of the girls don't have. I think she'll be fine."

"And Jessica?"

Peggy chuckled. "She's quite a firecracker. God's blessings must have been on you to run into her. A lot of grit in that girl. She's a survivor."

Jessica's words returned to mind. *Just survive, Mike. That's what I always say to myself. I just gotta survive.*

When Peggy turned and walked outside, I brushed a tear away and whispered, "Thank God for grit."

"Mike." Deborah pointed toward the motel doors. Jessica and Emma stood near Emily, shifting nervously as they glanced between the shelter van and us. "I think they're waiting to say good-bye."

"Good-bye?" For some reason I didn't even consider that they might leave for the shelter. "Deb. They can't go."

"Did you tell them otherwise?"

"Not exactly. I just thought ..." I had no idea how to finish.

"You thought they should stay with us. And I'm all for it. A hundred percent." She extended a hand. "Let's ask them."

I grasped her hand and rose from the chair. With her holding my arm, we walked toward the girls. As we drew close, Jessica nudged Emma. They straightened and gave us forced smiles.

Deb took Emily's hand and whispered in my ear, "Just share your heart with them."

I nodded and faced the two girls. "Excuse me, young ladies."

Jessica's brow lifted. "Yes?"

My throat tightened. I had to spit out my words quickly or I would lose control. "I was wondering if you'd like to stay with us."

"I thought you'd never ask." Jessica threw her arms around me, leaned her head against my chest, and spoke through sobs. "I love you, Mike. I love you so much. Thank you. Thank you for everything."

Emma squeezed in and hugged me. "Does that mean you'll be our new father?"

"Your new father?" I patted them on the back. Choking up again, I whispered, "That would be an honor."

When the van pulled away, Deb, the girls, and the two armed citizens were the only people remaining in the motel, though Alan stood outside talking to a few other officers while a crew photographed everything and collected evidence before stowing the corpses in a van.

Soon I would have to talk to Alan about the charges against me. Surely it wouldn't take too long to clear my name, considering that I had acted in self-defense in every case, though my last bullet in Vega's face might raise questions. And going to the station would give me a chance to start a search for Mahoney. With Vega dead and Spencer gone, that might take a while.

I sat again in the chair and gave the two local men a nod. "Thanks for staying so long."

The John-Deere man took off his cap. "Pleasure's ours. We'll stick around until you're safely on your way."

Deb withdrew the minivan keys from a pocket. "I'll drive."

"Good idea." I pushed against the chair arms and rose to my feet. My wounded leg throbbed terribly. "But there's one thing I have to do."

"What's that?"

I spread my arms toward Emily. "Will you forgive me?"

She nodded and ran into my embrace. I cried. She cried. For how long, I don't know, but I relished every moment while taking in her wonderful scent. As it filtered in, every vestige of my headache washed away.

Emily drew back, pulled a round green object from the pocket of the jeans she had received from the shelter, and grinned. "I'm not sure Rupert forgives you, though."

I laughed and scooped her into my arms. "Let's get out of this place."

"Mike," Deb said. "Your leg."

"Nothing's going to stop me from carrying Emily this time." As I walked toward the entrance, I basked in the electric touch. I finally filled my aching arms. I carried my precious daughter after stupidly refusing three years ago. And it felt like heaven.

Jessica opened the first door, Emma the next. Deb curled her arm around mine, and we walked together from the stable. This mad quest was finally over, and I was back at this wonderful woman's side with Emily in my arms. Without Deb, all would have been lost. She was my hero. And I would be there to tell her so for the rest of my life.

CHAPTER TWENTY

I stood alone at Fred's graveside while Deb waited nearby. Frigid air breezed past, sending my breaths toward the sky. The rising streams of white raised a memory. Hadn't I first met Fred in such a chilled cell of sadness? His beloved Amy had been spirited away from his fatherly embrace. Now Fred's spirt rose to the sky to find solace in the embrace of his heavenly father. And helping me, even after his treasured daughter returned to his arms, was the reason for his premature departure. My failures led to his demise.

The awful truth wilted my stiff upper lip. I dropped to my knees and wept. No words filled my sobs, though I hoped Fred understood my silent lament. We were both fathers. We both loved our precious children. And we both knew the bitter bonds of self punishment. The whipping strap of guilt cut deeply. I deserved nothing but scorn.

Deb laid a hand on my shoulder. "Maria says to take your time, but she and Amy want to give you something when you're ready."

"I'm ready." I rose, brushed tears from my cheeks, and straightened my coat. The cemetery had emptied of people. Only grave markers and snow-speckled grass remained.

At least I hadn't caused a scene. Since so many people still doubted or even despised me, we had stood at the outskirts of the crowd in order to avoid notice, and we paid our respects after the service was over. "Where are they?"

"At their SUV." Deb's gloved fingers intertwined with mine. "I'll be at your side."

With Deb's arm around my waist, I limped toward the graveyard's access road where the Horowitz's 4Runner sat parked next to the curb. Maria and Amy stood on the thin layer of snow bundled in coats, gloves, and boots. Amy held a purple canvas bag at her waist. Although her flowing blonde hair made her easy to recognize, the glorious smile she wore during our previous meeting was tragically missing.

When she saw us, she jogged ahead and embraced me. As I held her close, healing warmth overwhelmed me—forgiveness, pure and sweet. I whispered, "I'm so sorry about your Daddy. I know how much you loved him."

"I still love him." She kissed my cheek and drew back. "I have something for you." She pushed the bag into my hand and unbuttoned her coat, revealing the sweatshirt I had given her. "I'm keeping my promise."

I opened the bag and withdrew Beans, now bright white and wearing a purple bow around his neck. New sobs threatened to break loose, but I forced them back as I hugged the bunny to my chest. "Thank you, sweetheart. I'll keep my promise, too."

When they departed, I looked down the road where I had parked our rented minivan about twenty paces away. The rest of my loved ones milled around on the pavement near the driver's door waiting to leave this field of sadness—Emily, Jessica, Emma, and Tommy. He had flown to

Spokane with Paula a day earlier, though she had to return on the next flight to attend classes.

Just a few steps beyond our vehicle, a green sedan sat next to the curb, two people visible in the front seats. Maybe they were unable to start their car because of the frigid weather.

When Deb and I arrived at the minivan, I extended a hand toward Tommy. He smiled and held it as I looked at the females. "I'll be ready to go in a minute. The folks in that car might need help."

The sound of a closing door made me turn. Two teenagers, male and female, stood next to the sedan and looked at us. They wore jeans, sports shoes, and black sweatshirts. A logo on each sweatshirt's front depicted a winged-angel silhouette holding hands with a child at each side. A caption under the logo said, "I Am a Guardian Angel."

I gave them a nod. The boy thumped his chest with a fist and nodded in return. The girl formed an "I love you" sign with her hand. Then they reentered their car, started the engine, and drove away.

As I watched the car shrink in the distance, a new tear crept to my eye. These two understood—the mission, the urgency, as well as my need for privacy. Maybe their generation would live to see the evils of trafficking come to an end.

I withdrew the key fob. Just as I set my finger on the unlock button, a horn honked multiple times from far away. Another vehicle appeared down the road, a full-sized van closing in quickly.

Deb, Tommy, and the girls gathered around me and watched as it drew near. Jessica squinted. "I can see the driver, but I don't recognize him."

When the van arrived, the driver's door opened. A black man jumped out and strode toward me, a hand extended, a splint and bandage wrapping his pinky finger. Standing at least six-foot-five and sporting a muscular build under his short-sleeved polo shirt, he looked like a professional athlete. "Garth Mahoney. It's good to finally meet you, Mike."

"Mahoney?" I slid my hand into his and shook it, careful to avoid squeezing the injured finger. "How did you get here? The police couldn't find a trace of you."

"The two goons who kidnapped me took turns driving all the way from Fort Lauderdale." He gestured toward his van, a late-model conversion cruiser. "In that sweet ride there."

"And they just let you go? How? When?"

"I can tell you the gory details later, but when we got to Spokane, we stopped at a bus station, they told me where to find you, then they got out and took off. So I drove straight here and saw all these beautiful people standing around." Mahoney nodded at the others. "Nice to meet all you beautiful people."

Deb smiled. "And you, Garth."

I crossed my arms and stared at him. Chill bumps covered his skin from wrists to biceps. Too bad my coat wouldn't come close to fitting his massive frame. "Any clue why they brought you here?"

"Only this." Mahoney handed me a small brown box with a sealed note taped to the outside. "It's safe. I saw what they put in it, but I won't spoil the surprise."

I peeled off the note, opened it, and read it out loud. "Mike, thanks for saving my life. The van's yours. You'll find the title in the glove compartment. Also, I'm sure you've wondered why no police officers or bureaucrats have contacted you about Jessica and Emma. I called in some favors at the state office. The girls can stay with you indefinitely, so you're free to pursue custody or adoption at your leisure. Maybe now we're even. For your sake and mine, I hope we don't meet again. Special Agent Reese Spencer."

Jessica bumped fists with Emma and turned to me with a sly grin. "So ... Daddy ... to celebrate, I'm thinking a dramatic reciting of Jabberwocky and mugs of hot chocolate. Are you game?"

I gave her a wink and a smile. "Definitely."

"Let's see what's in the box," Tommy said.

"Sure." I handed the note to Deb and opened the box. As everyone leaned closer, I withdrew the contents—an empty Sugar Daddy wrapper.

Deb peered at it. "Mike, what do you think it means?"

"A symbol of victory, maybe? We exposed Vega. He's dead and gone." The wrapper's words, red emblazoned on yellow, looked like a flashing warning sign. Danger ahead. I folded the wrapper and pushed it into my pocket. "But then again, if Spencer's responsible for Fred's murder, it's more likely he's kissing up to us to hide his true objectives."

"To be the next Sugar Daddy," Deb said, "but one who's not so obvious. A coat and tie instead of a clown suit. A different wrapper."

"That's a chilling thought." I fished the minivan key fob from my pocket and extended it to Mahoney. "I assume you want to get some warm clothes. Put the charge on my account. We'll take the other van and start a new journey."

"Oh?" Mahoney took the fob and the box. "Rescuing girls with the whole family? That'll be an adventure they'll never forget."

"And I'm going to try again to track boys." I patted his arm. "Still want to be my manager?"

"As if you had the option to get rid of me. But I'm setting up a mobile office." He lifted his bandaged hand. "Broken fingers mess up my perfect body image."

"Yeah, we all need to get out of the spotlight. Deb's our new disguise expert. I'll tell you that story later."

Mahoney turned to her. "What about your computer store?"

Now holding hands with Emily and Emma, Deb smiled. "I'm selling it. A friend of mine took my place there for a few days and loved it. He's getting together with some buddies to buy me out."

"Excellent." Mahoney pressed the button on the minivan key fob and unlocked it. "I'll drop your rental off at the airport and fly home. And don't worry; I'll put the airfare charge on your account. But first I'll see about outfitting your new ride with some state-of-the-art communications so we can be in constant contact." As he scanned Deb, Tommy, and the girls, he flashed a brilliant smile. "With your wonderful family, I guess you could call it heaven on wheels."

"Heaven on wheels." I let the words echo in my mind. "I like that. I like that a lot."

"Well," Mahoney said as he handed me the new van's keys, "where are you guys going first? It's a big country out there. Lots of hurting people."

"I don't know yet." I held Emily's hand on one side and Tommy's on the other. Deb, Jessica, and Emma linked up at the ends and formed a circle. I inhaled deeply and took in their lovely scents. The aroma of love was sweet indeed. "Maybe I'll just follow my nose."